Indemnification

Carroll Dean

Copyright © 2023 Carroll Dean

All rights reserved. No part of this book may be reproduced or transmitted in any form or by any means, electronic or mechanical, including photocopying, recording or by any information storage and retrieval system without permission in writing from the publisher.

Hearts Lock Publishing—Lockhart, TX
ISBN: 979-8-218-16531-4
Library of Congress Control Number: 2023903662
Title: *Indemnification*
Author: Carroll Dean
Digital distribution | 2023
Paperback | 2023

This is a work of fiction. The characters, names, incidents, places, and dialogue are products of the author's imagination, and are not to be construed as real.

For everyone who knew him, it seemed like my brother changed and became someone else they didn't know. No one would have ever dared question the effects of such tragedies that he went through. I don't think they looked at him with any sort of blame, just compassion, and I feel that was a misjudgment about his experience. I don't see that he ever changed. What everyone got to see, was something that had always existed within him. It was always in his inner character, as I believe it is written into the code of all men. Most are too scared to look upon it, and if they do, rarely will any of them allow it to emerge. My brother, although forced into seeing it, didn't just discover who he was, he committed to who he was.

Matthew Richards

Chapter One
The Decision

The room was filled with the discussions of a busy day. The people were packed in such great numbers that the faces seemed to blend unrecognizable. Every person was engaged in their own conversation, unaware of the situation that sat in their midst. Each individual speech was important in and of itself as volume became competitive. The noise in the café was so loud that to someone alone it would simply become a numbing constant tone.

Camouflaged to the people sat one individual that wanted no company. Dulled to his surroundings, he seemed invisible. At the moment, no one seemed to pay any attention to him.

Clutched to his cup of coffee, his hands steadily remained almost unbearably hot. The breaking of his concentration was untouchable. Even his utter dislike of cigarette smoke wasn't provoked by the thick haze being tossed about by the ceiling fan. He was a man zoned into an element and a place outside of his dwelling.

Shut out of his surroundings he raced past memories of the life he had once cherished. It was a life that had stopped so suddenly, when all had seemed so perfect. Now, feeling empty, the task at hand would at least provide a bit of closure to a grim state. Dr. Joseph Richards had been patiently waiting for this day. A day when he anticipated delivery of at least a portion of restitution.

As his eyes wandered, he looked around his present setting. It brought about a sentiment of abhorrence. His story was so far above any of the useless drama that fueled his surroundings. Anger, frustration, and bitterness clawed inside his core like the slowest and most deadly cancer. He wanted it to be as though it never happened. He so desperately wanted her back. He wanted to forget the pain and have it all go away, and yet not lose the memories of what was once a perfect life. He wanted a guilty conviction, with the harshest of punishments. He believed in a life for a life. It would be fitting if the man got the death penalty. This tyrant had done everything to deserve his life as payment. It wasn't as though he was a person who had made a mistake. This was truly a worthless soul, needlessly occupying a piece of society.

The time he had spent living showed no consideration for anyone but himself. His was a life who seemed to forfeit its right to live. He was a danger to others and had proven it many times. On and on the doctor's mind reassessed the various outcomes that were possibilities in today's age. With the clock being one of Dr. Richards' concerns, he wondered if the jury would even reach a verdict today. Emotionally he was drained. A calloused numbness had seemed to establish itself on his outward man. He was tired, and it needed to be finished. His wife's murderer had not received what he was properly owed.

Time had continued moving with its own purpose, excluding the doctor. It was like winding a clock of expectancy for peace and the hand never reaching any release of torment. Patience is a virtue, was just a thought without hope. It had been two years since her death, and now he had to dredge through a trial that was taking over two and a half months. The level of stress was compromising his self-control. He knew in his heart that he had to remain collected for the memory of his wife. He also felt he had to do something, but what? There was an intuition inside him coveting an exploit. He knew above all things that he must maintain his calm. He had been brought up in a well-respected household, where standards meant everything. He was not about to stoop to the level of what he saw as a lost society. This hopeless age of character was beneath his integrity, but justice was not. He was desperate for answers but feared he might not get the ones he wanted.

"Would you like a hot up?" asked the barkeep behind the counter.

The doctor found the environment even more undesirable with the man's approach. It had only proven convenient. He did not want to engage in conversation with anyone. There seemed no better place to hide out than in an overcrowded, over spoken diner where everyone was preoccupied with their own conceits.

"Sir, do you want any more coffee?" the elderly man said, this time a little louder.

Dr. Richards didn't say anything, only acknowledged him with a nod indicating no. He looked at the man and with extreme judgement giving him credit for owning the establishment. Animosity had begun to become instinctive with the doctor. By looking at the patrons, he thought this man had been cut from the same cloth as those he served. The doctor was not impressed with anything he saw. He accounted all of them unworthy. His loathing of the world had come as a reaction to his unfortunate loss. What a dive, he thought. He began to have second thoughts about coming into the place.

As he started looking around the room, he noticed people making eye contact with him. He received the occasional nod or half smile man is programmed to perform when eyes meet. The bias he had placed on the crowd didn't accept these gestures with open arms. It had proven to not be a good choice for remaining obscure. Neither did it aid his character in practicing compassion for his fellow man. He knew his heart had fallen and bitterness dwelt within him, but it was beyond his control at this time.

With his current situation, this environment only helped create disgust in his heart. Under any other circumstance, he never would have stepped foot in there. They were all a part of the world the doctor now despised. Since the horrific murder of his wife, he had removed himself from the world and its workings. As far as he was concerned this was what life was to become. It was what he would be up against from here on out.

The picking of this place was determined out of its location. It happened to be around the corner from the courthouse, and his walk was only minutes. The doctor glanced at his watch. It had been two hours and thirteen minutes that the jury had been deliberating. His brother hadn't called him to come back. Why so long? Everything that was said, was clear cut. How long would it possibly take? He knew juries tend to deliberate extensively, but the evidence was overwhelming. It shouldn't take those jurors any time to see the truth. This individual on trial was tripe. His only need was to be sent to the chair with no mercy. The doctor had positive thoughts convincing himself of a conviction. At the same time, doubts about leniency wouldn't escape him as encouraged by the condition of sickness the world had incorporated. He abhorred what it had become and blamed it on the moral decline mankind had embraced. It was a breakdown in the family. People weren't accountable for raising what they made. He feared the corruption of this world had a chance to run its evil straight to the jury's heart. What if he goes free? What if he gets a light sentence? What if the jury is a bunch of ignorant people? Worse yet, what if they are stupid? His father had always left him with sayings of enlightenment. One he remembered was "people are born ignorant, but you have to work to become stupid, just as it takes a conscience effort to be smart." The doctor was desiring a morally intelligent jury. If only others had his upbringing.

As the doctor was advancing in thought, he became more convinced of people in general preferring a selfish, ego centric, maniacal lifestyle compared to his recollection of yesterday. It was a simpler time he was fond of; it seemed as though it had been abused and thrown away. He felt that he was a part of what the world was trying to discard. How can justice ever be served in a world like this? He wanted to know. He longed to see it. It was a highly stressful meditation that he was working through. Judgement sat atop his head, as his hands remained tied behind his back. The man who tried serving him before began coming his way again. This time with the coffee pot and a cigarette in his mouth.

"Need a little more coffee there fella?" he said with the smoke rolling out.

"I'm good," the doctor said, as if having no patience.

"How about an ear, you look like you have a full chest," the waiter said as an attempt to make conversation.

Dr. Richards wasn't about to divulge his complicated circumstances. This man, as friendly as he attempted to be, wasn't capable of understanding such matters as the doctor was experiencing. Conversation wasn't going to take place for the two. The doctor's problems would remain protected within himself. He felt he was so far above this man's intellect that it would be wasting both of their times.

"I can see you don't want to talk, so I will leave you alone. I hope things get better for you. Sorry about your troubles," the waiter spoke kindly, as if nothing could offend him, and then walked away.

This caused the doctor discomfort. What in the hell made him say that? Why would he attempt to be nice at a time like this? Why didn't he just deal with all the other people in here and leave the doctor alone. He didn't know what the doctor was experiencing. The pain that had been mounting for years was now becoming unbearable. To make matters worse was the kindness from the old man. The hatred for his wife's murderer, clashing with a stranger's benevolence, in the midst of a world gone wrong was a train wreck of emotions insufferable. The reliving of that horrible night for the last two and a half months had reopened all the wounds and was making the doctor feel unstable. Here the doctor was, embraced in anger, waiting for his answer, wanting to be left alone, and an act of kindness appears. Whether it was the thought this man had something of value to offer Dr. Richards or just the actions of a good attitude, the doctor took offense to his gesture. He felt as though this man was curiously intruding. It was accidently arrogant. He knew by looking at the man, he really didn't qualify for any conversation of worth. He determined it was just good old fashion nosiness. Although, Dr. Richards couldn't blind himself that the old man did it with a good heart. The waiter's simple comment was like a hot coal being placed on the doctor's head. It was a burn he couldn't remove. It stayed on a constant.

As Dr. Richards sat with great anxiety, two men began an argument at the end of the bar. The two men were quarreling and quickly their demeanor became excited. As their volume began to rise, not many seemed to notice, until without warning, both men suddenly squared off inside the place and proceeded to tussle about.

One would have been taken back from seeing the waiter as he jolted into action. For a short fat man, seemingly out of shape, he dashed around the counter and positioned himself between the two men in a compromising situation.

The yelling was as profane as one could imagine. Even though it was a substandard establishment, it was still a shock to witness the event. The doctor sat in amazement, now even more disgusted by society.

The two men began throwing punches wildly. Both men, with more anger than skill, threw their fists around. They made contact but seemed to miss their intended target like two out of control apes. The old worn-out waiter was doing his best to diffuse the situation, but to do that was to take a beating his body could have only taken years ago.

A few barstools turned over as people scurried to remove themselves. Glasses and cups were knocked off the bar, and shatters were heard between the hollering of the crowd.

"Call the cops!" a shout sprang out, and as quick as the fight had started, it seemed to end.

One thing both of those two men knew, was that running away was better than going to jail. Grabbing their possessions, both scurried off like rats into the streets. Just as the noise reached capacity, it died out to a low level. People began to make phone calls. Some were calling to tell the story while others were calling the authorities. The cops would be showing up soon.

In the middle of the floor lay the waiter who was bleeding quite heavily on his face. He must have taken a couple of direct hits, and by the amount of blood pouring out it looked serious. Although the doctor had been in his own world of analysis, he never lost the reactionary engagement function that was drilled in him during his internship in the ER. It was as if all his previous thoughts about his surroundings escaped for the moment and allowed for his inner practitioner to emerge.

The doctor had almost an instinctive response to come to the man's aid. Immediately he ran to his side.

Hollering to anyone who could assist him, he yelled

"Get me some clean towels, and water, NOW!"

A young girl, who must have been an employee, came running around the bar with towels and a pitcher of water.

As the doctor began wiping off the man face, the man was breathing heavily with a slow sort of choke. Aside from his nose pouring out blood, his mouth was bleeding without intentions of stopping. He was coherent, but in a great deal of pain.

He spoke to the doctor, "Thank you sir."

Dr. Richards wanted to administer to the man's needs but was limited to just cleaning him up and looking for obvious trauma. He had practiced medicine so long he could separate himself from any emotions when working on patients. This time was a bit different.

He knew not to give way to sympathy when working on anyone. It has a way of compromising the professional judgment. Hardly ever is it a concern in an emergency room, as the sufferer is an unknown. This however was a bit dissimilar.

This man had just shown the doctor kindness and was received from the doctor with a judgment. A sentence was given of inadequacy. It was just moments ago that he thought of this man as not worth much. He had decided this man was below him, not worth his time and was a part of this society that the doctor was learning to hate. As the doctor continued to clean and feel for any obvious broken bones, he tried to stay inside the task at hand and alleviate himself from what he was realizing. The doctor's heart had been hardened by the loss of his wife, and he hadn't been able to come around to wanting to help people anymore.

He hadn't been in practice since his wife's murder. All the thoughts that had been bottled up and under a slow fire began to let go of some steam, and perhaps removed a bit of haze that had been collecting for some time within him. Maybe it was the kind words from the old man. Maybe it was the judgement the doctor had placed on the old man. Maybe it was the fact that those kind words the old man spoke, were piercing deep into his ego. Maybe it was the hatred for a worthless society and acknowledgment of mankind's dependent nature, wrestling about inside the doctor, that was causing pause. Whatever it was, Dr. Richards was about to embark on a life-changing journey. He wasn't aware of it, but this was a beginning moment of clarity he would reflect back upon in the future.

As much as was going on at that moment, the doctor began to realize that perhaps it was all bigger than him. His heart was being shown the need to have mercy, due to circumstance. It was the old man's kindness taming unwarranted prejudice amid the doctor's pain. Dr. Richard's felt a bit of remorse. Maybe he hadn't learned it all. Maybe he still had the purpose in life to heal.

As the doctor wasn't prepared with a medical kit, he continued to clean the old man's wounds and analyze any damage. While assessing any wounds the man might have had, his reflection upon the importance of healing was emerging. This was part of the creed he was introduced to in medical school. He was so far removed from his younger days. Since his wife's murder he was even more separated from that philosophy. He had been harboring a hate that had impeded his ability to visit that passion he once held in his heart. Tending to the man was now showing him the importance of that need again.

As he continued wiping off the man's face, it was obvious the man was going to need stiches above his lip. His skin was likened to wrinkled crape paper. It only looked tough.

"I'll be alright, just help me up," the old man said reaching to hold the side of his head.

"No, you need to lie here until medical care arrives. You are going to have to go to the hospital to be attended to," the doctor explained.

The old man began a back-pedaling of excuses, "I am not taking an ambulance ride to any hospital, do you know how much that costs? I will heal up just fine on my own."

Dr. Richards felt for the man. He was aware of the welfare society that generously spent other's moneys, but this man needed help.

"Sir, I am a medical doctor and if I was able to, I would dress your wounds properly, and give you an examination. I want to rule out any trauma to your head as I saw you receive many hits. I am in no position to do so, but I advise you seek further treatment. Please listen to me and go with the EMTs when they arrive," the doctor said, professionally.

He knew that the man being old might factor into the extent of his injuries. The man still being persuaded by the fact that money was an issue, declined the doctors advise.

"Thank you, but no thank you."

Perhaps Dr. Richards had misread the man's character. He felt as though the man wasn't being stubborn, although one could argue the point. He was a man who made his own way and wasn't about to be a burden on anyone. Not having enough for something, was doing without that something. Whatever the case may be, doing without was fine for him.

One thing he did have, was the satisfaction of knowing that he wasn't a burden. He wouldn't put himself upon anyone, except as a friend. A friend was something the doctor could use, even though he wasn't privy to that thought. Perhaps this encounter was providence.

A faint siren could be heard gradually increasing in volume. The people who had been watching and waiting to see the excitement from the police and paramedics, ran outside the door to watch them arrive. Almost three hours had passed since the doctor had arrived and he wanted to check back at the courthouse of any news.

He waited for the EMTs to enter so he could have a few words with them. The paramedics came in with their medical bags in military style. They looked to be young and in excellent shape. This was probably nothing out of the ordinary for them as they rushed in unaffected by the disrupted scene.

"Excuse me, I believe the man you are here to see is going to refuse you taking him in for an examination, but I am a medical doctor and it is my professional opinion he needs to be checked out at the hospital. He took a few massive hits to his head."

Dr. Richards didn't want this man to succumb to any injury later. One paramedic said he would try to get the man to go with them, but if he refused they could do nothing unless he went unresponsive.

The doctor settled on well enough because he had to go. He was truly concerned about the old man but had another issue that took precedence over this one. He had to leave.

Stepping out of one stressful condition only to enter another was all he needed. He looked around one last time with shocking disbelief about what had just happened and walked out the door.

With all his steps toward the courthouse he kept thinking of the well-being of that old fat man. He never even got his name. What was his name? He remembered the name of the place, it was Dean's. Was that his place, or did he just work there? Maybe his name was Dean. How old was he? What were those two awful men fighting about?

Mixed inside his thoughts was a deeper concentration. I wonder if the jury has come to a decision yet? I wonder what Jeremy Williams is doing? I hope he isn't getting fed or watching TV. I am longing for a death penalty. I'm sure they would have called my cell phone to let me know of any news. His mind began to migrate back towards the business at hand.

Having been moved by the witness of an old man being subjected to disrespectful battery, he began calming as he approached his destination. One might still be quite upset from all the excitement he witnessed, but the doctor was becoming more focused on the case as he entered the courthouse grounds.

The doctor thought about his dear sweet wife not having to endure any more of this world. At least in the grave she could be free from all this corruption, until the time of her awakening. The doctor knew in his heart he would reunite with her one day. It just hurt to live without her anymore, even though he only hurt for himself. He was content about her whereabouts. She would sleep for now.

If only these ones who did the acts that caused such pains were made to experience their own destructive nature, life would balance itself out in peace. If only they were taught a lesson from their own playbook, they might have a change in attitude.

The doctor contemplated the imperfections of this world and what it needed. His emotions became a bit excited again. It was much for him to focus as so many variables were surrounding him. Without a solid ground on which to stand, confusion can begin to swim under your feet without being seen and redirect your walk. He reached back in his heart to stroke the strings of aversion. The doctor had so many things racing about his mind, that he was bouncing sentiments off reason.

Man's law had only shown to fail. It is slow, incorrect, misleading, and works according to the sway of society. This culture had been malignant for some time now. What does man know? He was never meant to govern himself anyway. The doctor began dissecting the legal system and its flaws. He criticized the outcome of its rancorous society. He wondered, was there any hope for justice?

As Dr. Richards re-entered the courthouse. He could see his brother Matthew speaking to a family friend. The doctor had been constantly surrounded by family and friends since the trial began and had been attempting to create space to allow for normalcy. His family knew and respected his wishes and did their best to oblige him. Everyone wanted to help by saying something to ease the pain, but the right words just didn't seem to manifest themselves in this time of extreme trial.

When Matthew saw his brother, he immediately came to him and updated him.

"Joey, where have you been, I tried calling you about thirty minutes ago?"

The doctor looked at his cell phone. It was on silent.

"I had silenced it earlier in court and forgot to turn the ringer back on. What is it, do you have any news?" The doctor asked apprehensively.

"The jury is about to come out from deliberating, and I think they have reached a decision," his brother spoke with optimism.

The doctor began feeling uneasy as a sudden rush of anxiety hit him. It began causing a pressure, which created within him a pessimistic attitude toward the awaited decision. It was as if he began to want the decision to be halted. He feared of hearing an unjust sentence. He was convinced the death penalty was the only action that completed truth and justice in this case, but first he must hear guilty of capital murder. It was going to be an uncomfortable verdict to witness.

One of the state's attorneys came up and approached the family. He seemed rather young and anxious.

The trial had gained much news coverage and was worthy to any lawyer who could seal a deadly fate for such a public menace.

"It's good to see you're back. If you will, you can take your seats. The jurors have reached a decision and will be coming out in a minute."

This was it, the doctor thought. *Now is mine. I must accept it, no matter what. What if I can't,* he worried. *What will I do,* the doctor kept his thoughts racing.

Everyone began sitting down. Most of the people were quiet, but a few were speaking as softly as possible. As conversations were continuing, they began to increase in volume.

The unlocking and turning of a large heavy doorknob cracked all words to silence. A door opened, and the jurors walked in. They all had emotionless faces, as each one walked with a pace of patience. The doctor took note of each one as they sat down. He had been examining them from the beginning. Four women, and eight men comprised the twelve. All races were present, with the majority being white. Would that help at all? This was a white-on-white crime. None of them seemed very old. None of them had ever shown any facial expression throughout the trial. A seasoned jury was what the doctor had hoped for. It was his desire that they wouldn't have trouble with a judge sending him to the chair, thus finding him guilty of capital murder.

The age of the suspect was twenty-seven and sometimes juries consider that when weighing the balance of justice. It was out of the doctor's hands now. The doctor couldn't worry anymore. As the jury sat, people in the courtroom began talking again, without being too noisy.

A loud and commanding voice startled the room as the bailiff announced the judge's entrance.

"All rise. The honorable Joyce Hendricks is now presiding."

The judge's presence made those watching anxiously anticipate the verdict. With the victim being a female, would a female judge overseeing the proceedings have any effect?

She was a handsome woman, professional in all her body language. She appeared to be as tough as any old western hanging judge, and yet someone any man in the courtroom would desire. The uncomfortable silence hung heavy in the air. Would justice be served? How would the jury see things? The defense had used a lot of emotion to attempt chicanery in the hearts of the jurors. Their case was the usual victim of poverty, victim of location, victim of circumstance. There was no accountability for anyone's actions anymore. It was always someone else's fault for people's wrong doings.

The state relied on the victim speaking for herself. The absolute brutality of the crime ought to be all the proof the jury would need. It should prove to be an uphill battle to convince people to have mercy on the merciless, but it had been done before. The possibilities were confounding. Dr. Richards needed to have this matter finalized.

The courtroom doors were closed, and the bailiff handed the judge a paper from the foreman. She read the paper without showing any signs of the decision and handed the paper to the bailiff to be handed back.

"Would the foreman please rise and render a verdict?" The judge spoke, allowing no one time to guess an outcome. "In the case of Jeremy Williams, murder one, how do you find the defendant?" A brief pause passed over the room.

"Not guilty." The foreman's voice was like a dagger being pierced into the heart of Dr. Richards. His family and friends were stunned, and a few cries and gasps went out from among them.

"Quiet," the bailiff hollered.

The judge spoke again, "In the case of Jeremy Williams, murder in the second degree, how do you find the defendant?"

The foreman's response seemed even faster, "Not guilty."

It was now that hope was all but gone.

"In the case of Jeremy Williams, charges of manslaughter, how do you find the defendant?"

The doctor was numb and emotionally drained. He had used all he had.

"Guilty."

The jurors had helped to twist the knife that had killed the doctor's wife right into the very heart of her husband. This sentence carried with it a maximum of twenty years. This would hardly pay for the unrest caused by this monster. In all probability he wouldn't even serve the entire time. The doctor knew that the jurors had fallen for the boy's story. The fact that he was on drugs and that his defense claimed he only wanted to rob them, convinced them that the murder was an unintentional act. They never considered the real victims in this tragedy.

The doctor sat too exhausted to feel. His mind had consumed all it was going to for some time. The doctor's brother began crying and hugged him. Dr. Richards leaned his head towards his brother but failed to pick his arms up.

For the next twenty years, this murderer would receive the comfort and care given by the state to rehabilitate, if they decide to keep him that long. He would have access to books and schooling. He would be able to completely change his life, come out in the world at a relatively young age, and start a new life for himself.

This was hardly justice for the doctor, who had made the correct choices. He and his wife did the right things to build up their lives. They were productive, meaningful people with purpose. They had done their best to make good of all they participated in, and at fifty-four her life was taken without cause.

Where would the doctor's rehabilitation come from? Where would he rebuild his chances? His story was broken in two. How do you start over at that point in the game? There had to be an answer. His energy was spent. He knew it was going to take time. This was something he knew he had. He stood up and told his brother he was leaving. Not much was said as Matthew knew his brother's character.

As Dr. Richards walked off, he just ignored the sympathetic comments coming from the people in attendance. He just didn't care. He was drained. He averted any contact with the news or press. He would leave the lawyers to answer any questions. He knew he could only complicate matters by being vocal.

A determination was becoming manifest inside his mind. There was a storm that was developing within him. It was of great magnitude and would carry with it change. It would create rehabilitation like none before. He would seek to find restitution entering a flawed justice system and allow for all to understand the error of their ways. Something had to be done, but what and how.

The doctor would find his resolve in his strict adherence to life being right. It would all become business with no regrets. He would become determined to make a difference for the good, for his wife, and most especially for the ones doing wrong.

He was about to embark on an adventure that would renew his old passion in life. He was born a natural healer. His purpose in life was to heal. To make the sick well. He would be determined to show men the error of their ways with a most unpopular side of love. He would use a mirror, not only to reveal what they were, but reveal the effects of their crimes. It was time to help people make the right decision because they want to, and the doctor would soon discover a cure that would work. It would become a new justice.

Chapter Two
Fare Well My Love

Two weeks seemed to disappear just as if they had never existed. Practically all of Dr. Richard's time was spent staying busy around the house. He had developed a systematic routine that continually reciprocated a need to do, with no end. Still desensitized by the inconsideration that society had placed on his wife's life, his only course of action was escaping into the mundane things of the day.

It was constant work until nothing seemed left undone, and then do it again. It was striving for a purpose that just didn't seem to be there. He knew he needed to do something, but what? Staying active might allow for clearer thinking and eventually cause thought for something to come along. He would work things out in his own mind. His heart still being hardened, he wasn't ready to talk with anyone. His phone was set directly to voice mail. He just couldn't be bothered by anyone right now. His thoughts were enough to self-process at the time. Most everyone knew his character and respected that. If nothing else, at least the ones that mattered knew and left him alone.

He just continued working around the house doing things again and again. It was as if he wished to find something that needed attention or an answer to his void. His lifestyle was one that required a project. There was nothing that wasn't clean or in its place. He was staying busy to stay busy. He desperately needed something to occupy his time. His lack of having anything to do had him searching for an answer that just couldn't be found.

Inside of all of this, he knew what he wouldn't be doing. His career as a doctor wouldn't be returning. He had decided back after the death of his wife, that he wouldn't be returning to his medical practice. Now, more than ever, he didn't see the need or significance to ever go back. He was well to do for the rest of his life, despite his lack of enthusiasm. It didn't seem worth it anymore. It was supposed to have been good, but that was then, and this was an entirely different outcome than was planned.

During their years of work, he and his wife had managed to invest, and it paid off for them both. They were on course to retire within a year before her death. All the planning that had been done was preparation to a dream they had mapped out collectively. They had spent many days and nights forecasting a future after retirement. All their time would be spent together, fulfilling their true obsession. There was nothing that could have changed their direction. Perhaps things might have been different if they had been able to have children, but that was never an option.

The reason for this was outside of their control. It was one regret his wife had always held under her surface. She had struggled with acceptance of her condition since children had always been a definite choice for her.

Her development of endometriosis in her younger days had forced the hand of a hysterectomy, and therefore ruined all chances for a family of their own. Her inability to bear children was hard on her at first, but they managed to focus on the opportunity to help others. Someone to care for seemed to be what drove them both.

They would often entertain the thoughts about the possibilities of what their prodigy would have looked like. Sometimes their evenings would extend with romantic indulgences of fantasy family planning. They would talk of the things they loved about each other. They would laugh about the quirky things each other did, and then pick on each other's faults. Mixing the best quality traits with the silly things they loved about each other, they imagined exactly what their children would have been like.

One might think it torturous to think such thoughts, but to them it helped to fill a space that would never become. To love was what they dreamed of. To the doctor and his Love, it helped to drive who they were.

Their role in life was to direct, heal, help, and to love. It helped them in creating their goal, and purpose for what they were working for. Since they had no children to invest in, they would find others to invest in. It was to become a target based on a passion they both shared. It was a common theme that drew them to each other. Each one's love for healing had been discovered by the other in a chance encounter during a weekend visit to an elderly home. So fond and powerful it never went to a memory of the past. It was always as though it was just yesterday.

The doctor was in his fourth year of medical school, and his soon-to-be wife had just finishing achieving her teaching degree. Both were visiting a grandparent and happened to cross paths at a vending machine. For those who find nostalgia in fairy tale chance meetings, this might not have been the classic setting. However, the encounter was priceless and was the start of a beautiful thing. Now that she was gone the doctor would often replay their chance meeting many times in his head. He remembered thinking, *She was just standing at the vending machine so undecided. It must have taken her three minutes to not decide whatever it was she didn't want.*

"Hello, can I help you?" The doctor was a bit apprehensive to speak but decided to anyway.

"Well, I don't know, can you, and with what?" she spoke with a commanding look of a woman with much experience and yet at the same time exhibited the delicacy of a rose that had bloomed that very morning. She was an enigma, as her body language displayed a humble confidence. After words had exchanged, the doctor was a bit taken back. There was no mistake they were attracted to each other. She was young and fresh with a face that flowed strength and professionalism.

He remembered thinking that this medical student, in all his grandeur, was about to play one of the most challenging hands he had ever faced. He perceived she was worth the effort. Women were not something the doctor had ever spent much time looking for or chasing. He would often avoid them and keep to his own, but something about this time was different. It was a thing called fate.

Upon the first glance, he had seen something that he desired greatly and would attempt to catch her. Her voice only complicated matters for the doctor. Watching her facial expressions and hearing her voice together was almost intoxicating. She was infectious in the delivery of her speech. How can someone be taken back from such small words is sometimes a mystery, but it undoubtedly happened for him. He was never given to witty conversation, but in no way was he about to see this as a missed opportunity. He remembered how he was so attracted and intimidated at the same time. This proposed a challenge that he had never faced.

"I can see you are having trouble deciding what to pick."

She looked at him with a sort of grin and with a slow return, politely questioned, "What would you suggest?"

Immediately the doctor knew from her demeaner she was ready to play with him. He would have to develop a good answer if he didn't want to walk away looking foolish. He thought for a moment and responded.

"From the looks of you, I would suspect that you don't eat anything unhealthy, and if I were you I wouldn't." One might take offence to that comment, but she was wiser than that.

"Everything in here is pretty much unhealthy, so what do you propose I pick?" She just sat there still holding her grin with style.

"I would pick the filet, smoked gouda cheese grits, fresh spring vegetables, and a glass of wine."

It was bold, but it was also the elegant move the doctor was waiting to make. He didn't know if the conversation would get to a point where he might be able to make a move, but it did, and he took it.

He had mentioned his favorite meal down at Angelo's by the Lake. It was one of the most down-to-earth, quaint, and yet elegant places to enjoy some of the best food he knew of. It was a perfect pick. It was just like her.

"I don't see that in the glass, perhaps you could show me where it is?" Her answer left him knowing that his invitation was a score.

"I would love to, if you are free tonight and you would like to go out. I can pick you up around sevenish. I'm sure you are going to go home to get ready, although it won't take much." The invitation was accepted, and things went better than he had hoped for. Their personalities were a perfect match and their bantering played on into the night as they never looked back.

Their marriage didn't seem to come fast enough. Their love was one that started with attraction and grew into a mature enduring love. They had experienced their true love for the first and only time together.

Life also laid out its agenda. Medical school was a priority along with careers. It was him working in the hospital and her job as a school counselor that passed many of their days, but all their remaining time stayed in dedication to each other.

They had plotted out a course and laid its mission to pursue the truth and love in life that they were growing in and learning together.

Upon retirement they had planned on traveling and visiting many remote places in the world. Included in their plans was charitable help for people of less fortunate circumstances.

It was imbedded in their innermost core. His profession in the medical field and her career as a school counselor had brought them to a natural conditioning for wanting to help and heal those with problems. It would be that in retirement. Wherever the road took them, they wanted to make a difference. They would set out together to make a change and leave their mark for making things better.

Unfortunately, this all came to a screeching halt, and adjusting to the change hadn't been easy. The monotony of searching for things to keep him busy had its own consequences. At times it was as if he was losing control of himself. He would have to stop and channel in from the abundance of discipline he and his wife had managed to construct. The order he and his wife had developed was so polished, that his exhaustion was a result of continuing to go, do, and be productive, underneath the weight of trying to lose the pain of his loss.

Dr. Richards was driving himself crazy and hadn't found anything to occupy his time. He would need to find something to work with in order to function. Sitting on the couch, he glanced over on the side table, at a framed letter his wife had written to him on their 20th wedding anniversary. Feeling himself begin to indulge in some much-needed rest his eyes began to slowly shut.

He was finally listening to his body which was letting him know he was wearing down. Rest was at least a moment in peace. He could drift off and enjoy a brief escape from the real world and its horrors. He needed to separate from the pain that hadn't seemed to subside. The soft sounds around him were lulling him to sleep, when the sudden ringing of the doorbell jolted his hypnotic state.

The doctor sat up for a second and wondered who could be coming over. As he began to remove himself from his seat, he moved with the utmost steadiness and stealth as if to take enough time for whoever it was to go away.

"Hello?" a voice he did not recognize came from the other side of his door accompanied by another ring of his doorbell. "Hello, Dr. Richards. Are you home?"

It was a young energetic voice of a lady. This propelled the doctor to the door. As he placed his hand on the deadbolt, he looked through the peephole and saw a very attractive woman at least 25 years his younger. He wondered who she was. Was she with the press? He was not in the mood for an interview, and certainly didn't want to engage in conversation that might be upsetting. He wondered if he should just not answer.

"Dr. Richards, if you are in there, I would just like to leave you with some information."

This couldn't be anyone from the press, he thought. *Who could it be, and what information do they have? They probably wanted information about the case*, the doctor thought.

Either way the doctor had to start dealing with these situations. He decided to move her on her way.

"One minute please, and I'll get the door."

He could have opened it immediately as he was at the door, but he wanted to wait to allow his thoughts to settle. He was not opposed to people and their good will efforts, it just didn't seem like enough time had passed for him to open up.

Finally, as he opened the door, he did it slowly, to receive a better look.

"Good afternoon, may I help you?" The doctor was not retaining any kind of attitude with regard to helping anyone but said so to be polite.

"Hello, my name is Denise Wilson, and I am a social worker with the Tarrant County Sheriff's Office. We provide various services for our community in a wide range of areas. If you have time, I could sit with you right now and go over what we do, and the services offered free of charge for people with challenging situations like yourself." She spoke as though it was a requirement to memorize her lines.

The doctor presumed her to be a newcomer to her job and perhaps a bit nervous. Maybe the fact that his wife's trial had gained much press was her reason for seeming uneasy. Either way the doctor still thought to move her along.

"No thanks, I'm a little tired, but I do appreciate you coming by."

Was this the first of many of these visits? The doctor wasn't wanting this to become a familiar event. He stepped back to close his door, and she spoke again, but this time not so rehearsed.

"Doctor, if you could give me just a minute, I think I might be able to help you. I would like to try at least."

She was persistent, due to the fact that anyone would have been able to read the doctor's lack of interest. Maybe it was just routine to ask again, but her second attempt didn't seem to have much more of an effect.

"No thanks." He turned his head.

"Doctor, I don't want to sound intrusive, but I asked to come to your house. I have followed your wife's case since its beginning, and it has had a great effect on the community as well as myself. I learned about her case while I was going to school for my criminal justice degree. I did everything I could to follow your situation, up until the verdict a couple of weeks ago. It was devasting to our community. More than ever, I now want to make a difference after learning about your circumstances. I don't want to sound presumptuous, but your situation has given me a lot. I believe I have developed into a more conscientious adult, and I would like to give back to you if I could, in any measure."

Wow, what a statement. This was not what the doctor was expecting. The door should have already shut, but now it couldn't.

"I can only assume it would make your wife proud to know that she was still doing good work in her death. Her story is why I am here. Please let me do something, anything."

The doctor stood still. His eyes wanted to well up, but he managed to hold it back. The utter sincerity of this young girl had taken mountains of courage. This was something the doctor applauded. He saw his young wife's tenacity for a few seconds. It was overwhelming.

"You speak from the heart, and that is refreshing my dear. I wish it were true about most of the people I encounter. As for helping me, I'm not sure you can. I know I need to heal, but I don't think I will ever want to forget and that is the compromising part. Even though the memories are painful, they are still memories of her."

It was the young social worker who couldn't contain her emotions and a tear rolled off her cheek.

"Forgive me, doctor. We are told to be the strong ones for our victims, and here I fall short of that. Honestly, perhaps it might not have been such a good idea for me wanting to come here. My intentions of helping the situation might have been an overshot on my part. I thought that in working with you, I might be able to learn more from your situation and in turn help others. That might sound selfish, but it's true."

She was all but out of the thought that she possessed good intentions and had a cause worthy of a fight.

"Honesty is something I can use a dose of. It is not always the best tasting medicine, but it is truly the best for you. I am tired today, but you are welcome to come back for some coffee and a conversation whether it is for work or just honest friendship. I think I will enjoy your company."

The doctor felt a warming in his heart. This was something he had forgotten and hadn't felt in a long time. This breath of fresh youthful spirit felt like purpose to the doctor. He sensed it in her willingness of wanting to help others. He also saw within her, the drive and compassion his wife had expressed throughout their time together. The honesty and integrity that was within this young woman was in such abundance, that it claimed its presence without announcement.

This short encounter with the doctor made a connection that only fate was responsible for. She was someone he could relate to in this time. She was someone he could trust and knew this without having known her. Intuition wasn't something the doctor put much stock in, but when it is experienced, it only becomes apparent. It is not to be questioned, only accepted.

Outside of the fact that she was from African decent, he sensed for a moment that she displayed the characteristics he and his wife had dreamed of in a daughter they never had. She was built with the same inborn need to want to heal.

"You make the call. Whatever works for you Dr. Richards. I can call you, I have your listed number, or you tell me how you would like to meet."

The doctor hadn't been answering his phone lately, so he asked for her contact information.

"I will call you in a couple of days. Depending on the weather, we might go and have lunch somewhere."

She smiled and gave the doctor a friendly hug.

"I would like that very much, do call. I promise to be an ear more than a mouthpiece."

Dr. Richards enjoyed listening, it was something he learned to do as a doctor.

"We'll talk."

With that said, the doctor said goodbye, closed the door, sat back on the couch, and began a cry he was due. Looking around the room his eyes wandered to the letter his wife had written to him which was beside him. He picked it up and read it again for the countless times.

Years ago, we danced to a song called "The Keeper of the Stars." You chose this song for us to celebrate and start a lifetime commitment together. As time has gone by, I have become more aware of Love's

True Meaning. People are not truly "in love" when they enter into a marriage agreement. Love is something we learn as we build our lives around each other, until it becomes us. Couples who grow old together are blessed to experience this in life. I have no doubt that the love we have was set in motion before we met, and that the Almighty's Hand has placed His Blessing upon us. You are not just my husband, companion, mate, and lover. You are my favorite person. God has blessed us with 20 years, and if He is willing, the next 20 will only get better. Thank you for sharing life with me.
   Your Wife
   Melinda

The second 20 never came. He was crushed every time he read it. He was sworn to never forget her, and he felt as though he needed to do something. He would have to make a difference in this society that had changed all that for him. Maybe, this chance encounter with the social worker was it.

With the framed letter clutched to his chest, and tears already having caused his collar to be wet, he gasped. It was no more a time to cry. It was time to move on. He vowed from this point on to make a difference, and it would be in memory of his love. For her he knew no price would be too high.

Chapter Three
An Attempt to Assuage

The summer heat was starting to let up, and the dog days were beginning to be a vision in the rear-view mirror. The climate was becoming more favorable as autumn was coming into its own.

The doctor was laying in his bed taking in the changing conditions to the weather. It was the doctor's favorite time of the year. The temperature was a pleasant warm during the day, and yet nights could sometimes warrant a long sleeve shirt or even a jacket. This was the best of Texas weather, when it was cooperating.

An afternoon underneath the live oaks and a caressing southern breeze was enthralling. Like all things though, this time of the year wasn't without its imperfections. Anyone from the Fort Worth-Dallas area is well aware of the corridor it houses. Tornado Alley, as it is affectionately nicknamed, presents its surprising twists to the fall from time to time. It is like a thorn that lies in the midst of the roses. The weather can go from an absolute picturesque setting to swarthy skies and rolling thunder in just a matter of minutes. Nothing can always be the best. Perfect was something the doctor had come to know didn't really exist. He had learned this lesson under great misfortune. It was just something you are forced to accept in order to enjoy the best parts life has to offer.

Outside of the downfalls, Dr. Richards loved this time of the year. A small storm was even invited for its excitement and special smell it brought prior to the rains.

It reminded him of simpler times during his youth, when he would run about with his brother and cousins playing hide and seek. It was always more exciting if their game was surprisingly interrupted by the "devil beating his wife." His mother use to refer to the rain and sun's presence at the same time, suggested such folklore. To the doctor and his friends, it was elation. They would stay out and play in the rain despite their mother's adamant demands they come inside. This probably added to its excitement. He always felt like she would have enjoyed joining in on their fun, but her apprehensions wouldn't let her step out to enjoy such freedoms.

Some of his mother's traits must have been passed down to him, becoming more apparent since his life's tragedy. He too was a much more apprehensive individual now that life had delivered such a setback.

If only life could be simpler, as it used to be. Back then it seemed as though caring was only used for expressing love and not fear, as fear had no particular role it played in their lives. One didn't have to care about things in the sense of worrying. All was carefree and he cherished his childhood for those reasons. There was nothing he could recall that was bad in his upbringing.

He had many memories that he treasured, dating back to the time prior to his marriage. The life he had made with his wife was more than he could have wished for, but that was in no way to be compared to the time before that. They were both times of plenty. Love was abundant, and one did not think of their protection, as threat never presented itself to anyone.

Memories of yesteryear always brought about a smile. It was all the recollections of the abundance of family, music, food and south Texas produce. He remembered working in the family garden and all the vegetables that were in season during this time. Most of the kids he knew complained about the outdoor chores, but not him. A good work ethic was engrained into him early on. He learned to embrace the gratification earned through labor. He was taught that people who are given everything in life are really being robbed of their ability to appreciate. He also enjoyed the rewards of his labors, the vegetables they grew.

His father, Joseph Sr. had come up in a humble household that lived by the code of hard work. He made sure and raised his boys to not just know this way, but to value it as well. Reflecting brought about soothing sentiment. He thought about the bounty that was gathered and the food his parents prepared. Food, drink, family, and celebration was what life seemed to be lived for. It was the season of imbibing.

Hand in hand with the harvest was the cookout. This was the time of the year that people began to fire up their grills. Sometimes he would catch the sweet aroma of his neighbors lighting their pit and was reminded of those times. His recollection of his parents outdoor cooking was priceless.

It had been a while since the doctor had participated in that past time. He enjoyed all aspects about cooking outdoors. It was a tradition he had inherited many years ago. His thoughts about this time of the year and how it had seemed that some kind of event was being celebrated every weekend with a barbeque was set to truth as he became older. The truth was that family was the only excuse needed to gather and cook outside. Family was the secret to being special. The doctor needed that feeling again. There was nothing like searing food over an open flame and indulging on a cold beverage as the sun sets on a Lone Star horizon.

In his moment of pause he gave credit to those significant days of his youth. They helped the doctor have a flash of clarity. Reflections on our past sometimes helps us to understand our future. It can give one a sense of direction with regard to the path they want to take. This reflecting was therapeutic to the doctor.

This kind of thinking seemed to be helping with his healing process. It wouldn't serve to be everything, but it was helping with his healing.

His reflections made him yearn for the corruption in the world to be forced to know what was right. It was something, he felt, had to be attempted. Not knowing how, he was determined in making a difference in the damaged civility he saw everywhere. It would only work by creating a balance between mercy and discipline. He would somehow have to concentrate serenity and position it as a corner stone to this scale. Nothing, not even good intentions, should be allowed to compromise its weighing. His assorted emotions were finding this thought process challenging.

As the doctor considered these things, he looked at the clock. It was 4:47am on Sunday morning. He had woken up earlier than he wanted. His body clock was set automatically, and he had been waking up early.

There was not an issue about him not getting enough rest. He was just managing life with less sleep. His body seemed to be adapting to it.

He enjoyed waking up for a morning cup of coffee, as it had been a ritual with he and his wife for years. Back then, their days had been congested with work and it was the only time they could truly dedicate to each other without excuse. Of course, early to them was earlier than most. Mornings just hadn't been the same without her.

As he sat still lying in bed, he just enjoyed thinking about the time of the year and how much he favored it. He wanted his morning cup of ambition but waited instead of getting up, as he knew the pot was set to automatically come on at 5:00am. This morning, he was content to wait and think about simpler times. It was an exercise for him to focus on better thoughts, and possibly a brighter future.

Within reaching distance from him, was the piece of paper with Denise Wilson's contact information. He had called her previously and had brief conversations with her to continue their relationship.

Most of their conversations had been casual with each occasionally revealing some of their personal life to the other. They hadn't discussed anything too in-depth but began expressing themselves more and developing a fondness for one another. It was becoming a narrative towards a friendship more than a case. There was something about her he enjoyed that helped him escape his agony. He felt the need to keep in touch with her.

Her contact information had been set on the nightstand as a reminder to continue to call her, although he seemed to think about her often. He wondered if she was up. *Perhaps it was too early*, he thought. He was pretty sure she drank coffee, but maybe not at this time. She was too young to be up at this hour. Young folks stay up late. He was anticipating calling her as he wondered if she might want to come over today.

It was Sunday, and the forecast was sunshine in the low 80's. It would be good for the doctor to entertain someone. His thoughts about cooking out were not in vain, as he immediately surmised cooking steaks outside, upon her availability.

His taste was particular. He was partial to prime cut ribeye steak, preferably aged from the Town Square Market, where he had been frequenting for many years now. He began to plan the day, unsure if she would be able to come over. It would be splendid. It was football season and the 3:30pm game could be a background to their conversation.

Dr. Richards was impressed with the young girl's representation of her job. The doctor had much of an interest in Denise's work and thought it might be a good outlet to possibly become involved with. He could volunteer in the programs she administered. His interest of contributing in any way was also going to offer him a small portion of resolve. Assisting with others healing might allow him to figure things out about his own healing. Of course, the conversation would have to take place and an opportunity present itself for planting such an idea.

Not knowing if that was today, he would still try and set things up. Whether she was coming or not, he decided to get up and after coffee he would clean up and head out the door. He was going to enjoy the day as he did in his youth, outside. If she could make it, that would be great.

It was about 9:45am, and the doctor had gotten back from his errands. He had two inch and a half cut ribeye steaks, sitting on the countertop acclimating to room temperature. At the market he picked up some heirloom tomatoes and zucchini squash. The steaks and the squash were for the grill. The tomatoes he would thick slice and allow them to marry with salt in the fridge. Ice cold beer in a longneck was his choice of drink. He preferred nothing produced by a brew master, just cold and simple. It was how he always liked it. Possibly memories of his Nana liking it was what had made it a fond memory to him.

A twelve pack was in the cooler surrounded by crushed ice. He liked crushed ice because when you took one out it left a hole and the ice standing in place. A bit particular perhaps, but this meant cold. It was just the way it seemed best. Everything was in place the way the doctor wanted it.

He was thinking of what he would say when he called up Denise. There was no hesitation about calling her. He knew from their many conversations that she wanted to see him again. His anxious spirit wanted to spend the day with her. He picked up the phone and dialed her number.

"Hello" she spoke as though the caller ID let her know who was calling.

"Well, how are you Denise? This is Dr. Richards." It was good to hear her voice.

She responded with an alluring tone. Her personality was catching.

"Hello doctor, what a pleasant surprise. You called me at a good time. I just got back from my run." She was physically fit, so it made since to the doctor that she was a runner.

"That's good. You know I used to run. It was a habit I developed when I was a younger man. Of course, it took a back seat when Melinda passed, but I've been telling myself I need to get back in the routine of running now that I have the time." The doctor was being sincere.

Most people might say things for the sake of conversation, but not the doctor. He was thinking of things to help with the structure of his life. He knew running was an excellent way to maintain a discipline in one's life.

"I would love to have you join me. I run in the mornings at 6:00am on Mondays, Wednesdays, and Fridays. I am able to do that before I go to work. Sundays are a little more relaxed. I go for a leisure run after I get up, no pressure, it's a little more my style. But if you want to join me, you are welcome to do so on any of those days." She had a way of speaking that was inviting. That was why the doctor gravitated to her.

"I'll let you know when I'm ready." He said with intention, but his sights were set on the day at hand. "I was actually calling to find out your plans for today. If you weren't doing anything, I thought you might like to get together and extend our conversations we have been having." The times they had spoken before were pleasant to the doctor, but he desired more. Now he could have an afternoon dedicated to getting to know her better.

"Well, I need to clean up and change. Would you like to meet up for lunch somewhere?" she asked.

"As a matter of fact, yes. I was thinking we could get together at my house. I don't want you to presume me being forward with this invitation. My wife still holds my heart, but as we have been talking, I sense a quality in you that has attracted me to who you are and to what you do. I have reserved myself from much talk with others but feel I can enjoy hearing from you. I have planned out the day. So, if you say yes all that is left to get is your company."

Honesty was always the best policy. His interest in her was in every way platonic. He was leaning on the possibilities that she might fill a void of him never having had a child. He would like to see a relationship develop between them that would share in their desire to help others.

"Doctor, I know where your heart is. I know it belongs to your wife still and I understand what you are saying. I feel that same connection. Today sounds great. I can be over in a couple of hours, around noon. I hope you're a good cook, because Sundays are my day I allow myself to eat more than normal." Denise lightened the conversation with a laugh.

"I won't disappoint you. We can enjoy some steaks on my patio. I look forward to seeing you. Take care." The warm laugh eased his response.

"Good bye." And they hung up.

After prepping the vegetables, the doctor went out back to get a fire started to allow for the wood to make coals. It was a little early for him to start drinking, but he decided on a beer as he enjoyed the smell of the wood burning. He wasn't anyone given to drunkenness, so having one at this time wasn't a threat, just a treat. After lighting the pit, he sat down in his lawn chair. It was perfect. The sun hadn't reached full capacity and there was a bit of a breeze. He could hear a neighbor in the distance mowing the lawn. His fire was burning peacefully. The beer was cold and satisfying, and he was about to have an afternoon with someone that would soon have an impact in his life, one that he needed.

As noon approached the sound of the mowing in the background had ceased and the doctor's outdoor patio radio was playing. It was strictly seventies. Easy listening music would occupy the yard. This was the music that was about feeling good and enjoying life, something the doctor needed to start doing again.

His eyes had been caught by two squirrels playing in the trees. He chuckled within himself as the squirrels seemed to be engaged as a concerned married couple. He began remembering past conversations he had with his wife and imagined the two squirrels were acting in their place. It was kind of cute. The bantering between the two was a classic Honeymooners episode. The more they interacted it seemed they were teasing each other. The more he watched them he remembered his lost love. His wife just couldn't escape his mind in anything.

As his attention was embraced to their courtship it became interrupted by the doorbell. At last, she had finally arrived. The doctor drew his attention away from the two entertainers, got out of his chair and walked into the house. The backdoor had remained open the entire time he was out back. The weather was permissive for him to allow that. It gave an inviting, homely backyard feeling to the patio area when the house was open.

As he opened the front door, there stood Denise. A sight for the old, tired eyes that had spent some time in his chair drifting in make believe. She was dressed for a casual day yet looked good enough to go out. Suited out in capris, a spaghetti strap camisole, and sandals she was something to look at. She looked just how you would want to see your grown daughter dressed, pretty but not provocative.

"Well, I'm glad you came. I hope you like football. You know, the boys are at home today?" The doctor did like football but would rather spend the time learning more about Denise.

"Are you kidding, I grew up in a football family. Five boys and me. I used to play tackle with all of my brothers until they became too big and strong that they refused to let me play anymore. Although it was probably because of my father's warning about what would happen if they hurt me. I never let them know I knew that, though. I was always my daddy's girl. He wouldn't let anything happen to me. I just played along that they were afraid of me showing them up." Denise's expressions as she talked showed she had a deep love for her family.

"Sounds like you had a good upbringing." The doctor could see her appreciations for them.

"I did. I sure liked those days. It was always fun with my family growing up. We are all grown now, and I can honestly say I was blessed. My brothers have always been good to me, and since my father's passing, they have all stepped into that role in one way or another. I guess I should have been in charge being the oldest, but the men in our family tend to want to take care of their women." She conveyed her story in a way of transcending the true meaning of life.

She had a way of making the doctor feel good. It could almost create envy for someone else to hear her talk. She was full of all the goodness in life. You could tell her story was given with absolute respect for her family, and she learned the importance of giving it as well as receiving it.

"Well, where are my manners? Come in and let me show you around and then we can go out back and enjoy the yard."

They started slowly through the home, stopping and talking as they moved along. He enjoyed showing her his home. It was one of his humble prizes he always adored. He and his wife had remodeled the home that was originally built in the 1930's. Stained wood as far as the eye could see set the tone of his class and masculinity.

They walked about the house and he showed her the work that had been done throughout the years, but continually would stop at a picture on the wall, or a table, or on the mantle of himself and his wife. He would tell a story of that moment as if it had just happened, not escaping one detail. He was sharing with her all he had ever been.

Denise was an excellent listener. Although it had been well learned with her profession, she was captivated and moved by the doctor's zeal for the life he once had. It was allowing her to adore his character and realize how genuine of a man he really was. They eventually meandered to the back patio.

"Well, can I get you something to drink?" The doctor had been going on endlessly and was thirsty himself. "I have beer, or would you rather something else?" He wasn't sure if she drank or not.

"Do you have any wine?" She answered his question with her own.

He had some wine that hadn't been touched since his wife's passing. Wine to the doctor was good, but never a true passion as it had been to Melinda.

"As a matter of fact, I do. Are you a fan of Merlot?" The doctor had almost a full case.

"I love merlot," she said a bit excited.

"Well let me get you some to try." He got up to get her a bottle and a glass. Not that either one of them needed to be loosed for conversation, but now the party could begin.

The evening progressed with talk of each other's loved ones. They talked right through the football game, every once and a while commenting on a play or the score. As his grill had continued burning mostly for the ambience, he finally found the time to cook their food.

Dinner was continued conversation and the meal he had promised her. Denise was having a wonderful time as well as the doctor. The more they talked about their lives the doctor seemed to feel a greater connection between them. This sparked an interest in the doctor about her work. He knew she wasn't making a great deal of money but had managed to find a happiness in life that superseded that. He wanted to have that sort of happiness himself. It had the sound of an opportunity. Could this curiosity offer a possibility to becoming involved again in a work as gratifying as the medical field had been to him?

He wondered if there was something there for him. He thought about the good work he and his wife had done through their tenure together and was now looking to start a new chapter.

As the day was approaching its end and the doctor knew it was about time to wrap up this event, he asked her the question that had been piercing his interest for some time during the evening.

"Denise, as I listen to you and hear exactly what you do on a daily basis, I wonder if I could perhaps experience it with you, some of your appointments." The doctor knew that this was a shot in the dark, but he found himself attracted to the idea of working with her. "I would not interfere with your work. I would be there to strictly sit in as an observer. I would be willing to discuss my thoughts of the situation with you as it pertains to my experiences with what I have been through. It might be useful for you, or those going through rough situations. I know it will be therapeutic for me." The doctor was as honest with her as he could be. He knew it might not be an accepted idea, but he offered it anyway.

"Now that's an interesting thought. You know, you might be on to something. I can't say yes. I would have to get approval from my superiors." Denise knew this was above her signatory level, but none the less saw a certain potential with his offer. "They might want to vet you a bit before, but I will ask. I would love to work with you. You know, spending this day with you has shown me you have a lot more to offer in the way of wisdom. Much of what you say has been learned from long roads and comes with much thought. I don't think you are through with all your healing, but your constitution is so iron clad that your composure doesn't seem penetrable. As far as I can tell, you would be an asset. I'm all for it."

Denise had been able and allowed to see a side of the doctor that had been shut off for some time. It would be for both of their edification to have it exposed again. The conversation began to slow as the sun had already set. They both seemed to like the vision of working together. It was something they both saw as profitable.

"Can I help you clean up?" Denise didn't want to leave without helping.

"No, I can manage, besides I need something to do as I won't go to sleep early." The doctor enjoyed staying busy.

"Well, if you are good, I need to be running now, tomorrow I'm up early. You have my number. Call me anytime. I will get back with you after I speak with my boss." With a slow walk to the front door and a few more goodbyes, they parted, with anticipation of seeing each other again.

The doctor was finally becoming a functioning person once more. He hadn't felt the desire to be social in a long time, and now if everything worked out, he could do it on a more productive level.

Becoming a social worker was something he never would have considered up until this time. Helping others was key to finding peace. This would be a chance at a new beginning.

Chapter Four
A New Work

Dr. Richards' phone rang. It was a little after 9:00 am on Monday morning.

"Hey Joey." The doctor knew it was his brother. No one ever called him Joey, not even his parents in his youth. Everyone referred to him as Joseph or Dr. His brother was the only one ever given that pass.

"Hello Matthew, what can I do for you?" The doctor was always more formal with names, even in his family.

"I just wanted to check on you, see how you are doing, if you needed anything."

"No Matthew, I'm alright. Thanks for calling. I've been going through a lot of thoughts about many things."

"Well, relax Joey, you've been through a lot and stressing ain't gonna do you any good."

"Actually, I am feeling a lot better. I have been considering the idea of a new work that I believe is going to help me tremendously. It might not sound that good, but it is social work. I am thinking about assisting people that have become victims of crimes and it might help me to work out some of my problems. I have been talking with one of the social workers that was sent to check on me, and she has sparked a big interest in me." There was an uncomfortable pause for a second. Dr. Richard's was aware of the expected response from his brother.

His brother, the younger of the two, had lived a life less disciplined than Dr. Richards. It was no less privileged, though. He lived as a successful real estate broker and had managed to have an office with over 20 employees servicing the real estate needs of the Dallas/ Fort Worth area. He also was over spoken and extremely opinionated. The doctor loved his brother but was never someone he could really relate to.

"Are you sure that is such a good idea? If you go and get yourself involved with other people's problems, you are just going to create more problems for yourself." Dr. Richard's knew his well-intentioned brother's heart, but just didn't feel like arguing with him.

"Matthew, I'm not saying I am going to do this for sure, I'm just thinking about it." The doctor's intentions were more than just an inclination. "Maybe you're right, I just want to check things out."

"Well, don't go get involved with something that could cause you more problems than it is really worth."

"I won't. How's Karen?" The doctor wanted to switch the subject right away. He knew his brother would switch gears right along with him. He just needed a chance to throw in a different subject.

"She's good. She's visiting her sister in Houston for a week. I thought maybe we could go out for dinner or drinks sometime this week. Maybe help make things a little more normal."

The two talked for a while about getting together and gave a few laughs towards the conversation as it would remain short.

"Sounds good. Call me towards the end of the week, Thursday or Friday would probably work for me." The doctor expected Denise to get back to him before that.

"Sounds good Joey. I miss you. When Karen gets back, I'll have her cook something good and you can come over. Little Julie is in cheerleading this year and Matt is playing football. They will be glad to see their uncle. I'll call you later this week."

"Thanks for calling Matthew. Talk to you soon."

"Not if I see you first Joey, bye." With that the doctor hung the phone up.

The two brothers loved one another, but never really expressed it in their conversations. Dr. Richards was fond of his brother and his family. They just had a relationship that never allowed each other to truly know the other. Other than a few cousins that he didn't really communicate with, Matthew was all the family he had. Melinda had always been his everything. She had been an only child and with her parents both being gone, there was no one on her side he spoke with. His brother didn't come close to filling in any void that he might be feeling since the loss of his wife. This was one of the reasons he was attracted to working with Denise. She managed to manifest that type of feeling within the doctor. He would wait to see what she would find out.

The doctor wasn't forcing anyone in or excluding anyone from coming into his circle. He believed all things happened for a reason and his encounter with Denise was no accidental chance meeting by any means. It was something that was meant to be, as far as he could see.

Denise's schedule had been busy, causing her and the doctor's request to take a secondary position. She made sure her boss had the chance to hear her proposal, knowing she wouldn't get an immediate response. This was fine with her as she could take her time to make a subtle sale of it. She introduced the idea and left it alone, allowing them time to look at it. She wanted everyone to see it for what it meant to her, a worthy endeavor. Honesty had always been her only means to accomplishing anything, and she knew this was something the doctor possessed.

His credentials academically weren't in question, however his situation with losing his wife was the delicate issue. Denise knew this would be the concern of her boss. She believed in the doctor for his genuine compassion. She knew he strived to see all things good and for that reason she would do her best to sell their plan. She also knew he was in it truly for the work itself, as he had let her know, he would be working voluntarily.

Money wasn't of any concern to the doctor. He was there to help and make a difference. She wasn't aware of this type of arrangement ever having been proposed or even approved. The people they encountered were usually in sensitive situations and disrupting that was something they would want to avoid. Some of those situations involved people of questionable character. If not thought out properly, things could get out of hand and that would be devastating for the entire department.

Denise's supervisors and the Tarrant County Sheriff's Office were well aware of who the doctor was and his accreditations within the community. Their knowledge of who the doctor was went back in history, prior to his wife's slaying. As a doctor in the ER, he was well respected and adored for his many years of service. The entire department wept for him when they heard of his tragedy. That still didn't make granting this request automatic. Much consideration would go into determining this.

It took a few weeks, but finally enough conversations gave way to an interview and the doctor was called in. It would serve the department to get a real feel for the doctor now that he had experienced a hard trauma. Denise and the doctor had continued their relationship during this time, and she made him aware of this.

They invited him to come in and meet the staff Denise worked with. Along with her supervisors, they sat down for a meeting. Initially it appeared to be more informal than one would expect. Everyone, knowing who the doctor was, stepped up to shake his hand and gave him a comforting greeting. The doctor took to their warm welcome as best he could, but knew he was there to have his character examined.

He thought the process would have been more deliberate. It would seem logical when considering the ability of someone to participate in these programs that scrutiny would answer the door. That thought slowly faded and he realized he was just apprehensive about the whole matter. It was friendly and casual. Conversation was open and complete. The ice didn't break, rather it just melted.

Denise talked of him wanting to participate in programs offered out of her office, particularly pre-intervention/ child protective services. The appeal for his involvement sounded more like her request with the way she presented it. It was preached as an asset of a wise man, who could aid Denise in many ways. It was also brought up that she originally pursued him as someone in need of assistance, and that this might help him as well. Everyone was sympathetic towards his situation and the conversation was set to create a relaxed atmosphere.

Some of the discussion was spent asking the doctor about how he now viewed different classes of society, since he had been affected by a criminal element. He was asked his views on the justice system, and if he felt as if it were effective. This had to be asked as they worked hand in hand with the justice system. He answered them as truthful as he could. It probably wasn't a perfect score, as the doctor had reservations about justice, but none the less, he didn't sugar coat the matter.

He expounded on the fact that society had lost touch with true justice and had succumbed to a system of excuses. He also told them the main ingredient lacking in the American home today was love. He wanted to help put a little of that back in where it belonged. He would do this with Denise and pure determination of heart. One thing he valued more than most men was his integrity, and he let them know this. He let them know that it was this foundation of integrity that was missing in most people today.

"If it were different, most men would respect others because they would simply respect themselves." Many of the statements he made had the team realizing his character was solid. It was obvious that his standards were of extreme value to him. It was his core and foundation.

Through the conversation all ears knew it was in his heart to want to make a difference, and after some discussion, enough people saw this as a potentially good opportunity.

The doctor and Denise were fortunate in becoming the ones to successfully launch a volunteering program in the County for at-risk subjects. Some might have had lingering thoughts about possible failures due to the doctor's circumstances, but only those who are willing to risk can receive reward. It doesn't come by being stagnant, and that became the consensus. Approval was given, and the doctor would begin working alongside Denise.

Starting out, he would be an observer. He would take notes and become familiar with the cases. He would be joining Denise on a selected case she was already involved in. It was important that the ones they were working with remain in a stable condition. Adding a variable, such as the doctor, to their environment could produce unwanted results. This would place an importance on who they thought to introduce the doctor to.

Exchanges with other counselors within the department were also a part of the program, to monitor the state of mind of those dealing with these situations. This was common practice for all case workers. Checking everyone out was an insurance to the well-being of the whole effort. The whole process was set up to help others, and in so doing that, the entire team must remain healthy.

He was looking forward to the experience, even with the various challenges he knew it might pose. He knew he would be seeing people who were sometimes living in impoverished conditions. He would come across families plagued with abuses of all kinds. He understood he might be witness to victims that are mistreated by people such as the man who murdered his wife. Despite what he felt, he believed his desire for good would outweigh any evil he might witness through any of the situations. He wanted to help and was willing to do whatever it took. This was his first step towards seeing that his wife didn't die in vain. This would be his tribute to her legacy.

His partnership, working alongside Denise, would be second to none. His confidence in succeeding was based on his belief in his newly found relationship. The commonality he shared with Denise was a hatred of all things immoral. This coupled with the love he always had for his wife would be the drive to making it all a success.

It resonated positive thoughts in his being to know he would make a difference for those who were suffering. He was aware it was not going to be an easy task to help those with this type of need. Healing from the inside was something the doctor had achieved with many of his patients, but no knife or surgical skill could be used in this instance.

This inside to be healed would take patience, listening, care, compassion, and love. The love he would have to exhibit would have to be strong and sometimes detested by people. It would be a challenge to help pick these people up. He knew that nothing could be accomplished without building up, and sometimes before any edification process takes place, certain things need to be taken down. All that is corrupt and confused must be removed for sanity to reside. When those walls are torn down, and façade has no place, people can be real, and construction can begin. In extreme cases it might call for demolishing all of what is there. This would be the key ingredient for making the difference between progress and success. So, as it was, the doctor couldn't wait.

It was the beginning of a new week, and the doctor was leaving the house to make a new start. A drive down Main Street had him heading towards Denise's office for a briefing of a family. The subject was a thirteen-year-old boy who had seen the abuses of society his entire life. The doctor would need to learn about the dynamics of his family before meeting them for the first time. His eagerness had him arriving to the office thirty minutes early. He was excited for this new chapter.

He pulled over to pick up some coffee for himself and his new partner. He would need the added caffeine, he thought, to not miss any details. He wanted to make his first day on the job a benchmark, and from there hold to a standard. Not missing anything was a must.

He arrived just a few blocks from downtown, close to where she worked. When he walked in, he was greeted with many hellos. His coming into the office must have been known to the entire staff. There wasn't a single person who didn't acknowledge him. To some it might have been too much, like an over welcoming. The doctor invited it as a sense of belonging.

"Good morning doctor." Denise came around the corner smiling with her morning brilliance.

"Morning, I brought you a coffee." Dr. Richards was happy about getting started.

"Thank you, I was about to get some in the break room, but yours looks a little fancier. You are a little early, but we can go in my office and start going over my files on the young man we are going to meet. His name is Dillion Myers."

Denise and the doctor went into her office. It smelled like her perfume. Everything was in its place. This already impressed the doctor as he liked a clean workspace. She opened her computer, pulled out a file and began explaining who this boy was and what they would be doing on the doctor's first call.

Dillion was a troubled youth whose dysfunctional childhood had him shifted amongst family and foster care his whole life. He was considered high risk, meaning the propensity of pursuing a life of crime was almost guaranteed if he remained without any assistance. The bouncing from homes and certain family situations warranted Denise's department to become involved in Dillion's life.

Denise's education entitled her to work with children, which was one of her passions. She had been working with him for the past year, since he had been returned to his family. He was currently living with his grandmother and three younger siblings.

Trials had begun with Dillion at birth. His mother was an addict when he was born. He was immediately removed from her custody just after being born. Shortly thereafter, he was placed in foster care, as his mother was facing time.

Denise had a few choice words to express her thoughts about his mother.

"She is a piece of work. I don't make it a practice to hate people, but she is the closest I think I have come to feeling that way." The look on her face changed to a look of disgust as she mentioned Stacy.

"Is she some sort of drug addict?"

"That is just a tip of the iceberg. There is so much she is involved in; I'll get to that at another time." She continued explaining Dillion's situation and as she talked about his mother, it brought about anger inside of her.

She explained that through the years his grandparents would have him from time to time. They wanted to do all they could for their family, but just weren't able to. The task was too overwhelming for them. It seemed impossible for them to raise him with a total of ten grandchildren they tried to be responsible for. Their household had been a swinging door for their children's irresponsibility since they started having kids. None of their children were worth the effort it took to make them. They multiplied their parent's misery by making children and not caring for them. It was a cycle of corruption that breeds to no end. With some hope, this would be a stopping point for some of it. If they could start with Dillion, they might be able to make good out of the rest of them.

Dillion was the oldest out of all the grandchildren and had a huge challenge facing him in life. Outside of his family, everyone knew who they were. Most people he dealt with already decided for themselves they were all degenerates. It was a curse he was born into.

Education hadn't been that much forgiving either. He attended school in an alternate program as he needed special attention and had gotten into some trouble at school. He hadn't committed any crimes and had a clean record. Keeping his record clean was a primary focus. Once a person starts committing to a criminal mind, it only becomes easier for them to repeat as they enter a system they become familiar with. Soon they learn to embrace it as it accepts its own and owns what is accepting of it. Keeping him from making dire decisions would help him to preserve any decent character he may possess.

The school system saw so many problems that they didn't have time to address him properly. They focused on the children who were there to learn. It was standard practice to ship the bad kids through and let the law deal with them when they get out in society. This was done in part because discipline had long since been stripped from the teacher's hands. Most of the school faculty felt too underpaid to deal with other people's problems.

His attitude was challenging, probably acting out due to the stress, embarrassment, pressure, and hate that had been collected in his heart. It would become the task of stripping him down to the bareness of his innocence. Making him define as just a young boy wanting love in his life. He had never learned that, and if it were to come his way, he probably would have a hard time recognizing it. His guards were high, and he didn't like looking over them.

Many thoughts raced through the doctor's mind. Pity encompassed the majority. He had never lived with a lack of love in his life. The first time he experienced a loss of love was during the death of his parents, but he had his wife to help him through those days. The death of his wife had been a whole new challenge. Other than that, everyone he had in his life had only displayed what the doctor had considered a natural expression of their own brand of love. He couldn't imagine anyone not having this in their life.

Denise picked up some papers and looked at the doctor.

"Well, I hope that you don't have reservations about Dillion. He probably won't talk much. He usually just answers with no or yes. I will attempt to get him to speak up, but it is likely he won't say much. Well, let's go." The doctor got up, and with all that he had consumed on the life of this boy, he felt great pity.

"I want this boy to get what he needs. It is a shame that the world can be so cold. Denise, I know you already know this, but this situation needs to be handled with care."

"You are right, doctor. I'm hoping with you, we are able to make that difference. Let's go." With that they both walked out of her office and headed downstairs to the parking lot to go meet his first appointment.

Chapter Five
A Broken Home, a Broken Soul

The visit with Dillion had proven to the doctor that this undertaking would provide challenges of epic proportions. As gratifying as success can be through various trials, it also carries with it great risk. If they didn't handle this young man properly, they could contribute to his failure. Getting close with someone that has a potential to become destroyed, whether by someone else or self-inflicted, is always dangerous. Disappointment is just a word used commonly. It doesn't give due justice to all the emotions that can establish themselves inside of a failed attempt to heal.

Dillion's family structure would prove to be the biggest hurdle in his recovery. His mother, who had been stripped of all parental rights, still popped into her mother's house from time to time, when not incarcerated. This was probably the largest obstacle in Dillion's road to success.

Just like any child, they will love and want their parents no matter the condition or behavior they possess. This was the enigma corrupting this young impressionable mind. The system knew a total separation from her would be the best-case scenario, but legally she had the right to show up to her mother's house and carry about her business.

Mrs. Metzner, Dillion's grandmother, had been advised to keep her away, but being old and tired, her better judgement was generally trampled on by her own family.

Dillion's mother spent her time prostituting herself to fuel her addiction for drug use. She was much younger than she looked, only in her early thirties. Her passion for selling herself had little to do with men. She had forgotten how to love. She was in it to get high. Her faithfulness to drugs wasn't even that loyal of a commitment. She owed no particular drug any type of a devotion. It was whatever she could get, she did it. It was an escape from reality, looking to find a love she would never be able to recognize.

Dillion was torn between having a mother he loved and hating her lifestyle with a passion. His emotions were beginning to manifest themselves in his interactions towards others at school and home life. The need to keep him from making a life-changing mistake was the primary focus.

The anger released by Dillion was unstable but had not exploded to a crossing of the Rubicon. The criticality of saving him was at a high level. He was entrenched in a system that he had already begun to imitate.

This being the first assignment of the doctor's, he put effort into this with the determination of his achievements back in grad school. He would take notes about the discussions he would have with Denise and bring them back to his house for examination. He would research the subject of child behavior. He had purchased a couple of books written by renowned doctors on the subject, so not to be presumptuous he knew all there was to know about the topic.

That first meeting had set precedence in the doctor's mind about the challenges he faced. He kept going over the conversations Denise and Dillion had in front of him. He kept remembering how long it took for Dillion to talk, but when he did, anger camouflaged in excuses was all the little boy had harbored inside of himself.

"Dillion, what seems to be the problem? Why don't you want to talk with us?" Denise had been inquiring about a few incidents that the school had reported about his behavior in the past week. The doctor recalled Dillion's objection to his presence.

"Who is he, and why does he need to be here?" Dillion spoke without respect and seemed a bit embarrassed.

"I told you; this is Dr. Richards, he is here as an assistant to me. He is new in our department, and he will be working with me. I think if you give him a chance, he might be able to help. His reasons for being here are quite noble. I think we might be able to all help one another, if we try." Denise's voice had a sense of pleading inside of it. The doctor knew that Dillion had much of a shell that would need deconstructing.

"Well, let him go help someone else. He is a doctor. He doesn't know anything about my life. What kind of struggles has he ever had to deal with? I'm sure he has everything he could ever want, a fancy house, fancy car, lots of money. Why don't you just go home to your wife!" Denise looked quickly at the doctor for his reaction to the innocent mention of his wife.

The doctor remembered having a cold chill run up his spine and wanting to put the thirteen-year-old over his lap and wail on his backside until his arm tired out. Deep breaths and pause helped provide him some clarity. He slowed down and allowed himself to think. Rushing to reaction spurred by volatile emotions isn't a good choice. Denise looked at the doctor and saw he was contained, then focused on Dillion.

"You know, you speak words you know nothing about. Your world is not occupied by you alone. If you want things to get better, you must make the first move to make them better. I'm sure you don't want to continue on the road you're on. This is done by treating those around you in a compassionate and caring manner, no matter the circumstances, even yours. The words you just spoke were selfish and inconsiderate, even in your ignorance. This man has ridden a road of torment you know nothing about. He has been wronged by society and wants to make a difference, starting with the troubled youth such as yourself. His time is valuable, so if you don't want him here, we will put him somewhere he can be productive and appreciated."

Denise's words were harsh and truthful, yet showed she still was sympathetic to Dillion.

"It's up to you, say the words and he is gone." Dillion remained quiet with his head looking down at the ground. He only knew how to look tough, but inside was a shattered soul. Denise stuck her hand out and rubbed on Dillion's shoulder. "I want to help you. That is why I brought the doctor." Dillion's head stayed facing the floor, and Denise knew he wasn't about to raise it as she could see tears falling from it.

The pressures of Dillion's life were overwhelming for a young teenager. They caused him to lash out at everything, with no optimism of things ever changing. He was broken and had to be fixed and now was the time. This conversation showed everyone Dillion's weakness. The doctor knew they could get to the boy, as this breaking down of these walls was apparent.

The meeting continued and seemed to measure some small success with Denise asking questions and receiving answers that were short and to the point. They couldn't expect Dillion to fully open, but he showed to be a bit more comfortable and that was what they were aiming for. The doctor took notes and remained quiet for the entire meeting other than their initial greeting. As the meeting came to a close, Denise spoke.

"Dillion remember that we are here because we care about you. I want to see you become more than myself. If you do well with your life, you can help others with theirs. It is a process that continues when applied correctly." The doctor recalled Denise's words comforting Dillion with hope. He also gave credit to Dillion's character with what he said to him.

"Doctor, I am sorry for being rude. I don't know who you are, and I still don't. I don't want people getting involved in my life, but if you are Denise's new co-worker, I guess we will be seeing more of each other, so I'm sorry."

From that point on, the doctor set his sights on fixing Dillion. This would be his first assignment of healing someone since leaving his practice years ago. It would take a long time and much dedication.

Patience would be the virtue the doctor would need to internalize. Especially with the negative forces he would be battling in this boy's life.

The one thing that was leaving disgust in the doctor's gut that he couldn't remove was what his eyes were privileged to see, that fateful day, as they left Dillion's grandmother's house. His mother had showed up for a pop-in visit, or to ask her mother for some money. Whatever the reason, it was for herself.

She had pulled up to the house as Denise and the doctor had already gotten into their car. Denise had the car running and was jotting down a few notes as she and the doctor were talking. When Dillion's mother got off the car, the driver, a shady character, stayed behind the wheel with the engine running. There was no intention of an extended stay.

At first glance, she appeared to be trash, but one might be able to see that at one time she was probably an attractive girl. Those days had long since faded into the rear-view mirror. She didn't appear to be clean in any sort of way. It was as if she had been partying all night and was ready to continue.

The doctor had been attempting to customize his attitude to feel compassion for those in these dire situations. This one somehow seemed to escape his mercy. He only saw selfishness in her being.

After the talk and torment he had witnessed inside of her young boy's heart, he remembered he felt utter contempt for this woman.

This was the true battle Dr. Richards knew he was up against. How does one show mercy to someone like that? His internal struggles containing the death of his wife, forgiveness, mercy, rehabilitation, and love would eventually prove to be the biggest challenge the doctor would ever have to face.

Any conflicting thoughts that might have emerged that day were quickly dissolved by Denise as the doctor saw her shift her focus to him when they reached the office. She knew he had heard words that could have hurt him inside. She knew he was a mature individual, capable of handling a lot, but the mentioning of his wife might be a trigger of anguish. The therapy continued, not seeming formatted or part of any program. It was genuine and concerned, like an extension of a hand.

By this time Denise and the doctor had developed a close relationship. She knew the doctor didn't have much interaction with anyone else and wanted to be dedicated to this work. It was his commitment to his wife.

"Well, what do you think? Was it rougher than you expected?" He remembered how Denise spoke, with her hand extended, holding the top of his hand. "Sometimes people say things they know nothing about. Sometimes you must see conditions that repulse your wanting to care. I know today wasn't easy and if you need to give it a break, I understand. I will say this, staying the course long enough to see positive change makes it worth it all." Denise's positive outlook was everything the doctor could live for. The doctor took his other hand and placed it over Denise's hand and said words he was compelled to say.

"I don't think it is by chance we met. Yes, I want to make a difference. I want to leave good in the path of evil. I want to aid in making the crooked, straight. I want to do this as an honor to my wife's slaying. I feel it is my calling. I also have selfish reasons for my actions. You have filled a void in my life that I don't want to replace. I take nothing away from you and your family, but if I ever had a child, I couldn't imagine them not being you. You have brought me much comfort and peace." He remembered thinking how did he ever get those words out without crying, but in fact he did. His concentration was firm. Every word he said rose from his marrow.

He believed in their relationship outside of their work. She was more than his therapy, she was someone he loved. Denise was the one taken back by the doctor's word. He continued speaking as she seemed to be at a loss of words.

"I am sorry for making you cry, but you are growing on me in a big way." The doctor let her know how he truly felt.

"No need to say you're sorry. I understand and feel privileged to not just work with you, but to have your enduring respect and love as well." Denise couldn't get the words out without sobbing but managed to say them anyway.

Their conversation continued in their appreciation of one another but then slowly got back to the subject of Dillion Myers. The mutual fondness they had for one another would prove to be an asset for their steadfastness in seeing a true recovery for him.

That afternoon seemed to gradually fade into the evening. It was one the doctor would remember for the rest of his life. Their continued talks took them past the hour of going home until home began the calling.

"I better let you go." The doctor was the first to suggest it had gotten late. He was ready to retire.

"I thought you were trying to assist me in some overtime," Denise spoke jokingly but was ready to go home. "Call me tomorrow, I have a few things to do early on with another case, but I should be done by 9ish. It is not necessary for you to come in, but we can discuss that mid-morning." The doctor walked Denise to her car and said goodbye.

That put to rest his first day of work in the field. It also sealed a point in his life he never thought to see. From then on, Denise would be to him more than just a co-worker or even a friend. His heart had set apart a special place for her and he would do all to protect it.

That day left Dr. Richard's driving home, clear minded, reflecting on Dillion Myers and what his approach might be. Was it what he had expected it to be? He really didn't know at that point. How can you expect something without knowing what to expect? Life can deal a treacherous hand, but it was never meant to. An emotionally driven choice is sometimes the culprit in life's confusion, with blame and denial declaring it's non-existence.

Dr. Richards believed the Creator didn't complicate things. It was mankind that did. The gift of choice was given as a blessing, so we will be willing to do what is right because we want to choose what is right. When we allow feelings to dictate above what is right, unfortunately, right decisions are not always made, and the result is destruction left in a path of confusion.

The doctor and Denise had the undertaking of helping Dillion see these things for himself. The doctor grappled with why bad choices were made if the result is ruin. The hard truth he would eventually learn was that some just want what is bad. How to deal with these people would establish an answer to a question the doctor never thought he would have to discover.

His mind raced with these thoughts as he drove home that night. When he finally pulled up in the driveway his thoughts focused on food. Not being very hungry, the doctor ate a small amount of cold cuts and finished the day reading a few chapters of a biography he had started a few weeks earlier on Theodore Roosevelt.

This was a man he admired, not just because of his accomplishment and character, but because of the time he lived in. The adventures he pursued were somewhat of an affection to the doctor. The doctor liked reflecting on others, whose accomplishments were noble and worthy of learning. He felt that those who had made good decisions in their lives had much to teach, and that profitable knowledge was a compilation of those many lessons complimenting one another. Here a little, there a little, knowledge grows as we are inspired by words of wisdom. The hard work is putting them into practice.

The words of the book became heavy to the doctor's eyes, and he decided the day was done. He walked to his room, changed into his pajamas, lay in bed and said a prayer.

He thanked his God for everything he had ever had. He asked for understanding and guidance. He asked for forgiveness, not for just the things in his past, but the things he would unwillingly do the next day. He thought about his wife for a moment, and then thought about Denise. He thought about the young boy with all his problems and the broken soul he lived within, and then he thanked God for his sanity.

He rolled off to sleep that night knowing that the next day might become more challenging than the day he just faced, but not facing another day would be accepting life's ceasing and he was willing to live.

Chapter Six
Young Again

After a few scheduled meetings, the doctor's presence became more accepted to Dillion. The progress was slow, but the channels of communication began to open. Through conversations, the doctor could see that positive activities had been omitted out of Dillion's life. For the doctor, making time for recreation was not a much-experienced schedule that he had practiced in his adult life. He and his wife were always driven by purpose and youthful play didn't seem to find its way into their routine.

In his reflection of Dillion, he thought of all the things that were missing in the poor boy's life. Other than the few non-productive activities he pursued, like gaming, he had no one in his life to take him, encourage him, or participate with him in any sort of activity that youth his age should enjoy. While the doctor had done these things under the guides of his parents, he was far removed from his youth and the freedoms it possessed.

What a shame, never being able to apply that kind of environment to one's childhood. It is only received once and has a great impact on who we become. One's early years determine a large part of their expression in adulthood based on what they take in as they grow and mature.

The doctor was inclined to show Dillion what he thought was missing in his life. A day out with he and Denise, at a place where they could all be kids again and one of them for the first time was a pressing thought on the doctor's mind.

He looked online within the metro area, for a place they could spend the day without any cares. Although it was a bit outside of the distance he wanted to travel, he located a family game house possessing all that the imagination could want.

Located an hour away, in a small town, was a family-owned entertainment center. The website showed the place had bowling, movies, arcade, axe throwing and even an obstacle course. The doctor thought this was just the right kind of medicine Dillion needed to get him to become comfortable outside of the shell he hid in.

Thinking of the time to be had, the doctor began to enjoy the thought of he and Denise goofing a bit and having fun. He knew Denise's attitude and saw her reveling in the chance to swing footloose and fancy free for a day. While he enjoyed the thought of he and Denise having fun, the intent was to see some healing in the young boy's mind.

Price was of no concern to the doctor. He would gladly handle all expenses. He just needed to coordinate the day. Sundays would be his preferred day to have an outing and the coming weekend offered promising weather. Would it happen as the doctor envisioned? Was he forecasting liberties he shouldn't? He was just a volunteer, so would proposing this be seen as an overreach? He would never know unless he asked. A quick call to Denise would give him his answer.

"Hello doctor."

"Denise, how are you doing?" He spoke enthusiastically as she answered her phone.

"Doing fine, just doing some paperwork. I figured you would be calling soon since you aren't here at the office." The doctor usually came in but occasionally he would call if he wasn't going to be there.

"Yes, I have been thinking of doing something for Dillion and spent this morning attempting to plan it out." The tone of the doctor's voice was reminiscent of a kid with a surprise to tell.

"Am I involved in the planning? Sounds like fun and I haven't even heard what it is." Denise allowed her concentration to shift from her desk work and totally focus on what the doctor was about to explain.

"Absolutely, I wouldn't think it would be worth doing without you. I would like you, Dillion and I to spend the day at a Family Entertainment Center located about an hour away this coming Sunday."

There was a brief pause as Denise didn't know how to respond.

"Wow, that's a much bigger idea than I expected. Not that I object, just very spontaneous on a short notice."

The doctor began explaining to Denise what it was, how he found it and about the importance of what and why this boy needed something like this.

"Well, that sounds fun. I'm for it, I'll just have to get things lined up with the bosses, but don't think that is going to be a problem."

As Denise listened to the doctor, she was confident that he was the right partner to have. His intellect and care of all things was his driving force. He operated out of love and could control thoughts that might compromise that direction. This was his motive in getting Dillion out.

Denise was finding herself wanting to indulge in the events as he described many of the activities the place had to offer.

"Well, I hope you don't think this is going to be completely owned by him. I want some of this for myself." The doctor chuckled at Denise's response. He could see her as the real kid on the adventure.

"Don't think I'm not going to play a bit with you guys. I think I still have a little youth left in me."

"This sounds like fun doctor. I will see if I can arrange for Dillion to go with us. What time are you thinking?" Denise was planning on approval as she attempted to help with the details.

"I was thinking we could get there at lunch, eat there, then start in on whatever activities you guys want to do."

The doctor was looking forward to following the lead of the both of them. He was expecting Denise to express the fun innocent kid he knew she was and hopefully allow Dillion to discover the one that lived inside of him.

"Sounds great, you know you are the best partner I have ever had." Denise replied.

"You have never had a partner," the doctor responded with a smirk she couldn't see, but knew was on his face.

"I know, but truth be told, I already know this answer would hold true forever. I'll call you with a confirmation. We'll talk later."

Denise hung up and the doctor went back to his online searching. This time he was searching news articles of some of the city's crime stories.

The DFW Area had changed so much during his lifetime there. It saddened the doctor to see the degradation in society that the people seemed to accept. *Times have definitely changed*, he thought. The doctor would go through spells of elation after having spoken with Denise and making plans for Dillion. He would then enter into bouts of anger and realizations of the threats the world played in the lives of such precious souls as this youth. He wrestled with the idea of law vs. lawlessness, mercy vs. enabling and delight vs. disgust. Where would the balance be found to correct all things?

There were too many loopholes allowing for injustices and doing things the right way seemed wrong in many ways. Taking a step back was all he could do sometimes. This thinking process began to be a regular exercise for the doctor.

The day ended without Denise getting back to the doctor. Everyone had enough to keep themselves busy. Scheduling about the coming Sunday preoccupied the doctor and Denise had her share of computer time to knock off. Each of them knew the other was tied up and tending to their own business. It was with all confidence they expected the field trip would most likely take place.

The week passed quickly with the doctor's appearance at the office happening only a few times. His brother had made plans of getting the doctor out to spend time with his family.

Matthew wanted to do this for his brother and thought it might be therapeutic for the doctor. They would spend the day together out on the water. Friday was the opportune day since the kids were out of school and it was forecasted to be excellent weather.

His brother owned a 50-foot yacht, and it resided on a slip at Eagle Mountain Lake. It always proved an enjoyable time whenever he went out with his brother's family. If his brother and sister-in-law knew anything, it was how to have a good time.

They didn't spend the day riding the lake, rather they anchored the boat in an area where anyone could swim, fish, or just enjoy the setting. There was food, drinks, and each other to appreciate. His brother's kids adored their uncle as well as the doctor having an affection for them. However, his mind was occupied by the outing he would be having with his newly acquired subject.

Denise called him earlier in the week letting him know their plans had been accepted and they would be going out with Dillion. His mind seemed to stay saturated with the idea of giving this young boy a day of fun. It occupied much of the doctor's thoughts, even on the trip his brother had planned for them. He didn't have a lack of love for his family, he just knew that Dillion was living in a vulnerable lifestyle and needed his attention more. Looking at the comforts his niece and nephew had, made him realize all the more the susceptible nature of Dillion's life and the need to remedy its defenselessness.

"Joey, wake up, you haven't said much since we've been on the water. It's just me and Karen talking." The doctor's mind had been set on coast as he was digesting how fortunate his brother's family was compared to others. A part of him was reminded of the thought that

Melinda and he never had children. This would come to mind sometimes when others around him were enjoying those blessings. He understood things don't always work out the way people would plan them and thought that Denise's presence in his life might have been an answered prayer he and his wife asked for a long time ago. Melinda was just never to receive it.

"I'm just soaking in the day. Matt and Julie Lynn are getting my undivided attention." The doctor was laughing internally as he saw the two siblings compete in the silliest of ways.

"Joey, you want a drink?" Matthew had already been drinking a few beers. His wife Karen, who was quite attractive, was sitting in the sun enjoying a Mexican Martini.

"Yea, get something to drink Joseph. You're making me think I'm doing something wrong." Karen didn't have to have anyone do what she was doing to make it acceptable for her, but she genuinely wanted the doctor to join their fun.

"I think I'll try what you are having, it looks good with the olives."

"They are, let me make you one. Do you want the rim salted?" The doctor generally watched things like that and made the small wise choices to deny those extra indulgences, but not for this drink. It looked to have a flare that was worth all the extras.

"Absolutely, and extra olives."

"Joseph woke up honey." Karen shouted at Matthew.

"It's about time. Hey Joey jump off into the water with the kids."

"No thanks, the drink will be all." They continued to talk as the doctor opened more to the conversation. Matthew and Karen were a lot to keep up with as they lived a lifestyle that required many amenities. The doctor was just as well off as his brother's family, he just enjoyed life differently. He wasn't as flashy as his brother; however, he appreciated all his brother extended towards him and had a wonderful day that ran into the evening as they talked.

They ate, drank, laughed, and loved. Karen even brought up the subject of his wife and the past times they had, even bringing a few tears to the table. The doctor knew he was in the presence of loved ones and appreciated all they had done to give him the attention and love they were extending. During it all he couldn't get the poor boy Dillion out of his mind. The good fortune around him kept reminding him of Dillion's misfortune. He was awaiting the opportunity to give Dillion the chance he was experiencing that day. Sunday couldn't get here quick enough.

As the day was drawing to a close, they began moving back to the slip. You couldn't have asked for a more beautifully painted sky as the boat coasted at a steady pace. Matthew, truly the captain of his own ship, didn't let the nut fall too far from the tree. Matt was standing right next to his father, wanting to take his turn at steering. You could tell this made Matthew very proud. Julie Lynn was cuddled up next to her mom about to fall asleep. A remanent of Karen's perfume mixed in her sunscreen still flavored the air as the boat slowed down to dock.

It had been a great day for the doctor. A day to remind him of the value of family. He was glad to see the happiness that surrounded his brother's life and wished that all people could somehow grow to understand it. He just knew that wasn't in the cards for everyone. He would work to see Dillion get the chance to taste it once. Whether he desired more would be his decision.

When Sunday finally arrived, the doctor woke up early, had some coffee, and went for a walk. He hadn't gotten as far as running yet but was enjoying some early morning walks and his plans were to get more physical as time went on. The walk was a bit brisk as he prepared to exert himself at the entertainment house.

His real ambitions were to see Dillion and Denise interact as youngsters. Dillion needed it as he probably never felt it before in his life. The doctor, seeing Denise as someone full of life, was excited to watch the day unfold with her interactions with Dillion.

He would skip eating this morning as he supposed it would be pizza, hot wings, and pitchers of coke to fill the lunch belly. Knowing this, he took precautions with an antacid.

The rest of the morning was spent with random TV shows, never really staying put on one channel. 10:15am came and the doctor called Denise to tell her he would be coming to get her, and they would pick up Dillion. This would put them at the place at precisely 12 noon. You could tell by her voice when she answered she was eager and ready.

"Yes?"

"I guess you are ready?" The doctor had her figured out completely.

"Yes!!" Denise was ready and excited.

"I'm on my way. You might want to give Dillion a heads up that we will be coming, in case something changes the plans."

"Oh I hope not. Let's not think that way. I'll call, he will be ready."

Something the doctor was familiar with was the unpredictability of things seemingly going right. He knew it was more than possible for a wrench to be thrown in the mix of the healing of this boy. However, he wouldn't dwell on that. His attitude towards the day would be positive.

"You're probably right, we will be on our way shortly."

The road trip was peaceful, with the radio on a low setting. The 70s were going to be the choice. The doctor offered to pull over for anyone wanting something to drink. No one was thirsty so the trip began for all of them.

The doctor and Denise spoke most of the way with Denise occasionally asking Dillion a question, to get a bit of interaction out of him. It wasn't a counseling session, and they didn't want it to appear to be as one, so all words spoken were around the edges and seemingly insignificant. That still didn't provoke Dillion to much of any exchange. For the most part, he sat back, watched, and listened.

Once they arrived, the place looked huge. As they stepped out and approached the building, you could see Dillion's eyes light up with anticipation seeing the size of the building and the signage out front.

"Wow, looks fun." Denise was the big kid in the room. Playfully she started to speak to get some sort of reaction out of Dillion. While walking up to go in she exclaimed, "I get to go first, I get to go first." She was pulling a bit on Dillion's arm and getting a slight smile out of him. The doctor was a few steps behind them and laughing quietly. He knew Denise was going to be the big sister Dillion never had. It was looking like it was a good decision to come here.

After walking in the front door, it looked even larger and so were Dillion's eyes. An arcade a child could only dream about was the first thing you saw. To the left was an obstacle course adorned with tight ropes only the brave would dare to test. Next to that was a bowling alley surrounded by big screen TVs. The lanes were lit in neon and blacklight. Around the corner from that was an area where one could play medieval with a challenge of axe throwing. The smell of all kinds of tasty treats came from a restaurant within the place and a movie theater topped the whole thing off.

The doctor was amazed by such a wonderfully set up facility. As they walked in, he admired Denise as she grabbed Dillion by the hand and began to wander ahead of the doctor. They had no intention of leaving him behind, they were just fascinated by the amount there was to take in as they saw the place.

The crashing of the bowling balls and the lighting of the lanes attracted Dillion and he asked a question.

"Can we go bowling first?" The doctor felt good about him feeling comfortable enough to ask.

"Absolutely, do you think you can beat me?" By throwing a friendly competition his way, he thought it might open Dillion up a bit more.

"I don't know. I have never played this game." It was a real eye-opener to see the things that he was missing. Despite these realizations, today wouldn't be dwelt on sadness. The doctor started making his way to the line to sign up for some lanes.

"I am willing to bet you." Denise couldn't help herself. She was the competitor. "We used to bowl quite a bit when I was young. My father was in league for years. Two of my brothers still bowl. If you are up to it, I'll take you on. What should we wager?" Denise was up for making it fun.

"Denise, I figured you were pretty good but I'm not that shabby. It has been a while, but I used to regularly bowl over 200. Let's get through the first game and compete on the second or third, depending on how many we play." Dillion was watching the bantering between them and smiling the whole time. It was a healthy exchange for him to see conversation like this existed.

"I would like to start with two games, we might want a third. I'll let you know after the second and three pairs of shoes, please." The doctor asked the young girl working behind the counter for a lane. "I need a size 12, 9 and a women's 8. Does that sound right?" Looking at their feet, the doctor made an educated guess. "Is that right?"

"I'm a 9." Dillion spoke up knowing the doctor picked his shoe size out."

"7 ½ for me." Denise laughingly enjoyed the doctor being off.

"Well 2 out of 3 ain't bad." The doctor was enjoying this play.

"I'm sorry ma'am we don't have half sizes." The girl behind the counter helped make the doctor 3 for 3. He was on a roll and knew it.

Turning towards Denise he inquired about the unfinished business.

"You never said, what's the bet?" He was curious as he knew Denise's nature. There would be no money involved rather some sort of task for the other to do.

"If you win, I will wash your car. If I win, you have to run the obstacle course with Dillion and I." The doctor had seen the course when he walked in and thought it would be a great idea for Denise and

Dillion to engage in but didn't fancy the idea for himself. Any healthy exercise of overcoming fears is always an essential part of character building, but the doctor thought he needed none of this today.

"I like it." Dillion's excitement from watching all the communication between them had him speaking out more. He seemed to be developing a comfort zone around them.

For the first time, the doctor saw Dillion interacting as if he wasn't affected by his circumstance. It was as though he had forgotten who he was and could just be a kid for once.

"Here you go, sir." The young girl handed the doctor their shoes. "That will be $54 and you are on lane 21. Let me know if you need help setting up the scoreboard." The girl was most courteous. The doctor, focusing on two conversations and still knowing he wasn't in favor of the proposition, couldn't refuse the bet now.

"You want to see me scared, or do you think either one of you are better than me in bowling?" He was glad to see this lively conversation unfold. He knew it would be enjoyable just as it would be productive. His goal would be to play competitor and coach at the same time. Competitor so he wouldn't have to climb the obstacle course and coach to truly show Dillion how to bowl a decent game. "Let's order something to eat while we play. Dillion look at the menu and figure something we can all eat. Just keep in mind, I don't eat pork or shellfish."

"What is shellfish?" Dillion asked with a confused look on his face.

"Things like shrimp, clams, lobster, but they probably don't have that on this menu."

"Are you allergic, doctor?" Denise was now the one with the confused look.

"No, I keep the dietary laws that are in the Bible. It is something that my parents taught me at a young age and was confirmed in my adulthood when I began my studies to become a doctor."

"Ok, interesting, I've heard of people following that diet. I do try and eat healthy but haven't explored that." Denise took what the doctor said with accreditation, but then turned to Dillion to get lunch ordered. "Go ahead and order something." Dillion still looked confused, so Denise looked at the menu over his shoulder. "I'll help you." She and Dillion began to pan over the menu. There were so many choices. Dillion was reluctant to order as he had never been given permission to even such a small thing as this. "The doctor asked you to decide. What do you like?" Denise edged Dillion knowing the doctor wanted to give the liberty to him to decide.

"I don't know, I like wings, but this pizza looks good, so do the cheese sticks. I'm not really sure."

"Why don't you order them all? We are three people and if we don't finish anything, you can take it home with you." The doctor wanted to show generosity to the boy. Dillion wasn't sure how to react as he had never been shown this type of affection.

"Are you sure?"

"Yes, I'm sure and you need to order us all drinks, I'll have a Coke. Denise what will you have?" Denise was already putting her bowling shoes on. "I would like a Dr. Pepper."

"Me too." Dillion ordered the same. As Dillion ordered the food, their eagerness of playing was excited while they listened to the crashing of the balls into the pins of other lanes.

Time flew by as they bowled a less than average first game. The doctor and Denise over anticipated their skills as it had been awhile since they had any practice. Despite the doctor's bowling, he did give good advice to Dillion on how to play. Dillion was able to develop a slight curve in his delivery. It needed control but you could see he enjoyed being able to perform well.

Throughout the first game their food was delivered and they ate. The doctor was enjoying giving this opportunity to Dillion. He was also reassured of the reason he loved Denise so much as he watched her own this moment with Dillion. As their game wrapped up, Denise just couldn't let the fun die down.

"Ok, second game doctor. We play for keeps on this. Are you in?"

"Yes he is." Dillion pushed the wager with his two cents. The doctor looked at him.

"Who said you could do that?" The doctor was surprised and gave him a puzzled smirk. Dillion had nothing to say but busted out with a big laugh.

"Yeah." Denise added to the outburst to force the doctor into saying okay. The doctor was locked in by circumstance.

"Alright, you got me, but you might be disappointed." The competition was on.

Even though it was a friendly event, faces became more serious when one stepped up to bowl. Everyone had a mind to win. It was a hard played game and while surface talk was on the table, everyone was concentrating. Even Dillion, without a dog in the fight and the least amount of skill, was competing in his own mind. He didn't pose much of a threat but did manage to bowl two strikes during the game which was a thrill everyone enjoyed together.

The concern came down to the doctor's final tenth frame. He was in a neck-to-neck battle with Denise. He needed to make a clean strike on his final bowl to beat her.

"You think you got this turkey?" Denise wouldn't say anything distracting while he was on the lane about to bowl. She did her taunting before he walked up to approach the lane. While it was a competition, they knew the rules. A win achieved when trash talking distracts, doesn't redeem full bragging rights.

"I think I hear a gobbling going on." The doctor had been doing well and had confidence in his game.

Dillion was having such a good time. You could see the suspense captured in his mind. His choice was for Denise to win. It wasn't a vote against the doctor, rather it was for the doctor. He was becoming fond of him and wanted to see Dr. Richards join he and Denise in walking the obstacle course. He also was delighting in the satisfaction and reward of success, so a small portion of him wanted to see the doctor overcome the odds of a loss.

The doctor finished wiping off the oil from his ball and approached the lane. Both of them went quiet. Two lanes over there was a family with small children. They were taking in a day of fun as well. The children weren't privy to bowling courtesy and had been stepping up to bowl while others were already set to bowl. This hadn't bothered their game, but this last deciding factor was worth the wait. The doctor paused and came back off the lane and took a drink of his soda.

"What happened?" Denise knew the doctor's reason for stepping back but wanted to rouse the challenge a bit.

"No hurry for me. I'll get my strike." The doctor stepped back up once he had no disruptions and gave a classic delivery. The ball looked to go towards the gutter for much of its travel and three quarters of the way down curved beautifully across the number one pin and stuck a Brooklyn strike. "Yes!" The doctor shouted as his excitement couldn't be contained. Dillion's emotions were high as he jumped up and went to make contact with the doctor with a sort of high five arm grab.

"Well, good job. I should have known you would pull it through. And when did you jump over to his team?" Denise shifted her conversation looking over towards Dillion.

"I wanted Dr. Richards to lose so he would have to run the course with us, but man that was a good shot."

"It sure was, oh well, I owe you a car wash. Let's you and me go have some fun." They began taking their shoes off to turn them back in and move towards the obstacle course.

"Well, I thought about it, and I can't let you two work the dangers of that high wire without some help." Dr. Richards was having too good of a time to sit on the bench now.

"You're gonna climb up there with us?" Dillion's eyes lit up as he asked.

"Yes, I can't quit now. Denise, you still owe me a car washing but I think I would like to run the course with you two." The doctor looked at Denise and smiled.

"Good for you, doc. I had a sneaking suspicion you might change your mind."

If days could be measured by the expressions received in them, this one would have held enough reserve for a lifetime. It wasn't just the connection but seeing the connection where one had never been. There was hope for this young boy. Keeping him connected would be the challenge. It would all be worth it.

The obstacle course was laughter and trust built into an adventure. It had its place in the making of the fondest of memories. Time throughout their day went too fast and eventually they had to go home.

The drive back was much like the drive there. There was not much talking from Dillion, but for another reason. Denise turned to look at him 15 minutes into the ride and he was dosing off.

"Dillion's asleep." Denise let the doctor know.

"Good, that means we got all we could out of him today. Hopefully he sleeps good tonight and wakes up feeling the same."

"I hope so. I had a blast too. I hope that is not the last time we do that. I really need to tell my brother Desmond about this place. Now you want to talk about people who would like that place. His wife, kids, all of them would have a great time." Denise was trying not to talk too loudly but at the same time was talking a bit fast. She was still on a high.

"We'll have to do that sometime. I would like to meet your family, even if it wasn't here."

"They would love you. They are really good people. You want to see me when I was little, Desmond's daughter is my mini-me." Hearing Denise talk about her family created a desire in the doctor to want to meet them. Her honesty and genuinely sweet nature was definitely a trait that is taught. He knew the rest of her family would be of that same quality.

The road trip ended with them waking Dillion and walking him to his grandmother's front door. It was a sad note to drop him off, as they could hear the yelling of his younger siblings. The house seemed messy, and it was obvious the kids weren't monitored that well. Something less desirable had been cooking and was still lingering in the air.

"We will have to do this again. Dillion, you rock." Denise wanted to give encouragement to him before leaving.

"Dillion, thank you, I had a terrific time. Denise is right, we will do something again."

"Thank you, sir. I had the best time. Even if we don't go again, just hanging out is good for me." Perhaps Dillion just wanted to start making some positive commitments, either way Denise and the Doctor were going to be committed to him.

"Thank y'all for taking Dillion." Dillion's grandmother, too old to really do much, was truly grateful. Everyone said goodbye, Dillion put his arm around his grandmother, and they went inside.

Driving off the doctor and Denise both had a sense of fulfillment. They were able to reach into the boy's heart and show him what was in there. They were able to show him purpose in life. They were both woefully aware of the fact that purpose could be preached in another light. They still had a huge competition with keeping the boy's mind right. It would prove to become a dedication in the coming days to see about the boy's change. It would also prove to those helping, that change might be coming their way as well.

Chapter Seven
The Syndication

Working with Denise on the Dillion Myer's case proved to have much more to it than just the repair of a young boy. While the sessions with Dillion were gaining much ground, there was a deeper element that would have to be dealt with in this equation.

Dillion's family, namely his mother, was causing a considerable hindrance with the progress being made. Dillion would show interest and commitment to the services being provided to him. However, the threshold of his understanding was hinged upon what was being taught by his mother when she was present.

On occasion, some of the successes that were being accomplished would become stagnant and question the progress being made. Stacy Brown was Dillion's mother's name. She still carried the surname of a man that she was once married to many years ago. It was her first and only husband. He left her after just one year of marriage. It had been a match made in hell. It was set to destruct from the beginning. Drug abuse and infidelity were the cornerstones of the union's inception and destruction. Her husband moved on to better things and improved greatly in life, she however managed to continue to degrade.

Relationships with men became the proverbial swinging door. It was in one of these encounters that she became pregnant with Dillion. His father never proved to be worth much. Any chance to demonstrate worthy parental qualities was taken away from him. A drug fueled car crash sent him to an early fiery grave.

Since his death, Dillion's mother had managed to make three more children from three different men, none of which she had custody. She pretended to be a mother but didn't even qualify as a lousy friend.

Stacy's presence in Dillion's life was a real distraction against the work being invested towards his development. She would compromise Dillion's emotions with spouts of false love she pretended to show him. This was done in between her sporadic appearances and altered mind. Everything she did was self-directed and done with selfish reasons.

Her arrivals were presented with an over-announced professing of love for her family. Soon to follow was an even deeper expression of the disgust she had for the law and what they had done to tear it apart. Never did accountability seem to enter her mind. She was addicted to her pathetic condition amongst various drugs as well.

She despised the mirror of truth. Whether it was family, the law, or in one instance Denise attempting to explain to her the detriment she was causing her kids, she would viciously scratch back with a rancorous attitude towards any criticism. Excuses were an automatic default. There wasn't much hope for her, only the longing for her permanent departure.

The removal of Stacy out of Dillion's life would have to come as a circumstance she would create. Denise knew she was limited to Stacy's careless lifestyle establishing a route to forcefully remove her out of Dillion's life. This was something Denise awaited, being aware of her involvement in criminal activity.

She discussed with the doctor the many things she knew about Stacy she had learned by working with other departments. Dr. Richards despised this mother for her lack of care towards her children. It was one of the things that tore him in life. The thought that someone like her was given many children and he and his wife weren't, was agonizing. As the doctor became more involved, he became more vocal, and he began to let Denise know the thoughts that were dwelling within him.

"Why don't we force the hand of law enforcement to keep her away from Dillion?" His passion expressed deep concern to rid them of this nuisance. He was beginning to have those old feelings of hatred emerge.

"Trust me, we have tried. All my contacts with the blue have told me, she is untouchable, at least for now. Even with their knowledge about her connections to Luis Maldonado, she manages to stay out of trouble. He does a large part to protect her."

Denise referred to one of the most notorious criminals in the city. This was a part of Stacy's life she had been avoiding talking about. Any connection to such a man, meant trouble. Her interest was that Dillion was protected and kept from the persuasions of going down that road. There was always that fear that he might choose that life, and keeping her mind closed to that fact didn't guarantee his fate. Enterprises like that can't be ignored, especially with the things they can offer. The power that can be wielded is made from two equal collaborators, profit and destruction. Men like Luis annihilate all that is before them by commanding its occupation.

His name had been in the papers, and everyone knew of his existence, although few had ever seen him. Luis Maldonado was a crime boss, involved in drug trafficking and prostitution for the past few decades. His infamy was riddled with strong arming, violence, and murder. He was no one to be trifled with. Stacy was a drifter that would work for Luis from time to time. Their arrangement was such that Luis owned and used Stacy as a rancher might own cattle. They simply see fit to send those to slaughter which they choose. She was a degenerate to him. He fed her habits, as it wasn't much of a cost to him, and when he needed something done, she was obligated to comply. Her trade ranged from trafficking to prostitution, to setting people up for collection, or any other job Luis needed done that he thought she was capable of.

There is no loyalty amongst thieves and there was no difference inside this enterprise. Love was for self. Stacy was embracing a false devotion which only led to death. She was a lost cause with loyalty only to herself.

Denise began to explain all the dark secrets that had been unknown to the doctor. His mind had never contemplated the severity of circumstances surrounding this young boy's life.

"Isn't there something we can do outside of our boundaries to keep her from him?" The doctor began to contemplate thinking outside the box to solve issues that were only right to do. His mind wasn't considering acting outside the law, only appealing to her vanities. If he could pay her to stay away, would it be worth it? "I'll pay her."

"Doctor, I know, I have thought about doing something, anything to keep her away, but what and how long will she remain tied to any agreement? She's not even capable of making a promise to herself." This was not the first time Denise had wrestled with this situation.

"Can we find out more about the people she is involved with? This Luis character, what about him? Can't we do something about him? Even if he is a threat, I'm willing to do whatever it takes for the sake of Dillion. Finding out about these people might show us an advantage. We might not be able to do anything, but the power of knowledge leads to better thinking." The doctor knew the key to success would be in relieving Dillion of his mother. To achieve this would be to understand everything about her and to use her life to lead her away.

"I can see what I can find out, but too much searching might cause flags to go up. Some people might see it as overstepping our boundaries. Let me see what I can come up with."

The doctor was in disbelief. How could the law be set up to allow this fragile child's life to be compromised by such blatant actions? Who cares if it is family? She must go.

The doctor had made a few friends in the police department back during the investigation of his wife's murder. He thought to call one of them up to inquire about a solution to this problem. Perhaps the doctor might have some influence on him, having gone through what he had experienced. He wasn't thinking about using his wife's murder for receiving any favor, but instead an opportunity to make some good out of his unfortunate situation. He would gladly pass that benefit on to a desperate teen like Dillion.

The officer he had in mind was Detective Marlon Crawford. Detective Crawford was the one who followed the trail and caught his wife's murderer, Jeremy Williams. The detective was a determined man, driven by gut and instinct. Never would one imagine the doctor favoring the detective's company, but in fact he was quite fond of him.

The doctor was dapper in all appearances, while the detective was much less groomed. He took on the form of a newer aged Columbo, where his work took precedence over any facade. The detective's exterior probably kept most folks away, but this didn't bother him at all as he was not a man given to many words. He was however, given to continued smoking and caffeine addiction. He was a stereotypical Dick. This most assuredly was adopted through his career and left him time to do his job well. Inside he had a heart of gold that many never got to discover.

The doctor had become good friends with the detective over the course of the investigation. It was his good heart that allowed him to see things others were blinded to. There was much confiding that took place between the two during those dark days. This was what compelled him to think about the detective. The doctor felt he could call on the detective for help. He didn't want to take advantage of his relationship with the detective but knew they both shared a zeal for justice. If the detective was available, the doctor would meet up with him for a few words. He stepped away from Denise's office and called the precinct where Det. Crawford was stationed and asked to speak with him. A receptionist answered the phone.

"Dallas PD South Division, may I help you?"

"Yes, I am looking for Detective Crawford, is he in?"

"Hold please." The receptionist didn't say more than was needed. Police work in the inner cities becomes routine and programmed. It is not to say there is no caring involved, but thin-skinned people should understand business is business.

"Hello, Detective Crawford here." His voice sounded as though it was conditioned with gravel. The doctor hadn't heard him in almost a year.

"Marlon, this is Joseph, Dr. Richards. How are you doing?" The two had developed speaking on a first name basis. Most everyone that knew them, called them by title. They had set those precedents themselves as sometimes things work out differently when relationships develop.

"Joseph, good to hear your voice. How have you been?" The detective seemed happy to hear from the doctor.

"I'm doing fine. Listen, are you busy? I would like to come see you and discuss something I am having an issue with. It might take a little while. Maybe I can take you to lunch." The doctor just didn't want to pop in and ask a favor. He valued the detective's friendship more than that.

"Is this about the case?" He was referring to the doctor's wife's murder.

"No, that chapter is finally over, and I have put that to rest. I'm involved in social work now and this has to do with some of the people I am working with, or rather people that are around the people I'm working with." The doctor didn't want to get into much detail on a phone call. He knew that time and business would cut the conversation short.

"Lunch sounds good. Does the old place still sound good to you?" He was bringing up a mobile lunch car they had frequented back during the days of the investigation. The detective wasn't for going into restaurants as he never paid much attention to his dress. He preferred the affectionately called "roach coaches" and outdoor dining for the more on-the-go lifestyle that he lived.

"When would you like to meet?" The doctor knew exactly where he was talking about. It was called the "Greasy Cheese" and it was located on the south side of town in a parking lot dedicated to mobile food vendors. The Park was nice enough, and they could sit in an area to discuss matters in an uninterrupted way. The doctor wasn't impressed with the choice of eatery but would go as he understood who Det. Crawford was.

"I'm busy for the next two days, but I can meet you on Thursday at 11:00am." The detective was an early man just like the doctor.

"Sounds good, see you there." It was refreshing to speak to the detective again. Hopefully he could be of some assistance, or at least lead them to a place where they could receive help.

The doctor walked back into Denise's office and told her he might have someone who could help them with their problem.

"Be careful doctor, we don't want to do anything we shouldn't. If my department thinks we are doing something out of line, you might not be able to work with me anymore." Denise wasn't disciplining the doctor, just concerned about passion driving him outside of good decision-making.

"I won't do anything unless you know about it first. A good friend of mine is a detective and I want to find out what he might know or what he can do, if anything." The doctor had no intentions of overstepping his boundaries. He liked and believed in his newfound work and didn't want to risk his involvement with it.

"Ok, let me know what you find out." Denise sounded content.

"I will. I think I'm going to go home. I'm beginning to get a headache. This work can be stressful." The doctor felt as though he could use a nap.

"You're telling me. Go ahead and go home. I'll talk to you tomorrow." The doctor got up to walk out.

"You're the best Denise, I'll see you later." The doctor wanted to say something more affectionate, but didn't as he was ready to be in his home inside his own corner of quiet. He just wanted to escape the troubles that he was seeing that were inspiring all the confusion in the world. He grabbed his coat, coffee cup, notebook and left his work for the day.

The next two days were filled with short conversations. The doctor and Denise were being led to the same roadblock, Stacy. It was frustrating but that was to be expected when dealing with these kinds of people. The doctor, not being tied to a paid job, had the freedom to come and go more than Denise. He decided to stay away from the office and allow for clearer thinking.

It entered his mind to locate and follow Stacy around the city hoping to find her in a reportable offense. While his efforts might lead to her being incarcerated for a time, he knew this wasn't his job and furthermore Denise would likely be opposed to it. Although intrigued by the thought, he would wait to see what Det. Crawford had to say.

Thursday showed up and the doctor called Denise. Her voice always comforted the doctor.

"Good morning sir."

"Hello dear, I wanted to call and let you know I'm not coming in this morning. I am going to meet with that detective I told you about, but I will try and come in this afternoon to fill you in on what he said." The doctor didn't feel like driving to the office and then leaving from there to go meet the detective.

"That's fine. I figured that was what you were going to do when you first told me about him on Monday. I'll be here until 4:00 pm. I have to leave early for a dental appointment. So, if we don't see each other today, I'll see you on Friday."

"Sounds good, talk with you later." The doctor was still having some coffee. He was developing an extension to the hours he indulged the beverage. It was probably due to working with Denise. The whole office drank coffee throughout the day, and it was becoming a habit for him. He would sit and think about some of his past meetings with his old friend as he sipped through his drink. Those days of horror were conversations that required patience. He learned discipline by having to wait. Today, anticipation for a solution to another matter would require that same mindset.

The doctor had a great appreciation for Detective Crawford. He possessed a character of true commitment. He wasn't interested in things that weren't of much importance. Dr. Richards liked the fact that the detective didn't care much for appearances, and that it gave him an upper hand on those who judged him prematurely. The detective was highly intelligent with an exceptional sense of intuition and a near perfect memory. This was what made him extraordinary at his job. The doctor respected Marlon very much.

As the time for their meeting approached, Dr. Richards drove to their choice location. When he pulled into the parking lot it was

10:40am. He could see Det. Crawford's car was already there. The detective wasn't in it, and the doctor didn't see him anywhere. The doctor thought he must have gotten there early, as was his custom. He assumed he probably went walking around as he was a curious type.

The doctor wasn't drawn to the idea of looking for him, so he stayed in his car waiting for his return. Appearing anxious to see the detective wasn't what he wanted to portray. He knew he would be back before 11:00am, so waiting for him was no big deal to the doctor. He thought about how he would present this issue to his friend. If there was any chance for him to assist them with this problem, there would have to be an agreement as to its importance. The doctor wasn't even opposed to the detective nosing about people's business to make them suspicious. Perhaps a few visits like that and people take hints and trouble goes away. The best-case scenario concerning the doctor was that Stacy simply went away.

Down on a walking trail leading up to the parking lot, he could see his old friend. The detective was walking in his direction. It was probably the most exercise he had gotten in a long time. The walk didn't stop him from smoking; hat was how the doctor spotted him.

Along the trail, amongst the joggers and pet walkers, was a man in a trench coat, billowing out a cloud every couple of steps. The doctor chuckled inside, not at the detective, but at the healthy people that undoubtedly weren't enjoying his exhale as they passed him by. The doctor stepped out of his car to be noticed by the detective. As he approached within shouting distance, the doctor hollered out.

"Marlon....Marlon!" The doctor tried to get his attention. He was looking off in another direction. Finally, when he got a little closer and turned his attention towards the doctor's direction and he could see the doctor waving at him. He waved back to acknowledge seeing the doctor.

As he approached, the doctor could smell the smoke before the detective was upon him. Switching the cigarette to his left hand, he extended his right to shake his friend's hand.

"Hey Joseph, how are you doing. It is good to see you." The detective seemed a bit winded. That was to be expected since smoking and walking weren't exactly a good match.

"Good to see you. What's it been now, over three years we been knowing each other, and I never knew you exercised?" The doctor jabbed in a friendly way at Marlon.

"Yea, I keep that part of my life a secret, mainly to myself." The detective had no shame in admitting he wasn't one for working out. "Well let me do what I do best and get something to eat, are you hungry?" Marlon began to move towards the food cars.

"Sure, I really didn't eat much for breakfast." The doctor wasn't hungry for this type of food but would sit down and break bread with his friend anyway. There was an agenda on his mind.

They both ordered food from different cars and sat down at a picnic table that was away from the others and the doctor began to fill in his old friend on what his situation was. Det. Crawford seemed unaffected by the story the doctor was explaining, dedicating most of his time to the cheeseburger he was enjoying. This was his usual personality. He was listening and the doctor knew this. The gears always turned in the detective's mind whether he appeared to be giving his attention or not. Many people misjudged him on that, accounting him as an uncaring type, but to their discredit he was a dedicated listener. This was apparent when the doctor mentioned the name Luis Maldonado. The detective's eyebrows raised, and he put his food down.

"This is one bad guy. No one has been able to nail him for all he is responsible for. If your intentions are to mess with someone tied to him, you might have a lot of trouble to deal with." The detective's tone changed as he showed an emotional attachment to the abhorrence he had towards this man. "This guy is lawyered up better than a politician. If you go after him or anything he is involved in, you better have your ducks in a row. Honestly, to take him down, one would have to jump in his arena, and do it illegally." As strange as it was, taking down a criminal as powerful as this man was hardly possible through the law.

The doctor felt a moment of despair as his friend seemed to take every bit of wind out of his sail.

"I have wanted to see something happen to Luis for years. Every time his name is connected to anything illegal, he takes a legal approach to his innocence. Then he uses people to take his falls, and is willing to murder those who won't. This guy should not be allowed to live. Not that I would ever do it, but if he were shot down, I would be fine with it." This response from the detective didn't surprise the doctor. He knew Marlon would operate within the limits of the law, but also had strong convictions about what was right. "I will tell you what Joseph, I know you want my help and your problem seems to be with this Stacy Brown. I will look into who she is and if there is anything I can find out about her or what she is doing so that we can possibly shake her. We can even follow her around for a while, but that must be done with caution. If she is involved with Luis as you say she is, that might lead to bigger problems. It would create a whole new situation as he might decide to protect his investments, legally or illegally. I will help you. Just know that getting too close might pose a problem." The doctor was learning the depths of a society that had no limitations.

Outside of the things he saw in the ER, his first taste of crime personally was his wife's murder. Most individuals perceived these types of events as just low-lifes and bad upbringings, never expecting them to touch their personal lives. His level of understanding hadn't considered the calculated complexity of a syndicated crime world. It ran deep into the fibers of our society, touching and negotiating against our morals. Would there ever be an end to this madness? The doctor simply wanted to get rid of this poor boy's mother who was no good for him. She seemed to be significant in causing them difficulty with Dillion's success, but insignificant in the way of being a force on her own to be reckoned with, and yet the problem ran deeper than he could imagine.

"Joseph, I'll get back with you if I learn anything or am able to pursue any avenue. Until then, keep working with the boy and hopefully either she will go away by herself or by us initiating it." It was almost 12:30pm and both men needed to be on their way. They committed to staying in touch even outside of anything work related, but work was both of their main focus.

Dr. Richards was back on the road driving in his car. The radio was playing softly. He dialed up Denise's number. She answered and her voice was comforting to hear.

"Hello, how'd it go?" She had spent the morning busy with other cases, but the doctor's visit with the detective never escaped her mind. "Did you learn anything helpful?" Her question felt inquisitive. The doctor, not wanting to create false anticipation, answered more indirectly.

"Well, it was good to see my old friend. He hasn't changed at all. He is going to look into a few things and see if he can help in any way." Denise responded to the doctor in the same manner. She read the doctor well and could carry on the conversation the same as he did.

"Sounds good, I would like to talk with you, but if you're planning on coming into the office, I won't be here. I have a dentist appointment later and I worked through lunch so I can leave at 1:30 to run a few errands. We can talk tomorrow." Their conversation was brief, and so the doctor began making his way home.

With much of the afternoon left he thought of taking the leisurely route home. He decided to just drive by Dillion's grandmother's house as it was still early in the day. It was out of his way and not in a favorable part of the city, but his interest in the case had him wanting to go anyway.

His luxury car going through this neighborhood would definitely be out of place and most likely perceived as a dealer. None the less he would maintain an anonymous detail. The neighborhood was located miles on a crow's flight to the county landfill. That was always prevalent in lower income areas. Factories, dumps, and wastewater plants tend to be close to the undesirable neighborhoods regardless to which made its claim to the land first. The doctor switched his air to recycle so as to keep the outside smell out. A bit of pity fell upon him as he ingested the circumstances he was riding past. There were cars with their hoods open, trash littering the yards, and bars on most of the decent houses. It was all he could do to not feel sick.

Although he had been here before, today he was alone with his thoughts and able to truly analyze the environment. He could never imagine a life lived in these conditions. He counted his blessings as he rode through a world lived by those less fortunate than he was. He was also not blind to the fact that many of them were contributors to it. They had become accustomed to accepting this way.

His compassion was short lived when he made the turn onto Mrs. Metzner's street. There he saw Stacy standing by a car parked on the curb and smoking a cigarette. He wasn't alarmed as he knew his car and tinted windows would provide a concealment of his identity. It was unlikely she had memorized who he was either.

As low class as she was, she understood the finer things in life and his vehicle didn't slip past her sight. She kept a hard inviting stare as he drove by. Her provocative nature was attempting to sell something that had long since been spoiled. The doctor drove in no hurry. He was reviled by the audacity she displayed. Without words, he knew everything he needed to know by seeing her. He had often heard it said, "You can't judge a book by its cover." He had even put stock in this philosophy at one time. He was slowly learning that this had become a tool by deplorables. It was an attempt to make people deny truths. He knew she was trash. She looked like trash. The doctor didn't feel pity for trash, so why should he feel pity for her. Trash is to be disposed of.

There were many things the doctor was working through in his mind. It was people like Dillion's mother that were causing him much frustration with the collateral damages they create through their selfishness. He felt compelled to find some sort of cure for the insanity that plagued his world. Dillion would be his first endeavor. He was worth saving. He hadn't become trash yet. The potential was there, but so was the potential to become great.

The doctor drove out of the neighborhood, caught the interstate, and headed for home. He turned up the radio and enjoyed the music of past decades. He wanted to think of other things. Thinking of the people he despised made him feel dirty if he let it fester.

Soon he was reciting the words to some of the familiar tunes he knew. It was already approaching 3:00pm and he decided to pick up some food before returning home. It was too early to eat, but once he got home, he had no intention of going back out. He stopped at a local market and picked up a piece of salmon and a salad. Something light would hit the spot with a glass of tea. He was planning on a couple of glasses of whiskey as he cooked the salmon. Today, he needed something to take the pressure off. He was coming home early but felt as if it had been a long day.

The doctor knew that tension was something that can age a person if not handled correctly. As a doctor he knew stress and was familiar with how to deal with it. This brand of stress carried a whole new tension level the doctor wasn't familiar with. He was ready for home.

After unloading his groceries and changing his clothes he attempted to unload his thoughts. With a drink in his hand and the fish in a skillet, he was ready. It was just after 6:00 pm and he knew Denise was probably close to home. He dialed her number up.

"Hello doctor, I just got home, what's going on?" The doctor smiled as she spoke.

"Not much Denise. I'm feeling a bit better now that I'm at home about to eat. Today has been stressful just thinking about things." The doctor wasn't about to tell her about driving by the house. He mainly called to hear her voice.

"Well, you know if things are becoming difficult, you can take a break." Denise assumed the doctor wouldn't want to but offered it to him anyway. She knew him to be a man of dedication.

"Thank you, I appreciate that, but I actually just called to say thank you. You have done more for my sanity than you know." She was a shining diamond to him in a world that had many dark secrets. He was learning these things and treasured being in her life. Their conversations were commonly becoming more heartfelt every time they occurred.

"Doctor, you have become a special person to me. I am thankful for having you in my life." Those words eased the doctor's stress more than the whiskey.

"I thank you for that. Look, Denise, I'm going to let you go. You probably want to relax, and my salmon is ready to come out of the pan. I love you dear, goodbye."

She responded back, "I love you too, goodbye doctor." They hung up and went their ways knowing that they had each other's back through it all. His fondness for her had him tearing a bit as he sat and thought about her.

The doctor took his time eating while continuing to read a book he had started. He cleaned up his dishes and went to get ready for bed. He had intentions to read a little more in bed, but after he showered his eyes became very heavy. After locking up, a short prayer, the doctor called it an extensively long day and fell fast asleep.

Chapter Eight
The Beat

The challenge of police work is sometimes having an abundance of knowledge but no evidence that will sustain in court. It can cause a sense of hopelessness with many, feeling enslaved to a failed justice system. This is where intuition conflicts with the processes of detective work. It is looked at as an invasion of civil rights. It is called guess work by the attorneys and the law substantiates this thought in court. This is where many policemen struggle in their noble cause to see justice accomplished.

If only there was a way to prevent crimes from happening, how better off would the world be? Instead, the system allowed one to go about with ill intentions, seeking what is wrong and setting themselves up to commit a crime and until the crime is committed, there is nothing that can be done. Having to react to crime versus being proactive to bad behavior has left in its path rights granted to those in society who self-serve at the expense of others. Subtly, over time, protective barriers have been provided for the criminal to set a defense up before they commit a crime. The only real way to be effective in achieving a just society is to have laws with consequences that eradicate injustice. This creates not just a letter of the law, but a spirit in man to desire justice.

Detective Crawford was no stranger to the current justice system's charade. He was seasoned to 27 years of it. He allowed its abrasion not to bother him, although it did consume a lot of space in his mind. He gravitated to things happening in their own time with higher powers calling the shots. He knew his limitations and respected the work he signed up for.

With Stacy Brown now in his sights, he knew he would have to work on this carefully. He knew what the doctor needed and how he felt about the situation. The primary focus was to help the young boy. His mother wasn't of any concern to the doctor, other than her interference with the progress that was being sought with her son.

Whether she knew it or not, she had decided a long time ago, on her own, that she wasn't worth anything.

Being involved in work that aids in people's welfare, compassion is generally the driving force. Inside of that thought, realizations of truth must be considered. Her worthlessness was apparent by her own actions. This they knew and were unapologetic about acknowledging it. She was responsible for her decisions and that was the truth. It seemed as though the truth was what was beginning to offend a sub-culture in society. What most people were failing to realize was that living without truth, one focuses on living in a world that doesn't really exist. Lying to yourself wasn't going to change things. Nonetheless, the truth about Stacy was that she had to be removed.

The job at hand was to see to it that she didn't ruin anyone else, namely Dillion. If this didn't stop here, there were younger children who were next. Det. Crawford shared in the doctor's sentiment. That was reason alone to act, but there were also his feelings for the doctor and his situation with his wife. He would make the effort for that reason as well.

Marlon's first step would be to review Stacy's record, searching to find any recent arrests or charges that might be pending. Opening the door to him being able to approach her within the law would be the most ideal situation in resolving the matter. If a conversation could take place, persuading her that she needed to not interfere with Dillion, it might be all that was needed. It was a long shot, but police work can involve persuasive conversations that make people rethink their choices. With Stacy, she had shown that she was content on the course she had set, so approaching her with this could toss results either way.

Det. Crawford popped his head into the records room and asked the young secretary to pull any files they had on Stacy Brown.

"Yes sir, give me just one second."

The department had just hired a new high school graduate. She was a young lady, who was going to work for the department while attending school to get a criminal justice degree. To call her attractive was an understatement. For this reason, every young officer working out of that precinct always seemed to be needing her assistance with something and it was obvious why. She remained over busy. She was good at multi-tasking and had a lot of tasks handed to her. It was her curse for being attractive. Detective Crawford decided to go looking in the files himself.

"I'll get to it detective if you give me some time. I'm working on something right now for one of the patrol officers."

He was aware of what was going on and knew his seniority could override any frivolous office play going on but decided to look in the files for himself. He wasn't upset in the least. He appreciated the youth he worked with and knew they had good intentions.

"Detective, you are going to have let me do my job. If you are going to go through the files on your own, what good is my job?" She was respectful and at the same time wanting to pull her own weight. The detective liked the young girl. She was a bit naive when it came to boys constantly needing her help. She probably could have refused some of the requests that came her way, as they really weren't her job, but she saw herself as a trooper earning her stripes.

"Don't worry about it dear, I'm really not all that busy. I just thought you might not have been either. I don't mind looking myself."

Det. Crawford started going through the files while having some small talk in the office. He found it amusing to watch. Just as he suspected, while he was in the records room, two young officers, at different times, came through in need of nothing much.

"Well, I don't see anything here other than old charges. I guess I'm done." Det. Crawford started on his way out.

"Detective, I wrote her name down when you first came in asking questions and if anything comes through here, I will be sure to let you know." Her eagerness was something refreshing to the department. She boosted the morale of that office.

"Thanks." Det. Crawford went back to his office where his coffee had gotten cold. He wanted a fresh hot cup, so he made his way to the break room. He always believed in not wasting things, so while walking to the coffee pot he slammed the remaining cold coffee out of his cup. It didn't taste that good being cold, but he didn't mind, he was just built that way. With fresh coffee in hand, he stepped out the door of the office. After lighting a cigarette, he made a call on his cell phone.

"Hello?"

"Mace, this is Det. Crawford. I was wondering if we could talk?" On the other end of the line was a man that Marlon had known for 10 years. He was well rounded in many circles and knew of many activities within the crime world. His name was Manus Ricci. He had managed to gain a bit of respect and a bit of a blind eye from the police force over the years. He had also gained a lot of respect in the world of crime. He was an entrepreneur by trade. Even though it bent a little outside of the law, he wasn't one who was ever forced to violence.

The detective never knew exactly what he had been involved in or was currently doing. Mace did well to keep his business to himself. This was the fine line he walked between what was right and what was considered wrong. Overall, he had a right mind for justice, although it was different than what the current justice system offered. He didn't like the innocence of people being offended, and thought those who do, should receive their dues more often and more appropriately. He was also of the mind that the government was too far overreaching in their thoughts to keep us safe. He liked free enterprise without the interference of the law. Although different in their perspectives, he and Det. Crawford had a mutual respect for each other.

Everyone that had ever met him called him Mace. When talking with him, he didn't display the sound of a typical bad guy. One thing they had in common was he and the detective agreed that Luis Maldonado was a bad man.

Mace had witnessed the destruction of lives that Luis was responsible for. He knew there was no limit to the level he would stoop at for personal gain.

"Marlioni, what do you have for me?" Mace had an interesting way of speaking as he was Irish Italian. Based on appearances, one might be suspicious of him, but he had no ties to any mob in his family history. In fact, he was raised in the strictest of Catholic homes. When he spoke, he always sounded like he was an Italian chef in a hole in the wall *osteria*.

"I was wondering if we could talk sometime," Det. Crawford wasn't sure if Mace was familiar with Stacy Brown or if anything might come out of their talk, but thought Mace was his best chance of learning something.

"Yea, you know, we can see each other for lunch, but I ain't gonna eat any of that slop you like. We are gonna have to figure on something else," Mace didn't speak with the intentions of being offensive. It was his natural speech to talk like he saw it. He knew the detective was calling for information. It wasn't always the case that Mace helped him out. He weighed the issues and decided if it was something he thought was right to do. He decided what to do as he was not a paid informant. He refused to take money from the department. He was successful in his own ventures and wasn't in need of any money. He looked at it as getting the bad guys out that didn't play right. He also figured it might give him a few liberties as well, and it did on occasion. What he received was a bit of confidence that he wouldn't get messed with as long as he stayed relatively clean, and as he and everyone knew, relative has a relative meaning.

"I don't necessarily have to sit down with you. All I want to know is if you know of a Stacy Brown?" Det. Crawford was hoping he might have heard her name in certain circles.

"Not to my knowledge. Doesn't sound familiar. Why, what's up?" Mace always asked questions for more information. This was how he stayed so packed with it.

"I'm asking for a friend, who is a social worker on a case with her son. She is causing problems with the help being offered to him. We just need her to stay away."

"What a minute Marlioni, I'm not one for separating families. You need to go find a rat for that." Mace was quick to show him the brakes. One thing he felt strongly about was the value of family.

"I understand your position, but she is no mother to him." Det. Crawford began explaining what he had learned of Stacy, letting Mace know, with a few choice words, what he thought about her and what she was doing to her family. He briefly mentioned the doctor and how he was involved with this case. Mace was familiar with the doctor and his loss, as was most of the city. "And the best part for you, she is connected to Mr. Maldonado."

"That piece of shit reprobate. That son of a bitch deserves to be dead." Mace had absolute hatred in his heart for Luis. There were many times that Maldonado's enterprises caused Mace to take a loss or lose out due to their ruthlessness. He was also aware of hits that had taken place in the past, sometimes for gain, sometimes revenge, and others for vanity. "Now that you tell me all that, I'm interested in this situation. I will ask around to see what I can find out about what she might be involved in."

"All I'm looking for is her to stay away." The detective didn't want Mace to become more involved than he had to with his disgust for Maldonado.

"Yea, yea all of them away. I know. Let me check. I'll get back with you." Their phone conversation ended, and the detective went back to his desk. The rest of the day was set in front of paperwork.

He wasn't currently involved in any investigation at the time. He was, however, reviewing old cold cases as was customary for detectives to do when they had time or when evidence in a particular case was uncovered. It was also one of the things he liked doing. He always thought that the answer to solving every case was right there, it was just that the line of sight was off. The thought was, one had to look at things from all angles until it became clear as to what happened.

Going through a couple of cases, he ran into the name of Luis Maldonado. His name was only written by cops in reports taken from the streets. Never was his name written under a sworn testimony or eyewitness account. Even those who didn't like him respected him. His reputation sent chills down most folks back.

He made a few more calls in the interest of knowing anything about Stacy Brown from fellow officers he thought might be of some help in the Vice. They were aware of her by name, but currently she wasn't wanted for anything. Marlon kept to himself for the rest of the day going through files and occasionally walking into the records room, although not for the same reason as the younger bucks. He attempted to put together as much as he could to get a better hold on the situation, but waiting to see what his friend could come up with was the best he had. With only a few minutes before 5:00pm, he walked out of the office early.

Detectives don't really have designated hours when working an active case, and outside of that their hours may vary. Marlon always worked over 50 hours in a week on the short side, so him leaving early was acceptable. He was feeling an urge to satisfy his addiction for fast food. Although this was a common act for him, he would often decide that he was going to give up his bad eating habits. The day to start just never seemed to come. The constant thinking his mind exercised, was the many cases he worked on, always set that thought to be postponed for another day. He never really stayed focused on taking care of himself. The week finished out with no news coming in and Marlon knowing it was going to take some time.

The weekend came and it was Sunday. The detective was at the mall pacing about following his instinctive curiosity that led him most of where he would go. He would go there sometimes during the weekends and walk around when he wasn't working. Dressed in his usual attire, all the youth that frequented the mall had figured out that he was an undercover detective. While a detective never really goes off duty, they couldn't have been more wrong. The fact that he didn't own any other type of clothing than what he wore to work was their first act of not knowing. Secondly, he was brought there by his curious nature and the food court.

He would spend his time eating something as he walked around watching the various people carry out their business, then go outside to smoke a cigarette. He would then come back to the food court for another snack and repeat the whole thing again until he got full.

Everybody seems to have crutches in life and the detective's were cigarettes, caffeine and food that was typically bad for you. The apprehensive teenagers just knew he was there for them. The conspiracy theories they came up with included the Texas Rangers, FBI and US Marshalls. It was always linked to a fugitive hiding out in the mall. Marlon was aware of their suspicions and the nickname he was adorned with, "Kojak." It didn't bother him. It was at least keeping them on their toes. In his mind, the mall was getting his services at "No Charge." In between one of his snacks, his cell phone rang. It was Mace.

"Hello, Crawford here."

"Marlioni, I got the news for you. Probably more than you want. There is a decent size haul coming in next week and Stacy is a driver in the route." Mace himself believed in the opportunity to make money on the free market, but because he knew the criminal enterprise she worked for, he didn't mind selling it out. Somehow, someway, this action would end up hurting someone along its way. It was the only way Maldonado did business.

"Do you have any details about time and place?" Det. Crawford had already started moving to the outside of the mall for better reception and less noise. Mace explained to the detective all that he had learned of the drug deal. It was clear that Stacy would be moving product and by the size of the load, it had to be for Maldonado. It was a win for the detective. He would give this to his partners in drug enforcement, knowing it would be a big win for them and at the same time take care of Stacy for his friend. "Thanks, I owe you one."

"Just one, Marlioni? You owe a bunch. Maybe one day I can collect. I'll talk to you later." Even though they were on separate sides of the law, they shared a common passion. They probably had more things they agreed upon than they disagreed. Marlon hung up his phone and called a sergeant with drug enforcement and filled him in on the situation. This would give adequate time to set up a good sting operation at the location where it was going to take place. All things looked good for the Beat. It seemed to be something to look forward to. With all things though, there can be a downside. They knew they would be initiating a fight with one bad player. As dangerous as they knew it might be, it was a risk worth taking.

Chapter Nine
The Gathering

It was the same Sunday that Det. Crawford was going about the mall, that Dr. Richards was cleaning up to go out for some Tex-Mex Food. Denise had planned this earlier in the month. The doctor was invited to go out dining with her and one of her brothers' family. Throughout their many talks, she quite frequently mentioned her family. The doctor could tell she was close to them and would comment how he would love to meet them. Denise heard that enough times and decided to set up a family outing in which she would include the doctor.

There had been a spot their whole family had been frequenting many years for fajitas and margaritas and Denise thought the doctor might like the atmosphere. The doctor jumped with enthusiasm at the chance to go with them. This would be his first time he would be meeting any of Denise's family. The doctor felt his life had made a huge healing due to his connection with her. Much of what he had been harboring towards his wife's murder was able to be set aside. He wasn't constantly bothered anymore. From time to time, he would have bouts of depression, but they were short lived as he now had something to replace the pain. It was the entire key to healing and maintaining a healthy attitude. The larger picture in the whole situation was what he was attempting to do with his newfound assignment for humanity. It was an attempt to help heal individual's minds. In the process he would be healing his own as well. Getting to meet more of Denise's family was "just what the doctor ordered."

It was close to 5:00pm and they were planning on meeting at the restaurant at 6:30pm. He had a bit of time to wait but was impatient with nothing to do. He had already cleaned up. He was even wearing a tropical designed shirt he had bought for the occasion. This was not his style or preference, but he had begun to feel like taking liberties he never would have after having learned of how life can be unexpectedly fragile.

The evening news was on and headlining the usual worldly events. It always seemed to be an attempt to receive better ratings by political bashing, victimization, horrible crime reports and the end of the world coming. If your relief during the news hour was a brief moment in advertising, it wasn't much of a comfort. These were the ones who paid for the air play and their stance wasn't much different. *If you have any of the following ailments, take this drug. If you suffer at all, take this pill.* This was always followed by, *if you have taken this drug and are now suffering from this call me and we will fight for your rights.*

The doctor was finally at a point he could chuckle a bit, without getting mad. The TV was ridiculous. What a mess, he thought. He just continued flipping through the channels to finish his time before leaving.

His phone rang and it was Denise. It was 5:50pm and she was calling the doctor to let him know she was headed out the door. It was approximately the same distance of travel for the both of them.

"I'm about to leave myself. If I get there before you, I can ask for a table. How many seats will we need?" The doctor knew he was meeting some of Denise's family but had no idea how many.

"Let me think, my brother, his wife, three kids and I believe one of them is bringing a friend. That is six, so with you and I, that makes eight."

"Good, that sounds good. I'm looking forward to it. I'll see you soon." The doctor grabbed his keys and headed out the door. The drive seemed easy. It was a Sunday evening when most folks are in the "take it easy" mode. The doctor had never been to this restaurant. He had heard of it, as it had many great reviews throughout the city. Its name was the "Pinchame' Taqueria." Its reputation was sold primarily on its fajitas. This was apparent when the doctor pulled into the parking lot. The smell of the meat sizzling on an iron griddle with onions, bell peppers and tomatoes filled the air. The aroma was so powerful, it entered his car before he could even open the door to get out.

Not only was it attractive by passing the smell test, it was decorated with the alluring landscape of a Mexican Paradise. The building was decked out to have that fiesta appeal. Water fountains and lush greenery surrounded a canopy covering a Mexican tile entryway into the restaurant. There was an adjacent patio similar to that for outdoor dining. The doctor didn't see Denise's car in the parking lot when he got there, so he assumed she was still en route. He decided to go in and ask for a table.

While waiting for the hostess, he noticed a family he suspected might be Denise's brother. The count was correct, a couple and four children. They also happened to be at a table with eight chairs. The doctor decided to just wait for Denise.

"Are you alone, or are there more people in your party?" The hostess, a young woman, asked the doctor about being seated.

"I'm still waiting for my party to arrive. Thank you."

"You may sit and wait at the bar if you would like." The hostess offered the doctor a better option.

"No thank you, I'm fine." The doctor was content to sit and watch his suspicions.

He was certain that was Denise's brother. He looked to be in good shape. His wife did so as well. At first glance he thought they were trainers of some sort. The children consisted of three boys and one girl. It was obvious to the doctor which of the four children was the friend. Two of the boys, looking to be around the age of ten and the oldest were the most animated of the bunch. One of them was Hispanic. This was the indication he was the friend. The next in line was undoubtably the younger brother, who was mostly laughing while looking at his older brother and his friend. He looked to be around the age of eight. You could see an appreciation for his older brother in the younger one's eye.

The parents were talking, already enjoying a margarita, with the occasional "Kids keep it down." In no way were the children out of line, as the Mexican music in the background was muffled by the many conversations at all the tables. They looked to be having an ideal family gathering.

What really stole the doctor's eye was the little girl. She must have been around six or seven, and not like the boys at all. They were carrying on like typical little boys, while she was poised like a young adult.

The boys were all wearing standard young boy summertime athletic gear, that most boys choose to wear. This seemed to be their own doing. They were probably playing prior to going out and told to clean up. For them that meant washing their hands and changing their shirts. That was to be expected for the boys, but not the little girl.

The little girl was definitely the family princess. It was obvious her mother had spent time putting her little outfit together. It was the cutest of dresses with a matching sweater, a little set of hose and some little girl dress shoes. Her hair was fixed up with ribbons and she wore a set of earrings. The doctor immediately knew what Denise must have looked like as a child. He was quite impressed with her level of maturity as she sat at the table conducting herself very differently from the boys.

Her parents had set her up with her own little personal bowl of queso and a plate with a few chips. She also had a "Shirley Temple" she was drinking as the doctor could see the cherry on top. She just watched her brothers and their friend as she casually took a chip, dipped it and enjoyed her own little world. Her feet, not touching the floor, would slowly swing back and forth as she was having her own time.

"Doctor, sorry, traffic was crazy. Have you been here long?" Denise surprised the doctor as she rushed into the foyer of the restaurant. "My brother's family is here. I spoke with him on the phone to let him know I was running late."

"I figured that was them," the doctor said as he pointed to the family he had been watching.

"That is them, you should have gone and introduced yourself."

"Well, I wasn't 100% sure, so waiting wasn't a problem." The doctor had already begun to follow Denise to the table to be introduced to her family. They could see them approaching and acknowledged Denise as they were coming to the table.

"Doctor this is my oldest younger brother, Desmond and his wife Cheryl." Denise gave pause for the doctor to shake both of their hands.

"Nice to meet you doctor, my sister has told us many nice things about you." Desmond stood up and had a stout constitution and a firm handshake, affirming the doctor's thoughts that his profession was in physical training of some sort.

"Nice to meet you Desmond, nice to meet you, Cheryl." The doctor was rotating to shake everyone's hand.

"Please excuse the boys, sometimes they are a little loud and silly." Cheryl had the motherly instinct of needing to speak on behalf of their boys in case they weren't on their best behavior. "You won't have to worry about Princess though, she just doesn't know how to get in trouble." All the children were paying attention and listening by this time. They were taught to give attention to their elders.

"This is their oldest, Trevor, next in line is William, we call him

Willy, and that one is Candace. We actually do call her Princess. This is Trevor's friend Xavier. You will hardly ever not see them together. They are on every team sport together. My brother coaches a lot of their sports." Denise finished all the introductions and they both took their seats at the table. They both ordered a margarita as the atmosphere was just too tempting for one.

The conversation consisted of the doctor getting to know Denise's family, and some interesting stories of their past growing up.

The doctor learned that Desmond and Cheryl owned a gym and a cross-fit training facility. They were huge competitors in the sports arena. Their children were all being raised to embrace the athletic lifestyle, except for Candace. She was a dancer, and ballet at that. The nickname "Princess" fit her on more than one platform.

The doctor enjoyed his time talking with her family. They did their best to make him feel a part of theirs. They were well aware of his situation, as anyone from the city would be. The doctor found great gratification and appreciation for what Denise's family was doing. They were a part of society that was doing things right. They were part of what was making this world worth living in. He enjoyed their company greatly.

As time was going by, they enjoyed their drinks and appetizers, and talked as if never wanting to end their time together. The laughter was infectious through the stories Denise and Desmond told on each other. The saying that goes "the apple doesn't fall far from the tree" has a lot of truth to it, as Cheryl would comment on their boys and some of the things they had done that related to Desmond as a child. Denise loved all of her family, but it was obvious she had a special connection to the one they all agreed was her little protégé.

"Doctor, when you see Princess, you are looking at Denise 20 plus years ago. Mama and Daddy always had her fixed up. That's just the way we Wilsons are. We like our baby girls to be our baby girls." Desmond was giving a compliment, but at the same time was smiling and looking at Denise as he did so.

"Alright baby brother, enough pampering." Their joking about ruly defined the closeness their family possessed. The doctor's phone began ringing. He looked down and it was Det. Crawford.

"Excuse me, I need to take this, I'll be back." The doctor stepped outside as he answered his phone. "Hello Marlon, I'm walking outside of a restaurant so I can hear you, give me a minute." It was too loud to be able to hear the detective inside the establishment.

"No problem, take your time."

As the doctor got out into the parking lot, he let the detective know he could finally hear good enough for him to speak.

"Go ahead Marlon. It was too noisy in there."

"Well, I think we are going to be able to remove your problem this next week. I found out some interesting news. Sounds like she is planning to do something that is going to get herself in a lot of trouble, and we are going be there to see that she gets caught."

"Fabulous news Marlon. I'm actually out eating with Denise and her family right now, but I'm not going to mention anything about that to Denise out here. We are having too good of a time for me to bring anything up right now." The doctor didn't want anything taken away from the moment he was enjoying.

"I understand, that would probably be best. You can let her know sometime later. I'll let you go; just thought you would want to know."

"I appreciate that, take care." This gave the doctor an incredible boost in the good time he was having. Finally, a chance for setting Dillion on a clean path to recovery might be in the cards.

The doctor went back into the restaurant feeling even better. All things were beginning to look like they were going in the right direction. Denise's knowledge in the matter would wait for a day.

Coming back to the table, conversation continued through another round of margaritas. When the fajitas arrived, they were sizzling in an iron skillet on a wooden base. The smell was incredible and not one eye averted from the table. Their discussions seemed to taper as they ate the food family style. Everyone plated from a few large orders centered on the table. Princess was the only one waited on. Cheryl fixed her up a little plate with all the trimmings, as she wasn't a picky eater. The boys were the ones that only fancied meat, tortillas, and Dr. Pepper. It was a wonderful time, had by all.

As they were finishing up, the doctor excused himself to go to the bathroom. On his way, he decided to go by way of the cash register. He wanted to pay for their night out but knew he would be refused to do so by Denise and her family, so he did it without them knowing.

After going back to the table there was a bit more of some small talk until it was time to leave.

"Well, it was sure nice meeting with you. You should come out and watch the boys one night. They are in a basketball league that I am coaching, and it gets pretty exciting sometimes. Cheryl is the Team Mom, and it is a family affair. Maybe you can bring Denise. She keeps promising she is going to come."

"Not fair baby brother. I have been to Trevor's and Willy's games, it's just been awhile. And last year I didn't miss one of Princess's recitals." While the two were going back and forth, Desmond was laughing and motioned to the waitress for the tab. When she came over she told them it was taken care of. Denise was the first to say something.

"Now, doctor that's not right. I invited you out here. I was going to pick your tab up, and my brother had his group." Denise was serious about not liking the doctor's gesture.

"I'm sorry, I wasn't doing it for any bad reason. I'm not sure if you all know how much of a blessing this is to me. I understand though, I shouldn't have done that. But that means there is a next time, and I won't pull this stunt again." As everyone had been getting up to leave, the words the doctor said were understood. It wasn't about putting his money out there. It was about being a part of something. He was wanting normalcy and his connection to Denise was somewhere he was finding it. They all began their goodbyes and were shaking hands again. He was truly in a happy place. He told all the boys he hoped they did well with their sports but was compelled to throw in their academics as he was a fan of scholastics.

"Trust me doctor, they know, no pass, no play." Desmond was a very structured father. "But we don't have any problems there. The boys are A B. Princess is all As." Cheryl spoke proudly of their family's accomplishments.

Little Willy even felt the need to speak of the grades. Laughingly he said, "Xavier made a C this year."

"Hush Willy."

"Boy," Desmond spoke, but it wasn't a second and everyone began to laugh as they were looking at each other for permission. Lastly, the doctor squatted down and hugged the little Princess. She reciprocated with a nice hug back. He told her that he appreciated having dinner with her and hoped to do it again sometime.

"Thank you, sir. It was nice having dinner with you too." Princess spoke so delicately, it just captured the doctor's heart. He was "in love" with Denise's family. He felt truly welcomed into their world.

This wasn't just a kind gesture some folks might do for spiritual flavoring in their lives. They were a genuine bunch, and he knew it. His instincts as well as Denise's actions let him know this.

Denise walked the doctor to his car as she would an older uncle.

"Will I see you in the morning?"

"Absolutely." The doctor was anticipating telling her the good news.

"Good, I'll pick you up some fancy coffee and won't take no for an answer." Denise was still uncomfortable about the doctor's gesture.

"How about a Danish to go with it," the doctor quickly replied while smiling.

"You got it. Drive home safe and I'll see you in the morning." The doctor felt like saying more but didn't. He was saturated with feeling good. They all got in their cars and went home.

Leaving an event such as that can, for a moment, make one feel down. Reflecting back on the day gave the doctor time to consider that there are things in life that can't be measured, they are simply virtuous, and their score has no limit. This was one for the record books as the doctor continued to add to the good times in his life.

Chapter Ten
The Briefing

In the business world, preparation means everything towards success. Whether you work on the good side or bad, both know the benefit of having a professional strategy.

Inside the top of Luis's organization were two henchmen that he had entrusted his life with on many an occasion. Although no one can ever be trusted in their kind of business, these men were the best examples of loyalty within an organization like this.

His number one bodyguard was his younger cousin, Manuel Consuello. He was more of a brother to Luis. He had been raised in the home Luis grew up in. A son of his mother's sister, he left his home at a young age and was brought up in his aunt's house assuming the role of Luis's younger brother. They knew of each other's secrets from their youth. Their spree in crime started early in the streets of Brownsville, where they managed to create many contacts with the Cartel.

Their innerworkings with these organizations brought them much respect as well as notoriety at an early age. This is where the number two henchman was met and began a relationship with the brothers.

Saul Robelo was someone they met in their early days in Brownsville. Their stint together started with petty theft and graduated to dealing drugs. In order to prove themselves as formidable in their trade, the young men all participated in their first murder together before any of them reached their twenties. It was a crime committed on an innocent man. They had mistakenly hit the wrong individual, which was rectified shortly thereafter. Their taste for ruthlessness was more than acquired. It was desired. From those early days, they stuck together, having felt they were committed to each other. Each one bowed to the devotion they all worshipped.

They managed to control a sizable network of men. Some were considered employees and others just contractors. Throughout the years, they proved their loyalty to each other by overseeing activities that resulted in heinous crimes.

Saul wasn't a relative to Luis or Manuel but was considered a member of the family, eventually taking a position as Luis's personal driver. Their whereabouts were generally unknown, but when they made any appearance, they were undoubtably together. People in the underworld knew that respect was in order when these men showed up. If you had done your assigned job without aversion or mistake, you could rest easy. You would be considered a value to their operations and compensation would follow. Crossing them, or even unintentionally failing at your job would showcase their true character. Their thoughts didn't consider twice on decisions concerning people's lives. Settling a score was as ordinary to them as a day at the office is to most men.

"The ones you have picked are good, se'?" Luis's question to Saul was more than just a casual inquiry on those that were assigned to this job. "You know there are *muchos ladrillos* to account for. I hope we have *dedicacion en mi operacion.*"

"The boys we have coming up from San Antonio, *leal. Puedo atestiguar por estos tres hombres.*" Saul knew that Luis would only accept men that were committed. He was vouching for them and that was his word that was on the line.

"*Bueno*, perhaps they can prove themselves with their lives if need be." Luis made no effort to hide his absence of mercy. He possessed no shame for concealing it. "What about when it gets here?"

"*Esa perra*, Stacy. The white girl. Better for driving up to Illinois. As long as she gets to Chicago, we are done."

No one in Luis's group cared much for Stacy. In their book she was "*basura*," trash, but offered an ability none of them held. It was who she was that they valued. This was her exploit. She knew it but didn't care.

"Make sure she understands *ninguna estupidez sera tolerada*, or she might disappear."

"I will do it myself." Saul had no issues with dispatching anyone, much less her. If they weren't in a position of using her, he probably would have killed her by now just because he didn't like her, and because she was aware of their business.

"Because she isn't worth as much as the load, let her know that." Luis would say his piece and let it go. He expected all to know his expectations. There wouldn't be any excuse for error.

The arrangement was that 25 kilos of cocaine was being moved from Dallas to Chicago. The driver, Stacy Brown, wasn't to know where it was coming from or where it was going. Drop off locations were all she knew, and those locations were given prior to needing to know. She would drive the long distance, while being followed, and that was her part.

Once this reached Chicago it most certainly was going to face getting stomped on. Adding one third of its weight to itself, they could increase the amount and charge twice its going rate in Texas. The drug industry was full of cheats and liars all standing to profit from someone's misfortune. They all knew this and despised others for the actions they would commit themselves. It was irony and hypocrisy in a battle of wits.

Just as they finished their consuming of the drug deal and its trimmings, the men began to carry on about a fishing trip that had been planned for some time. A deep-sea excursion out in the Gulf of Mexico to reel in some marlins. Their conversation turned on a dime from crime and murder to a peaceful and enjoyable vacation. Someone not privy to the first part of their discussion, and in earshot of the second, would think the world of these men. They sounded like old friends with great intentions and goodwill to great times. This was not to be misunderstood. Selfishness drove everything within their dark souls. A mere vacation was just because they wanted it. They fed their souls and their needs and nothing else mattered. They felt they were brought about for this purpose.

A much different setting was playing out to counter the actions of these men. All information known had been passed to the Narcotics Department to thwart the efforts of this deal taking place. Preparations were being laid out for a sting to counteract the mission. Manus Ricci had become aware of this through a friend of the girlfriend of one of the drop off men. His attempt to puff up his own vanity was the chink in the armor that exposed the plan. He was proud about having some "good" cocaine for a big party he was planning. His ego talked enough, even detailing Stacy as the one they would follow to Chicago. Hearing through the grapevine that she was no good, his pride let her name slip out. His girlfriend wanted to boast in her ability to have that party as she expressed that same sentiment to her friends. That was usually how it worked. Everyone wants notoriety, but no one wants to take credit.

This information was passed on to Detective Crawford and eventually to the Captain of Narcotics for the Dallas Metro Area. With a few informants being questioned and collaborating parts of the story, it was enough to set up a sting.

Captain Walter Ploetz was a 21 year veteran of the Dallas Police Department. Capt. Ploetz was well seasoned and had a successful record with handling busts in the City Limits as well as working with Task Forces in the surrounding counties. His journey had him starting in patrol and eventually working his way up the ranks to what he attributed to be the top, which was narcotics. Everyone in the department liked him. He was an easy-going man. This wasn't something you would expect from someone in narcotics. He managed to separate his job from his outside life. In fact, he separated it so well, none of his co-workers had much of a relationship with him outside of work. This is not to say he was an unapproachable man, but he didn't engage unless you did first. For that reason, many people misjudged his character. He was really the right man to be in charge because of his nature.

The location of the drop was scheduled in a parking garage that was in a lesser trafficked area. The Team of this operation consisted of eight men and himself. The count was Sergeant Benjamin Lewis who was paired with Guadalupe Martinez. They were to be staged inside the parking garage along with Officers Jonathan Wilke and Dominick Stevenson. They would provide surveillance and film what they could, in addition to being the first and closest to approach the situation. Both of these units would be placed on different floors of the parking garage where the transaction was scheduled to take place. The cars placed outside of the garage would be occupied by Officers Joel Brown and Michael Young in one vehicle and Officers Steve Handley and Buford Smith in another. This Team had been training and working under the coordination of Capt. Ploetz for about a year and a half. Their tactical training had kept them safe and, throughout all departments, regarded as the best.

"Settle in boys, I need to brief everyone on the information that has been given to us about a sizable load of drugs. An exchange is supposed to take place this coming Sunday, very early in the morning around 2:00am. We can expect to be set up a couple of hours earlier, the night before. It's going to take place in the Old Joske's Parking Garage. We are hoping for little to no activity in there. I'm sure there won't be if these monkeys have made any type of protections for themselves."

"Sir, if I recall this garage is primarily used by an apartment complex overflow that is one block over. It doesn't really fill up." Officer Handley offered up advice as he was familiar with the area.

"I thought that might be the case but wasn't sure," The Captain came back. "That was my next thing was to ask if anyone could confirm what the normal parking looks like. Thank you, Handley."

The Captain kept about his business going over the layout of the garage, complete with a map. They discussed where everybody was to be positioned based on the information they had and where the drop would take place.

It was estimated two men were dropping off the load. It would be loaded into Stacy's car. The Team was briefed on who she was and shown pictures of her to know what she looked like.

"Joel, wasn't that your date last week," Officer Martinez couldn't help himself. He was always known for popping off shots. It wasn't meant to start any type of scuffle, rather friendly joshing about.

"Wow, I thought that was your sister," Officer Brown retorted, playing right up to the line that you aren't supposed to cross."

"Alright, enough. We have serious business to discuss, and I don't feel like staying late because I feel you guys weren't paying attention. Listen, get it down and we can go home. This coming Sunday we need to be prepared." The Captain was a man of deliberation, not swayed by the things most men take into consideration. He truly found interest in only the things that mattered. This would be a huge seize for the department, but more so, it would be an incredible saving of many lives that might see a demise through an overdose, a gunshot, a stabbing or a heart attack. They would never know who or how many lives would be saved, but undoubtedly there would be some.

The difference between both sides was the strategy of the two different energies. One briefing consisted of self and the other of self-examination. What compelled one man on one side of the spectrum drove another man into action on the other side. These were the forces the doctor was having conflict with. Why was one so easily able to succeed and leave such a path of destruction wherever they went? The other was forced to be reactionary and would be stifled in an attempt to create order and to correct. Why did good have to anticipate and wait for evil to make a move? Evil waited for nothing but its own will.

Perhaps it was time for this rule to be re-examined. How much pain and suffering could be eradicated by eradicating the very thing that caused it? A proactive strike against wrong seemed worthy and yet society deemed it otherwise.

The minds of many in the world were wrestled out of good sense by their emotions. One would have to attempt an effort to change these things, the doctor was in the process of learning. He would have to remain with an optimistic attitude as the harsh realities of this world unfolded around him. It would be a matter of time that would force change to manifest real optimism. Under the current system, the best choices were hardly being made. Acceptances had their own crowds cheering and pushing forth their own efforts to promote their own will. Seeing to it that each side had a fight, and a chance was the determination of each. The doctor's conscience was exercising the thoughts of the powers that appeared to be around him. Time and planning would be the strategy for success from both sides. Determination and will would be the deciding factor for the victor.

Chapter Eleven
The Sting

Everybody was in position as the evening began to come upon them. The Team had been scheduled to be set up three and a half hours before the drop off. This allowed all things to look ordinary and minimized their movement when eyes might become suspicious.

Sitting in his controlling chair was Captain Ploetz. Being the tenured veteran with the Dallas Police Department sanctified his readiness. He and Det. Crawford had been long outstanding policemen working together throughout the years. Their relationship was built on a mutual respect for one another, so after receiving news of the exchange, Capt. Ploetz's department went to work coordinating the seize. Their planning that went into this operation was meticulous.

The five unmarked cars were strategically placed about the parking garage. The planning had estimating where the transaction would take place. The four-story parking garage, located in an industrial part of the city, now serving as parking for an overflow of housing, was probably reason for its location for this deal to go down. Surveillance cars were set on the third and fourth floors. From what little was gathered and skilled assumptions, the deal would be handled on the third floor. One of the cars was parked on the street close to the entrance of the garage, and the remaining two were in a parking lot across the street.

Captain Ploetz was in one of the cars across the street, coordinating the sting. Patience would be the challenge before the storm. Anticipation can bring with it fear. A lot of planning goes into police work, but no training exists for the unknown. Round table discussions of "what if" scenarios are scrutinized, but what will you do if the situation changes? What will you do if something unexpected happens? All possibilities are examined with nothing escaping the imagination. The end result being that you still don't know. The level of training is intense, and at the hour of deployment, it is sit and wait without knowing what is going to happen. Great training and a composed individual was what it took to run in this business.

"Is everyone tucked in for the night?" The Capt. came across their private frequency to all the cars in position. He was also checking all lines of communications.

"Yes sir, Handley and Smith here." The cars started a response in order like a roll call acknowledging that their ears were open.

"Brown and Young, we're good."

"Stevenson and Wilke, over." Every one of the officers were disciplined and on point.

"Martinez and Lewis here, goodnight John Boy." There always had to be one in the group. It was the young, only two years in the department Officer Lupe Martinez. Everyone liked Officer Martinez. He was always joking when it was appropriate, or so he thought. He was barely 25 and a newlywed with his first child on the way. Most of his colleges teased him as he was the rookie. He didn't mind it. His character seemed to ask for it.

"Watch it Martinez, or John Boy's gonna put you to sleep," The Captain's response was short, but in a playful manner. He wanted his men in a serious thought pattern.

Officer Martinez was in the car on the fourth floor with Sergeant Lewis. They had been partners since Martinez's start date.

"You know the Captain just loves it when I say things like that." Officer Martinez always had to have a conversation going. Sergeant Lewis, on the other hand, complimented him well as he was mostly a listener.

"Yea, I'm sure you're right." Sarcasm was also a trait he possessed.

The two kept about a small conversation, keeping their minds busy. The wait time was estimated, so allowing boredom to dominate could be conflicting to the mind. This wasn't a place or time for them to become complacent. Frivolous conversation lent its hand for that reason, but the obvious never escaped their minds.

It was no different in the other cars. They were having their small talk along with some snacks that usually accompany this work. The older officers tended to only have hot black coffee. Younger officers felt the need to bring a few things to snack on. Many times, these were a contribution from a loving and concerned spouse. Unhealthy eating was something they could afford in their youth, and the fact mama put it together for them was what made it so much more enjoyable. All the older officers would laugh as they knew they used to do the same thing, but age had now brought with it alterations. Sweets in a bag and sweets from home were taken in much more moderation with age.

Time seemed to go by slow. It was natural for talking and eating to help consume some of that. The arrival was what it was all about.

The information that was given to them laid out a specific sequence. A shipment of cocaine was being brought in from San Antonio. It had come directly from across the border and hadn't been stepped on, making it worth much more. It was of substantial size and value.

Stacy Brown would have 25 kilos she would be responsible for. It carried a street value of over a half million dollars. Her time committed would be about fourteen hours. Drive to the garage, have the drugs loaded for her, and drive the car to a determined location that would be given to her at that time. She would be headed for Chicago. She just wouldn't know until it was time to go.

Most of the tasks she performed had her driving across state lines. She would be followed to make sure she didn't stray from her directed path and to ensure proper delivery. In the case of any unexpected traffic stops, she was the fall guy. It was just standard operating procedure for large hauls to have sacrificial offerings. It was looked as something she should offer for the generous $25,000 payday she would receive.

With payouts like this, one could do jobs like this for a couple of years, get out and have a healthy early retirement. It never worked out like that. People in this business can't quit because they are either addicted to the money or something else that requires money. Managing in an effort to get out escapes even the smartest of criminals.

This money would eventually end up being partied away at a casino in a few weekends. She didn't care. It was all living for the moment.

The attack was to surprise them during the unloading and loading period. A chase would be avoided at all costs, especially to locations unknown. Controlling as many variables as they could, kept them best at determining the outcome. Dominating the occupation of the surroundings would need to belong to them. Once the cars entered the garage, surveillance would be a key component to building a case.

Martinez and Lewis were to exit their vehicle and take position and call for a surrender. The cars across the street would be called in by radio, just before a command of surrender was given, so that the element of surprise would overwhelm the criminals. All officers were armed with AR-15s and proficient in their operating.

The goal was to have it go down with no shots fired, but in no way, no one was to hesitate to shoot.

These men had to be deliberate in their cause and determined in their purpose. A common thought within this operation was that this work being done was coordinated by Luis Maldonado. While that could not be verified, there was no way this much cocaine could touch the streets and he not know about it. It was either his or someone would be in trouble for doing this in his town. It was a correct assumption to think he was involved. While it was known he wouldn't be the one going down, they would certainly be interrupting his operations at a costly sum. That would cause him great displeasure. It would be his cronies who would be taking the fall. Both sides were certain, snitching was highly unlikely. Doing time to not face a certain death sentence was a better option.

Time continued to unwind, going past its expected allotment.

"Is everyone ready, we should be seeing someone drive up soon," The Captain reached out across the radio. "Be sure to say your prayers before this all goes down." The Captain knew of the protocol society had forced on religious freedoms. When it came to talking about God in the workplace, some considered it a violation. He also knew they worked in a very dangerous world, where sometimes in a moment, in the blinking of an eye, things change forever. He meant what he said, and every one of his guys respected him for that. The men said silent prayers in their heads as they were God-fearing men.

"Sergeant, be careful, I want to keep working with you," Lupe Martinez gave a heartfelt send out to his Sergeant.

"I will. We need to just keep focused and do our jobs quickly and clean." Just as he finished speaking, the Captain came across the radio again. "I think our Mrs. Brown is going to turn in. She is driving the expected Ford Fusion, Color Red, License Delta, Edward, One, One, Six, Dog, Sam."

It was Stacy. She drove in the parking garage like she was going to a party. The officers on the third floor saw her headlights as she rounded the level of the garage floor and watched her park about 15 car spaces away on an opposing row. They had a clear line of sight but didn't know which side of her car the delivery vehicle would park. They weren't concerned about Stacy being a threat. Moreover, their unease was that the other vehicle would certainly be armed. That would be the challenge in maintaining control.

Accessibility to them was crucial. Stacy was seen sitting in her car, smoking and moving her head to the music. She seemed unfazed by the severity of the current situation. Officers Stevenson and Wilke were on the same floor as Stacy, recording her actions.

"She doesn't seem to be taking this too seriously, does she?" Stevenson mentioned to Wilke.

"I certainly wouldn't give her the job. She's a risk. That's good for us though." Officer Wilke was running the camera. He was a career officer with a large family. He enjoyed getting rid of the trash in the streets. He despised thinking these criminals lined the streets of the communities his children were coming up in. This line of work showed an element in society that most people don't even know existed.

These activities go on day in and day out under the very noses of people and they never know it. Good thought gives consent to doing things undercover as a best practice for concealment. Criminals have learned by not remaining ensconced, they can take advantage of a naïve society and conduct business and still remain obscure. Officer Wilke was ready to lock them all up.

"Looks like car number 2 might be coming." There was a brief pause over the radio. "It is turning. Lincoln Navigator, Color Black, Occupied at least twice, can't see in the back seat. License Bravo, Two, Zero, Charlie, Tyler, Four, Eight. Everyone get ready, this is going to go quick." The Navigator crept up the garage to the third floor and pulled in on the far side from the surveillance car, putting Stacy's car between them.

"They parked on the other side of the Ford. We will need Martinez and Lewis to have good positions before we exit." Stevenson came across the radio, assuming Martinez and Lewis were already moving out. Three men exited the Navigator, with only one moving to the back and opening the hatch. The other two were watching their surroundings and concealing automatic weapons underneath their clothing. The men were all dressed in black head to toe. This was unlike their associate. Stacy, who was more casually dressed, displayed a nature unsuspecting for a passerby. She popped her trunk without exiting her vehicle. This was to allow for them to load four large suitcases into the Fusion. By this time, the cars across the street had been running and were in gear to move forward.

Martinez and Lewis were both in a line of sight towards the two men flanked by the Navigator.

"We got a mark on them." Sergeant Lewis keyed up his radio and let them know they were in position. Just as they began to grab the merchandise to move it into Stacy's car, the Capt. gave the command.

"Let's move in!" The element of surprise was the luxury that had to be coordinated with precise detail to command control. If not executed properly, you can be the one surprised.

The cars across the street gave the first indication of action happening as their motors revved up and they sped into the garage. All the men abandoned the transfer and jumped into the Navigator. Simultaneously Officers Lewis and Martinez displayed their attendance with their guns pointed at the Navigator. The tactical lighting mounted on their weaponry created a blinding presence towards the Navigator.

"Stop, hands up. Freeze!" From the time they had driven into the garage to the police announcing their presence it took less than twelve seconds on a stopwatch. At this point Stacy was laid over in her vehicle, wishing she hadn't done this deal.

The men in the Navigator had a much different idea. Officers Stevenson and Wilke were positioned outside their car, taking precaution not to receive crossfire. As the cars were speeding to the third floor, the Navigator punched out of its parking space with a deafening screech of tires and a hail of gunfire towards Lewis and Martinez. Return fire became almost immediate from both of the men. Stevenson and Wilke were also taking shots at the car. The cars that had entered the parking garage stopped just shy of cresting the third floor as the melee held their positions back.

They exited their vehicles and placed themselves in cover for an attempt on the suspects coming down the garage. The Navigator's back doors opened and two men emerged with automatic rifles. They began thrusting themselves in the direction of Martinez and Lewis without any intention of suppressing gunfire. Wilke was able to take aim at one of the men moving towards his comrades, and with one calculated shot to his back, dropped him like a sack of feed. The other one, however, seemed to advance well towards his buddies, continuing to fire. The return fire now seemed to be coming from another point. Officers Handley, Smith, Brown and Young became engaged and were able to subdue the other gunman. Guns in hand and all senses heightened, things suddenly ceased and there were many unknowns. The smell of expressed gunpowder, burnt tires and a thick haze filled the garage.

"Drop your weapons! Get on the ground! Anyone moves and you will be shot!" Officer Wilke was yelling not knowing the fate of anyone besides Stevenson, who was beside him. "I said down, surrender your weapons!" Still charged with adrenaline, Wilke was shouting and getting no response. The silence from the Navigator gave way to his Team.

"Is everyone OK?" Sergeant Handley called out to everyone on the floor. He was next to Officers Smith, Brown and Young. They acknowledged their wellbeing.

"Wilke and Stevenson OK." There was no answer from Martinez or Lewis. Not knowing the fate of the driver of the Navigator or Stacy, the tactical Team approached with caution. They now knew there was a possibility some of their Team had been shot. As Handley instructed Brown and Young to sweep the scene, he and Officer Smith sat ready to provide cover fire if needed. None was needed as a result of the driver coming into their line of sight. He had been hit in the first exchange. He was slumped over the steering wheel showing major signs of trauma to the top of his head.

Stacy was alive and well, clutched in a fetal position on the passenger side floor board of her car. They only wished they could have said as much for Martinez and Lewis, as both men lay motionless with obvious gunshot wounds to their bodies.

"Martinez and Lewis are down!" Sergeant Handley yelled over the radio.

"EMS is en route!" The other officers had already turned them over and were attempting CPR. Stevenson and Wilke had gotten to the Ford Fusion and removed Stacy. Officer Wilke had one shoestring left holding his emotions together as he battled with the thoughts of his partners being down.

Even though Stacy was a female, that didn't override her being a "piece of shit" in his book. To place her in cuffs, he ripped her out of the car and slammed her, face first, to the ground, causing her breath to go out of her without intent of return. Although he never checked, he was sure she was uninjured by the resistance she gave on his attempt to remove her from the vehicle. She struggled to cuss at him but was unsuccessful as she was gasping for air.

Officer Lewis had a pulse and the Team kept breathing for him, throwing chest compressions in at the appropriate intervals. No one was willing to accept it, but Martinez seemed to have passed. His limp body had no pulse and the obvious shot to his head spoke volumes. Stevenson joined Smith in attempting CPR on Martinez. Deep down they knew it was useless.

As Captain Ploetz's car pulled up to the third floor, he was looking at the path that destruction had left. He looked around the entire scene and felt great disgust in his heart. The absolute worst thing for any commanding officer was to lose a man in any situation. It is a lonely corridor where few men can ever find a place to forgive themselves, even though they aren't holding any responsibility for it.

The sirens could be heard coming in the distance. Not a member of the Team stopped in their attempts to save their partner's lives. Stacy remained in the back of the police car within eye shot of the Captain. Looking at her, he struggled to resist the urge to hate.

When the EMS arrived, they immediately took over tending to the two downed officers. The main focus became obvious as they loaded Lewis into the ambulance and began to transport. A sheet was placed over Martinez's body. It was a solemn reminder of the oath they all took when coming to this job.

They had scored a big win in the war on crime, but the price paid was the ultimate one. They would want more than just Stacy, but getting more would be a challenge. Hopefully capital murder charges might convince her otherwise.

The determination would now be for Luis Maldonado. The original intent of removing a mother that was a bad influence had now turned into a useless murder. This would have to receive greater justice.

The gut-wrenching loss suffered by the Martinez family along with the unknown condition of Officer Lewis sat heavy on the hearts of the Team. Even though they had removed three crooks from the game, seized a sizable load of drugs and had one in custody, they still wondered, was it all worth it?

Second guessing and self-examination would lead them all to question themselves. Do I give an opportunity for surrender next time, or just shoot to stop it all? It was a threat to order. Law was the one in question.

When the law ceases to function properly, those who seek a just law will act accordingly to bring about order. With lawlessness abounding, this would become a more common question for those seeking justice.

Chapter Twelve
A Realization

It was a somber day in the offices of law enforcement for the DFW Area. As Monday crested and finally opened its eyes from the night's events, word of what happened spread like wildfire. All were feeling the loss of the young, dedicated Officer Martinez.

Officer Lewis looked to be pulling through, though it was going to be an uphill battle with expected lifestyle changes. In question was his ability to ever walk again. With one of the bullets piercing his spine, it was uncertain if surgery was an option. For now, his life was the pressing concern for his family.

The entire department was mourning their fallen comrades. The County Judge ordered all flags to be flown at half-staff. News media fulfilled their commitment to society with their generous attention to detail and informing everyone of the matter. There was a feeling of great contempt for the circumstances they were facing.

Despite the situation, there wasn't much talk in the offices where Denise worked. People kept quiet as words didn't seem to want to come out. Extreme depression was overlaid with a question mark. How was it that this could in any way be acceptable? Everyone involved knew of the risks they were taking going into this work. That was not the question. The fact that there wouldn't be anyone left to pay the price for this horrific event left everyone speechless.

Stacy Brown was hardly any restitution for the officer's death. The men who were wasted in the shootout were expendable by all counts. This left everyone knowing that the chief architect who coordinated the whole event seemed untouchable to receiving any punishment owed to him. It was a failed system and it seemed absurd. The law had turned itself against what it was intended for, to protect the innocent. It now acted as an excuse for the criminal. Dr. Richards was deeply affected by the death of the officer.

"In some way, I feel responsible. All I wanted was to help Dillion." The doctor was having difficulty dealing with the situation.

"It's hard on all of us. Don't look to explain why it happened, it just did. You had nothing to do with it." Denise knew the doctor had already dealt with the question of "why" in harsh criminal cases. She wanted him to remain healthy within his mindset. It was something that happened, and their work would have to continue. They had to stay focused on that.

For now, Stacy would remain outside of interfering in the process of correcting all things in Dillon's life. She would be going away for a considerable amount of time. To lose sight of that would make Officers Martinez and Lewis's sacrifices in vain. All parts salvageable would need to be made into gold. Dillion would receive full concentration on getting better. They weren't sure how he would take the news of his mother's involvement. Would it have a negative effect, as self-victimization was one of the traits she had always been proud of wearing? They would plan to sell it to him in the purest form of truth, hoping to appeal to the good they knew existed within this young boy.

In a different arena, the State would be focusing on her giving up her bosses. This was an unknown, but they would leverage all they had against her. No tactic would be withheld, in an effort to get to Maldonado. Would murder charges be enough for her to show her true disloyalty? They couldn't be sure as they knew she was in it for herself, which meant her life. Either way, the prosecution would be exploring every avenue they could to squeeze every bit of foul play to the surface.

Detective Crawford was assigned to be involved in the case of the killing of Officer Martinez. The interrogation process was a familiar territory for him. His expertise set against Stacy would hopefully get some sort of a confession as to Luis Maldonado's involvement. Her arraignment was at least a week out, but the detective's work would have to start early.

During the thought process of needing answers, Detective Crawford knew that all his information channels should be accessed. He checked back in with Manus, to see if there had been any talk about the killing. Knowing his friend would side with him, he guessed his call would be expected.

"Mace, this is Marlon. I guess you've heard what went down by now?" The detective wasn't one to show emotion but having had one of his own go out, it had taken a toll on him. He sounded a bit broken.

"Yea, I heard. I wish I hadn't. I know why you are calling. It's about Luis, isn't it? I still haven't heard anything, but if it was his load, which everyone knows it was, he is gonna want someone to pay for it." Mace's voice had a tone of anger in it. Even with his lifestyle riding on the borderline of what society deemed as criminal, he didn't approve of this happening and wanted the detective to know this. "I'll keep my ears peeled and if I hear of anything that could help you, I'll let you know." Mace wanted Luis just as much as the department. He knew they were wanting to pinch Stacy and anything that the department might have, could be crucial in making her talk.

"Keep in touch. I'll be the one interviewing the girl. I'm supposed to meet with her for the first time in a bit. Anything you might be able to give me, will be greatly appreciated."

"Will do, let me get back to you." The detective was going to be sitting in with Stacy. He was the primary interrogator. Her reaction to any questioning might open doors to their cross-examination.

He would propose to accomplish a feeling of trust, in order to get her to speak. By appealing to one of her vanities, victimization, he could possibly buy himself her dependency.

Stacy was transported to Homicide and awaiting her appointment with the detective. He sat amongst colleagues looking at Stacy in the interrogation room while he drank coffee and planned an attack. She was squirming in her chair, handcuffed to a bar on the wall. There was a table placed in the room to provide a comfortable barrier between her and Det. Crawford. She was provided a water and allowed to smoke, which she did continually. The show she was performing for them unsuspectingly spelled out nervousness. They wanted Stacy to be relaxed during the interview. Getting a confession of the whole truth was the goal. They would approach this with a blanket of trust being laid out before talks even began.

Twenty minutes of watching her on camera seemed an eternity. She had consumed much of her half pack of cigarettes, smoking them halfheartedly. After some strategic discussion on the approach, it was time.

"I'm going to go in," Det. Crawford announced. "Waiting too long might allow her to overthink and become shut off towards us." Marlon was losing patience and wanted to begin the process of extracting information. He grabbed a pen and notebook and entered the room. Only one officer would be in the room with Stacy. Causing a feeling of her being "teamed up on" was cautiously avoided. They wanted to derail any "lawyering up," which was a common practice among people familiar with the system. Recording something about Luis's involvement was the ace they were hoping for. Marlon knew he had to play his cards just right.

When he opened the door, Stacy's head moved from face down on the table to a desperate stare towards the detective.

"Hello, I'm Detective Crawford." He stuck out his right hand to shake Stacy's hand.

"Hello." She didn't say much and kept her free hand to herself.

"Well, I guess you know why we are here. I would like to hear your version of what happened." She remained silent, attempting to look away. "I would like to get to the bottom of knowing who all was involved in what happened in the parking garage. We know that you were working for someone else." There was no beating around any bush. The detective knew if they were going to get her to talk, they had to just open the door. She kept silent. "Look we know that this is not your stuff. Someone else is responsible for what happened, and we need you to help us, so we can help you."

"Can I get some more water?"

"In a minute, first we need to talk!"

"I'm thirsty!" Stacy's demeanor was beginning to look like she was going to break.

"Stacy, you need to talk to me. Don't you want to help yourself?" Shaking her head no, she lit another cigarette. Det. Marlon had no pity for her but had to remain calm. He also had to get to business before she shut him off. "We have four men dead, and one in the hospital recovering, with an outcome unknown. He is a family man and may never walk again. You need to begin telling us what you know if you want to salvage any part of your life that you may have left." Stacy was beginning to become flush. She felt the pressure and severity of the situation. It was laying on her like an unremovable weight restricting her breath. Shaking, she went to light another cigarette with one burning in the ash tray. Her lack of knowing what to do had her fidgeting about in the chair. She was backed into a corner. "You need to think long and hard, because someone is going down for all this, and all we have now is you." Detective Crawford began tightening the noose. It was an effort to get her to remove it by talking. His tactic proved too aggressive.

"I want a lawyer." Stacy heard more than she wanted to hear. Fear was eating her from the inside. She not only had the weight of the state on her back, but the criminal enterprise she was employed by considered her "still on the job." Not obeying them brought about its own set of penalties.

Detective Crawford got up and walked out without another word spoken. He was upset but knew the route they must travel now. It would be up to the legal system. He was sure Stacy would go down, but that wasn't all they wanted. They wanted to see the real threat society had been dealing with. They wanted the responsible characters to take a fall. It would stand to be a real challenge. Stacy was taken back to her cell to await a court appointed attorney to begin work on her case.

In another part of the city, Luis was well aware of the losses he was potentially facing along with the ones he already endured. His investment in the drug deal was cause enough to be upset, but now he faced the probability of Stacy implicating him in the deal. He was furious and would stop at nothing to liberate himself from this curse he had helped to create.

His motivation was like that of the devil. He didn't care about the damage he caused. He only accepted the results he expected, and anything shy of that was provocation to do all until his results came to be. The first course of action was to see that Stacy had good representation.

There was a well-known law firm that provided certain services for companies he was connected to outside of paper. Luis had this firm on retainer for situations that might present themselves when one is involved in the life he was. These men were known for representing the bad guys.

The firm was Lucas & Abrams. They were a high-priced firm that had earned their reputation as one of the best. They specialized in all criminal cases and had an exemplary record. They were a firm built by the team of John Lucas and Aaron Abrams. Both men had come from prominent Christian homes earning reputable honors throughout their childhood and professional careers. Hard working, hard studying, and respectable was the irony in their work. They knew the law and how to appeal to its flaws. They also had many inner connections in the political arenas with judges and politicians. It was a sad thing to know, but all their victories, no matter how much they might be in question, were done legally.

It was this law office that would be contacting Stacy, as she awaited arraignment. She would be instructed they would be representing her pro-bono. Everybody in the metro area knew of this law firm and what they were about.

Although there was never any communication between Luis and Stacy concerning this matter, nor would there ever be, she knew these lawyers were being sent by him. It was for his own protection. One thing he couldn't afford was to lose anything else in this deal. Protecting Stacy until he could get to her was crucial. Her foolishness would never tell herself this. She would never expect him to be angry with her. He sent in a team to cover her. Her selfish attitude denied her seeing just how evil really worked.

As word of the defense grabbed all those involved on the side of law enforcement, there was a shutter of despised revulsion. Everyone was familiar with this law firm and their capabilities. The very thought of a loophole presenting itself in this case would be unthinkable, and that was exactly what this firm did best. Only time would tell what the outcome would be.

Doctor Richards sat across from Denise in her office. They were preparing to visit with Dillion later that afternoon. On their last visit, he had seemed to make progress. That would all be in question now, since his mother had gotten into trouble.

Denise was anxious to get to Dillion before any conflicting emotions might unroot any progress they had been making. The next few encounters would be vital towards his growth. Overcoming the hurdle of his mother's incarceration would be a monumental milestone.

"I'm hoping this doesn't make Dillion think the system is working against him. He has got to understand his mother is a part of something he shouldn't want in his life. As sad as that sounds, it is something he must learn to accept." The doctor was becoming more "matter of fact" in all of his thinking. The cop killing had taken a hammering on his psyche. "It's good we don't have to deal with her anymore, but is that going to play on her son's mind?"

"I'm not sure doctor, we will just have to see." After Denise spoke to the doctor not sure herself, they did a bit of planning and then set out to visit with Dillion.

Their drive seemed long, with silence owning much of the time.

They were at a loss of words and full of thoughts. Prayers undoubtably were being sent out by them for a multitude of requests.

At their meeting, Dillion was surprisingly open. Not knowing how he would react, they let him speak. He did express a dislike that his mother was in custody for such a crime, but no way did he excuse it. He cried a bit during their discussion. As much as he disliked the situation, it was still his mother. He was connected by circumstance. Knowing this, they knew it would be a venting process. He would have to get much of his thoughts out there for them to address each one individually.

Denise encouraged him to set goals for himself, knowing that they could only be achieved with his mother's absence. He needed to learn it was ok to distance himself from negative influences, even if those influences were family. It was only natural for him to feel sadness. Breaking his heart were the ones where he had come from.

Their conversation continued for about an hour, with Dillion speaking a bit more than he ever had. This was making the doctor and Denise appreciate the power of positive thinking and what it can achieve.

"Dillion, I can say, Denise is usually the one who does most of the talking and I have steered from saying much to you, but you are an amazing young man with so much potential. For you to be able to see past the things you would want to change, but can't, and them being the closest thing to you, is remarkable. I know these things lie heavy on your heart and what we are seeing here today is what makes true character. It is the ability to discern correctly, no matter how painful the decisions are to make." The doctor felt confident that the outcome of Stacy wouldn't get in the way of their progress.

"I understand." Dillion seemed to run out of words, but his understanding was coming right along.

The doctor and Denise were relieved to hear that Dillion wasn't corrupted by this and felt at ease knowing he was seeing clearly. They knew this was a painful process, but he hadn't let it change his good judgement. That was what they needed to see.

All would have been well in the hearts of Denise and the doctor, but as fate would have it, Dillion asked a hair-raising question.

"Do you know if my mom was working for Mr. Maldonado?" The doctor quickly looked at Denise as his eyes opened to full capacity.

"Why would you ask a question like that?" Denise was

dumbfounded by Dillion's inquiry. "We don't know any of the details surrounding the case but how do you know this man's name?" Denise thought this poor boy's mind had been exposed to more than it should have.

"I have heard my mom talking before on her phone and whenever I heard her mention his name, I always got scared for her because I knew she was taking a chance of getting in big trouble."

"What do you mean by big trouble?" Denise had a puzzled look on her face.

"You know, drugs."

"We don't know. Many times, things are said. We don't necessarily know the facts; people speculate but it is up to the police to do their work. We are just here for you, so let's stay focused on that." Fear instantly consumed the thoughts of both the doctor and Denise. Sidetracking Dillion was a reaction towards his protection. Not saying a word about it, they both assumed the same thing. Although the connection was there, it was hearsay and circumstantial. The police would want to pursue it, but what protections would be guaranteed to a vulnerable boy in the event he testifies. It was another struggle in the battle of doing what was right. It might not fare out the way it is supposed to, and the doctor feared the writing on the wall.

As the both of them thought heavily about what they heard, they knew they would talk about it later.

"Do you know this man? Is he going to go after my mom?"

"Dillion, you're asking questions we don't have the answers to and you don't need to worry yourself with that. Your mother is locked up safe. Nobody can get to her, and she can't get in anymore trouble. You need to let all that go for now and we will keep concentrating on you. Remember WE are here for YOU," Denise finished by hugging the young boy. She could feel him crying as he was softly shaking while she held him. Raising up and looking at him he had tears but was wearing them with a painful smile. She knew they had his trust.

Before leaving, Denise and the doctor had a brief discussion with Dillion's grandmother on the overall situation. The grandmother expressed wanting for all things to be good but possessed no backbone to enforce it. Denise felt pity for her, knowing her situation. The power and possession of a good environment requires much more than just desire. It is actions of good will as well as efforts to remove all that is wrong. An assurance for things to remain good in Dillion's life would need more than his grandmother was capable of giving. This was why Denise and the doctor's continued support would be necessary.

As they were about to leave, the doctor took a liberty in asking Dillion to do something. With intentions of leaving the boy on a positive note for all he had been through, the doctor made him an offer.

"Dillion, would you like to earn a few dollars?" Dillion's eyes opened a bit more wide than normal and with confusion and he responded in a soft tone.

"Yes?"

"I see that your grandmother's yard could use a bit of cleaning up. If on the next visit, I show up and the place is mowed and all things are straight in the yard, I'll pay you for doing it." Dillion was surprised and replied in a positive manner.

"Yes sir, I'll do it." Dillion was aware he was a doctor, which translated to money in his mind. He thought that could add to a sizable sum.

The doctor wanted to see purpose in this boy's heart. As he set a different tone of conversation, the boy might be able to focus on other concentrations and have a purpose. The doctor was all too familiar with this philosophy. The doctor smiled as he knew that this progress was worth all that had gone into getting this boy's mind right. It was a small gesture given by the doctor to a boy he so desperately needed to save. The boy needed purpose and the doctor wanted to show it to him.

They got into the car and began the journey back to the office. Denise began in on the doctor. She expressed her disapproval of his gesture towards Dillion. Offering such things aren't a part of this line of work. She explained she knew his intentions were in the right place, but that it wasn't necessary for him to pay for someone's good behavior. The doctor obviously didn't see things the way Denise did and quickly explained his intentions.

"Denise, I wasn't paying for good behavior. I was simply wanting to reward him for doing something right, which he has never experienced. He knows that he can be rewarded for doing the wrong thing. His mother has shown him that and I'm surprised he knows all he does. He needs to understand that doing the right thing feels good as well. The good things we heard from him were well worth me wanting to reward him. On that alone I would have handed him something, but for it to be a lesson of learning, I asked him to do something for me. I think he is beginning to understand. Let's hope his mother stays away. On a more serious note, what do you think of his big question?"

"I don't know. I don't want to think about it." Denise's eyes rolled and she put her hand on her forehead in a sign of disbelief.

"I am going to talk to my friend on the force and let him know about it. He can decide if it is worth pursuing." The doctor thought it was a matter for the police to handle.

"I just don't want Dillion getting involved with something he shouldn't. If it isn't going to matter, why should we even get him involved?" Denise's concerns were for the well-being of the boy. In her mind nothing should compromise that, even getting to Luis. For now, she wanted to be content with Dillion's advancements. It was finally beginning to feel like things were progressing for Dillion, and Denise wanted nothing to get in their way. While the doctor was in agreement, he also liked the idea of allowing the system to work for once in taking down the bad guy.

As the state worked to make its case against Stacy, they held back no punches. They were seeking the full capital murder charge for the slaying of Officer Martinez. There was always wiggle room for a plea bargain if she was willing to confess on any level. However, the stakes would be high as the one they wanted was number one and no one else. This was the angle the state would approach the defense with.

The expectations were high for a confession. When considering that the death penalty is on the table, people tend to choose life. The state felt their case was set and they had expectations that a win was evident. What they didn't expect was the response that came from the defense. They were prepared to fight this one out all the way out. The District Attorney's office had no clue how they would propose to challenge them, and it was an eye opener to finally hear what they decided to hang their case on.

The defense's stance was that their client never broke any law whatsoever. For those emotionally attached to the officer's death, this was something no would have seen as even possible. Her lawyers, however, knew that was precisely what would get her off. Stacy was never involved in any drug dealing. She was at the wrong place at the wrong time. At no time were any drugs or money exchanged into her car or person. She happened to be sitting at a location when things went down, and there was a possibility she might be involved in a suit against the City for what happened to her, including a false arrest. All information that had been given as to this deal going down would be argued as inadmissible and circumstantial. The lawyers were ready to do battle, and everyone knew they were capable of winning. In addition to the false arrest, the way she was taken into custody would become a target for the defense as well. Everyone knew this was a complete lie, but it was one hundred percent doable in a court of law, especially with this firm.

Once news of this travesty hit, it set all of those involved in a tailspin of anger. Disbelief and disgust asked the question, "How could crime keep winning?" As the news hit Denise's office, she called the doctor to inform him of all she had heard. He was at home at the time and relaxing in his Lazy Boy. He sprung up, as if an electric shock had propelled him out of his chair.

"What do you mean, she can get off?" The doctor was clearly emotionally triggered.

"Settle down, I know what this means to you, but we have to let it run its course." Denise was just as upset as the doctor, but she was just running on more of a rational attitude.

"I'm not sure I understand, or if I'm even willing to understand. This is just too outlandish. Movies aren't even made this crazy. Something must be done. What about what Dillion asked us? That must show some involvement. I have to go Denise; I'm not feeling that good right now!"

"I'm sorry about this news doctor, but it is what it is and I'm not sure about Dillion saying what he said as carrying any weight now that this is going to be the defense's approach. I will talk to those I know that are involved in the case to see what they think." Denise was speaking in a compassionate tone, attempting to calm the doctor's unhinged nerves.

"Like I said, something needs to be done! This is getting personal to me!" The doctor hung up his phone and began going through a thought process he had never experienced until now. *What can be done? What is worth being done? What is the purpose of life if living is a constant threat? Is there ever a reason that justifies our actions to alleviating these threats at all costs?* The doctor began a litany of questions that appealed to his constitution of justice and questioned his conscience of law and order. Had we reached a point in life where a new law must take precedence? Had we bent justice so long that we lost all of the original laws that seemed to work? It certainly seemed so. These were some of the hard questions that the doctor refused to ask at the time of his wife's murder. He felt things happened for a reason. His newfound project seemed to be the answer, but now it was seeming to open doors of discovery the doctor never estimated opening. It was forcing him to ask deeper questions. He wanted to refuse the answers, but the more he saw, the more the questions became obvious. They refused to sit unanswered. It was only a matter of time before he would realize he needed to answer them.

Chapter Thirteen
A Target

A couple of months passed with the lawyers preparing their cases. Speculation within the community simmered about various outcomes. Most were relying on true justice to prevail, while others feared a more selfish outcome. Lingering in the ear of a concerned Luis Maldonado was the pressing issue of Stacy's son having been questioned by the police. Knowing how irresponsible Stacy could have been, he was on alert. There was very little trust he had ever placed in her and even that was diminishing as doubts flourished. What could she have said and what could the young boy possibly know? Was it a question even worth asking?

This business often asked, "Why take a chance?" This couldn't be left alone, especially if a testimony might reveal something detrimental to their operations. Looking into this couldn't be avoided.

Discussions began amongst his cohorts. What would be their safest approach in handling this situation? They were of the mind to see to someone's death if it could save them any trouble.

"*Jefe*, we can't really get to Stacy, but we can make something happen *con sus hijos o con su madre*, she'll get the message." Saul spoke with no emotion towards another's life. All that could be detected was shameless evil. While the others were just as ruthless, Saul possessed the ability to act on anyone, even a child. This was the true benefit of his membership. With him on board there was nothing they couldn't accomplish. They had no rules.

"I want you to find out more, *lo que el nino sabe*. If he talks, *no es bueno para el negocio*. See who all he hangs out with and what he does. This might be something we can handle, *facil con menos desorden*." Luis was brutal, but he was also a businessman. It wasn't good to make unnecessary moves, especially if it brought attention from law enforcement. The less violence, the smoother the operations. Manuel hardly ever spoke; he was your basic yes man. He didn't question the mission. He believed in what they were doing.

Direction would come after Saul and Manuel looked into the possibilities of the boy's knowledge. Digging about would be done carefully. They weren't cautious for sake of fear. They only acted to protect themselves.

"*Jefe, dame tu palabra* and I'll have a mechanic show up." This was the only way they worked. Luis always had the final decision.

Far removed from that part of society, was a concerned Denise. It was suspected that Luis could be apprehensive about Stacy's family. She had to continue her work on other cases, but her mind was concerned about Dillion as his situation had become potentially volatile. She was sworn to see that Dillion would be protected through this whole process.

One thing that was sure about Denise's character was her loyalty and her willingness to work for what she believed in. That was what attracted Dr. Richards to her. A part of that quality was also something he began to develop fears about. He was learning that a pure heart that sought to see good could be blinded to the threat the evil in this world presents. It was people like Denise who usually fell victim to its play.

An unsuspecting and loving heart is frequently trampled by those who work in a world of self. He didn't want to see her kindness violated. His past record had him losing a loved one in a most unjust manner and receiving less than an appropriate response from the justice system in place. He had been dealt a torrential downpour of unfairness with his reservoir reaching capacity. He was tired of seeing the just being abused. If Denise was to succumb to this type of harm, it would put him over the edge.

The payment that the world prescribed for such nobleness, wasn't what one of goodwill would expect. To the ones seeking only selfish endeavors, goodwill was a punishable offense. It was a proverb even in nature as a busy bee never sees that it is systematically and continually being robbed as it stores for life. When it finally strikes back, it results in its death. The arrangement of things seemed that the good guys just couldn't get ahead.

Days of contemplation would take the doctor on a rollercoaster of emotions charged by a yearning for legitimacy. Denise's character showed her to play by the books and go to bat for those she cared for. Blinded by her positive outlook, it acted as a shield that caused a naïve nature. Not being able to see things for what they truly were left her not knowing that things couldn't always be done the way she intended.

The doctor feared for her safety. She wasn't frightened by those she should be. She didn't understand how truly bad, evil people really were. She had a belief that good things happen to good people and right would always prevail. Thinking about her, the doctor sensed trepidation for her security. He wanted her kept safe and would avoid her involvement with his old friend the detective. He felt Marlon might give him something better to consider. Denise would be left out of any of these conversations. Her emotions wouldn't remain concealed with any revelation of criminal possibilities. He would attempt to maintain her safety as best he could.

The doctor made arrangements to meet up with Detective Crawford. His busy schedule made it hard to lock him down, but he was finally successful. Their usual spot for meeting hadn't changed and this time the doctor had no appetite. Detective Crawford, however, could eat in any situation. The "Greasy Cheese", still held in high regard by the detective, was still his go-to spot for discussion.

"Joseph, nothing for you?" Detective Crawford could see a look of contempt on the doctor's face.

"No, I'm not hungry. I haven't been able to eat much lately. All the old feelings of defeat seem to be creeping back inside of me. I'm worried things are going to spiral out of control. I am having bad feelings that Denise will make a mistake in trying to protect Dillion and get herself hurt and I don't like the fact that I am showing too much emotion, which might be getting hers uncalibrated."

"Slow down, you are going ninety to nothing. Look, I've been doing this a long time and you can't let your feelings dictate all your actions. If you do, you won't always do the right thing." The detective was well trained at doing his job within the limits of the law.

"Yeah but if my gut tells me something I know to be wrong, I'm not going to ignore it or lie to myself."

"So what are you saying, Joseph?"

"I'm saying, it is not going to be good for someone if I lose another loved one."

"Wait a minute. Don't let yourself become someone you won't be proud of."

"I think my pride might be gone if I don't do all to make things right for once. I was stripped of much already, you know that, Marlon."

"I know, it just doesn't seem right all the time." Walking up from behind them was Manus Ricci. He had information the detective might want and stopped to see him. He had been busy, but finally made time to locate the detective at his go-to eatery.

"Marlioni, catch you at a bad time? I see you are having a lunch meeting."

"No, I was talking with Dr. Richards. I don't believe you two have met before." Manus was looking at the doctor the whole time the detective was talking. He was aware of who he was. He was also aware that he had investigated the matter, asked by the detective, for the doctor. He wasn't about to acknowledge that or even act as if he knew him. This was a tactic used to create a better stance for beginning a relationship. Knowing is the advantage. What others know that you know can be the disadvantage.

"No, can't say that I do." The detective knew Manus knew who he was but allowed the conversation to continue in its current state.

"Well, let me introduce you, this is Dr. Richards. I helped solve his wife's murder back a couple of years ago. Doctor, this is Mace Ricci, a friend of mine." The doctor extended his hand to shake Manus's hand. He wasn't sure what he thought of him. His suspicions were definitely shady.

"Nice to meet you Doc. Sorry about your situation. I truly am. This town can be a nasty place. I'm glad the detective was able to solve things. He is good at his job."

"Thank you, I know. I'm still using him today." Hints weren't enough to open the obvious.

"Well, you let me know if there is anything I can do for you all. I gotta go, I just wanted to pop in and mention to you, Marlioni, that your boy is worried about that kid talking. You might want to let some people know." Manus knew the mention of this would get right to the doctor's concern. The detective would have rather Manus not mention things in front of the doctor, but he did, and the doctor reacted.

"Are you talking about Dillion and Luis?" The doctor wasn't going to stay reserved any longer. His thresholds had been pressed on too much.

"Yeah, sorry, maybe I shouldn't have said that." After the revelation from Manus, the detective shook his head as he held it in a downward position.

"I wish you wouldn't have." Marlon just kept his head down. The doctor refused to let this go by him.

"No, you're wrong Marlon, is this your contact that looked into Stacy for us?"

"Yes, this is, but we don't want to start making mistakes by doing things we shouldn't. Do you both understand?"

"Relax, Marlioni. Everything is ok. I don't think the doctor knowing me is a problem."

"I don't either, I just don't want it to become one. You do things your way, and I have my way of doing things. The doctor is still finding his way. This situation needs to be left in the hands of the authorities. I hope I have both of your commitments to that."

"You have mine, but we need to address this concern that was just brought to us."

"I need to address this concern!" The detective could see the doctor getting emotionally involved.

"Sorry if I confused things. I better go. I think the little kid will be alright. I just know that Luis is a piece of shit, and he will eliminate anything he sees as a threat. Right now, he is uncertain of what was discussed when the boy was questioned."

"The boy doesn't know much. He does know that his mother has worked for Luis and that she has been involved in trafficking for him, but that isn't going to be enough to tie him to her current situation." As if pleading a case, the doctor explained the boy's innocence.

Detective Crawford wanted everything clean, so if an opportunity to seize Luis came about, it would be able to stick. The doctor, however, took a fondness to Manus's understanding of things behind the scenes. He feared Dillion or even Denise might get caught up in a harmful situation.

"Would they send someone to question Dillion or make a move on his family?" The doctor directed his conversation straight to Manus. The detective worried it might lead to a friendship he would regret being a founding member of.

"Look, you two, I'm warning you, your good intentions might back-fire if you get more involved than you should. I can see where this is going. Don't do it." Detective Crawford stood up to show his displeasure with his two committed friends. "I gotta go. I'm asking you both not to do anything that will get you in trouble. I'm saying that because I care. That's all I have to say. Goodbye." The detective walked to his car and drove off.

Manus and the doctor sat for another thirty minutes discussing the matter. Manus described a side of Luis the doctor hadn't heard from the detective. Things that Manus heard from secondhand knowledge were put into the doctor's head. It was understanding things he wished he had never heard. The depth of evil this man's world swam in would be repulsive to the average man. He was for himself and himself alone. Both men had the conclusion that someone would eventually pay Dillion's family a visit. Even though the boy's knowledge wasn't enough to warrant action within the law, they would undoubtably act on it themselves.

"I have been wondering lately, if doing the right thing is even considered in the law anymore," the doctor spoke helplessly to Manus.

"Doc, I might not be the most law-abiding citizen, but I am a firm believer in doing what is right. Marlioni takes a bit of a different approach than me."

"Can you keep me informed if you hear anything? I don't want anyone to get hurt, but I am willing to protect those that I love."

"Sure Doc. You better set something up for that boy, so that he doesn't get caught by surprise by those animals."

"I am." The doctor and Manus exchanged phone numbers and left with a new trust in each other. They would place a certain dependency on each other. It was seeing this situation and maintaining the safety of those they were looking over.

The doctor's next challenge would be to get Dillion out of his grandmother's house and not rile up Denise with this newfound information. Not knowing her reaction might make things spiral out of control. People finding out his relationship with an informant that he met through the detective would only muddy up the waters. He might get himself ejected and then Dillion would be at the mercy of a failed justice system. It was all becoming clearer to the doctor. Justice would have to be found by him. He had to come up with a plan and fast. He called up Denise as he was driving home.

"Denise."

"Yes doctor."

"I'm wondering...I'm wanting to send Dillion to a summer camp, my treat, if he is willing. It is a couple of weeks long and I think it would be good for him to get away. I will show you all about what it has to offer." The doctor hadn't investigated anything. He had no prices or even an agenda. He was confident he would be able to find something to send the boy to. The important thing was to send him away.

"What are you talking about as far as price goes?"

"Now Denise, you can't tell me how to spend my money. I want to do this." The doctor's tone was stressed due to him not having an answer and not wanting to tell Denise everything.

"Doctor, you can't try and buy this boy's goodness. He will learn by us teaching him."

"I'm not trying to buy his goodness; I'm trying to save him!"

"We all are. Come into the office tomorrow and I will look at what you are talking about. Don't get so wound up. I can tell you are upset."

"I have a lot on my mind. I can talk to you a bit more tomorrow. I need to get home and unwind. I'll be there in the morning, so be ready for me."

"I will doctor. Remember, people love you like me, so calm down. It's all going to be ok."

"I know, I love you too. See you in the morning." The doctor hung up and began going through his conversation with Denise in his head. Dillion had to go on vacation. Wherever he could find a place for him to retreat, everyone must have complete buy-in. If Denise, for whatever reason, decides against it, he will be forced to divulge the information about Luis's henchmen planning on meeting with Dillion. What can he afford to say without Denise going crazy? He was tired but didn't foresee a night of good rest. His mind would be churning the unescapable path of needing only one outcome. Things must start going his way. He was determined of that.

Chapter Fourteen
The Rubicon

The next day the doctor arrived with plans set to send Dillion away for one month. He spent the first few hours of the day searching for a place where Dillion could escape. Finally, after much internet searching, he met his goal. With much of a persuasive tongue and no prorated discount, due to a late enrollment, the doctor managed to get Dillion signed up at an exclusive summer program. It was a cut above what was needed, but being that summer had already begun, these arrangements should have been done much prior. The important thing was seeing to it that he went away for some time. His protection was the concern.

He would come in to see Denise at 10:00am and bring with him Dillion's registration and paperwork. He would show her that the boy was signed up to attend a plush camp set in the heart of the Texas Hill Country on the pristine waters of the Guadalupe River. Dillion had already missed a couple of days of the camp which amounted to foregoing an orientation, a welcoming of the campers and the kids being shown around to see the different activities offered. The kids were then privileged to choose which classes they wanted to attend. This, of course, was not the main concern for the doctor.

Dillion would be assigned the classes that still had room for his attendance, which meant fewer choices, but the doctor was sure his experience would be appreciated by all, especially with his presence out of town comforting the doctor.

Upon arriving, Denise seemed to be busy with other work, but quickly gave the doctor her attention as he walked in.

"Sorry I'm late, but here is the agenda for his camp." Denise spent some time going through the literature.

"Now Doctor, I know this is costing too much for you to send Dillion to this camp. I'm afraid to ask how much?" Denise's eyes opened wide as she gave the doctor a look of non-approval.

"Don't ask, because that part isn't of your concern or business."

This was the first time the doctor had spoken to Denise with any kind of a parental authoritative instinct. Perhaps this trait was developing within him towards those he felt close to and could become vulnerable in his eyes. The wager to protect those he loved was slowly emerging as the realities of this world were seeming to increase. Denise looked at the doctor as an uncomfortable silence passed.

"Well, I didn't mean to touch a nerve."

"It's not you and then again it is you. I don't want to see anyone hurt. You must trust me on some things, Denise. I am willing to go the distance for you and extend myself as far as I can. Dillion needs to go away for a while."

"I get the sense you are telling me something without telling me something. Am I right?" Denise spoke with a questioning soft tone. She respected the doctor and could take on a role of trusting in him, knowing his character. She believed in him as well as he in her. "Don't say anything else. If you want to send Dillion to camp, I'll do what I can to make it happen. Just don't let me be blinded as I feel I am right now. I'm in this too, you know. I have a right to know as well." Denise stopped before it became complicated.

"Denise, trust me. I only have yours and Dillion's best interest in my heart. I think it would be therapeutic for Dillion as well as good for us, to allow him to go and come back with a vacation long overdue for a boy in his circumstances."

"You are probably right again, doctor. Maybe *I* need a vacation."

"You probably do. We all do. I'll tell you what. We can go out to the lake. My brother has a boat he continually tells me to take out. I never have, but now seems to be the time. While Dillion is gone, we can plan a day on the lake. Just a few friends." The doctor thought about planning a day where he could let Denise know a bit more about the involvement Dillion might be subjected to with Luis.

"Doctor, you keep forking out dollars and I am not comfortable with that."

"Ok, you pay, for what I don't know. The boat is my brother's. Maybe food and drinks for the day. I'm fine with that. You know what I drink. I have a friend I want to bring. I'm not sure what he drinks or even if he drinks."

"Doesn't sound like a close friend if you don't know what he drinks."

"Well, I have never drank with him, but that is not what trust is built on." The doctor was thinking of inviting his newfound friend Manus. Introducing the two might become a well-intentioned attempt gone wrong, but eventually Denise's curiosity would override her trust in the doctor and answers would have to be delivered. He sensed that the tenacity in her drive would force the issue. It was another one of the many attributes he admired in her and yet now was compromising the doctor's situation. Getting her together with Manus was inevitable.

"Fine with me doctor, just let me know what I need to bring." Their encounter would be spent less on drinks and more on discussion. Denise would have to understand the totality of this situation. It would bring about an urgency to be proactive as the doctor was beginning to understand.

"I'll set it up," the doctor responded with a calm reply.

With that said, Denise's work getting Dillion to camp was her agenda. She set things up with her office and Dillion's family before lunch and they were set to take him the next day.

The doctor's next few hours were spent getting his brother's permission to use the boat and thinking of how he would introduce the two parties. He called Manus to invite him on the outing. Manus agreed as he liked the amenities of the finer things in life.

"Sure, doc. I like boats. Maybe some steaks and some wine."

"I am not opposed to those things, but that is not my intention for this trip. I really want you to meet Denise. She is very protective of the boy, and I am protective of her. I don't want these guys trying to get at either one of them as it might cause me great torment and I'm not sure what might happen. I want them safeguarded and don't know how that is possible unless I make Denise aware of things." The doctor was at an impasse. He felt damned if he did and damned if he didn't. He had to make a move. It was paramount that his sale of Manus to Denise was successful. "Just know she may be sensitive to you and your personality."

"What do you mean? Everybody loves me, especially the ladies." Manus was making a joke, but the doctor was more serious.

"Don't be an imperceptive fool, Manus. I need you to act mature for this." The doctor had given himself to being more direct with people. Getting to the point seemed more important.

"Alright doc, no more jokes. We can do this. Just tell me when to meet you at the dock." They worked out the details and Dr. Richards would let Denise know when they would meet. He knew they were all focused on the idea of true justice and that would be the focal point of the conversation.

Character judgement might be a conflict. Denise, despite all her loyalty to fairness, might find it difficult to accept Manus. The doctor was aware of this. He mustn't make it seem they were proposing anything outside the law, yet protections were not to be sacrificed. The doctor wouldn't suggest any type of plot, just a commitment to justice. Whatever they must do, they must believe in doing. It wasn't an option to just accept the conditions anymore.

Getting Manus involved with them was an edge the doctor felt they needed. He wanted in place a guaranteed shield prior to any offense that may be aimed at them. Somehow, he would have to get Denise to understand.

In another part of the world, looking outside her window, Eddie Metzner was at home tending to the tireless job of raising her many grandchildren. As she was tending to picking up the days mess from the children, she noticed a blacked-out Mercedes-Benz slowing down to park in front of her house. There wasn't a blemish or speck of dirt that drew appearance to the eye, yet no eye could refuse something dirty about its presence. The car was flawless. She peered as she had no idea who could be parked out front. Her suspicions were that they were looking for her daughter. Stepping out of the car was a well-groomed Manuel Consuello. Saul was driving the car and stayed in his seat as today would only be an inquiry.

Eddie waited, watching cautiously as Manuel approached the door. Eddie stayed back and waited for the knock. It seemed to take a long time as her anticipation brought about a fear as to who these men were. A slightly soft knock was given on the old door that had seen better days.

"Hello?" Eddie responded with a weak, worn-out voice. She kept the door closed as she knew this wasn't someone that had come to help.

"Hello, I'm looking for Dillion. Is he home?" Fear ran through Eddie's old, tired body. She wasn't capable of defending anyone. Her instincts had her wanting to protect, but her spirit had been wrung of all it had once possessed.

"No, Dillion is gone." Dillion was in fact home. He was asleep in his room and Eddie was just hoping he didn't wake up and come walking in to be heard.

"Well, if he comes home, tell him Don needs to talk to him. I need to ask him a few questions. Let him know I will come back later." Eddie was beginning to have cold sweats as she knew this wasn't a visitor of goodwill. She was aware of her daughter and the dealings that consumed her life. She felt broken to the fact that it was filtering down to the level of her grandchildren. She felt helpless in a sea of madness.

"Ok, I'll let him know."

"Good, that will be good to let him know." Manuel wanted to leave a strong presence behind. He had suspicions the boy might be there, so letting them know he would return might scare them and convince them to comply with his demands.

Eddie's life was left in continual pain that never seemed to leave. Manuel walked slowly back to the car, turning around twice to see if anyone would dare move the curtain. He wanted to make an impression. This was common practice to make a way for someone's loyalty towards them in order for that person to save themselves. They didn't care how or why, just that people didn't cross them on any stance.

As Dillion slept, he couldn't imagine the totality of plans being made for him by two different sets of people. One sought to protect and send him to a kid's paradise. The other with intentions of greed to seek their own protections. Inside his own head were slow dreams of just wanting a chance. They were set to goals of low potential as aiming high hadn't been exercised in his mind. Little did he know, his current situation would have him learning to make decisions that would be forged in leadership. The camp he was destined to attend would become pivotal in specializing and honing this skill, even though it wouldn't be in one of the classes assigned to him that he would learn this.

The next day the doctor washed himself of any reservations he may have had the day before. He showed up early as he and Denise were set for a road trip to take Dillion to the Hill Country for his month-long retreat. It was a better part of four hours, one way. They were looking to get back to town around 9pm. Dillion was packed up and ready for them to pick him up at 7:30am. It would be a long trip, but with the other outings they had already gone on, it was something they looked forward to.

They would be stopping at a cafe for lunch. The doctor insisted on a full-hour lunch. He believed in getting where they were going, but also believed in a good lunch. Denise brought a book she would be reading for part of the trip. The doctor was content on driving the whole way. He felt obligated as this was all his planning. Dillion had things to occupy his time, but Denise thought it was a good idea to bring him a book as well.

"Do you like to read?" Dillion looked at her with a face that seemed to question if she was serious.

"Not really." He didn't hesitate to reveal to her he had no desire to even open the book.

"You really should give reading a chance. It is a good habit to get into. I have been a good reader my whole life."

"She is right, Dillion, reading is a way to exercise your brain." The doctor added to Denise's statement as he knew it would be an advantage for Dillion if he was planning on going far in life.

"What did you bring me to read?" Dillion asked with a less enthusiastic voice.

"This is one that I have read twice. I like it. It's called 'The Pilgrims Progress. My father gave it to me when I was a teenager. It was written by John Bunyan in the 1600s. It is quite an interesting read, not too difficult." Denise wanted to give Dillion something that could make him think as well as enjoy at the same time.

"Ok, I'll look at it. Sounds pretty old." That was Dillion's way of accepting Denise's gesture.

They settled in for the ride and before anyone got a chance to look at their watch they managed to get a hundred and fifty miles behind them with a fair amount of quiet in the car. Denise and Dillion were reading as the doctor drove in a soothing meditation.

"Well, you two, I'm going to stop up here in Temple for an early lunch. If either one of you want breakfast, they should still serve it."

"Good I'm hungry, let's stop." Denise began to put her book back in a carrying case and looked back at Dillion. Surprisingly he had been reading and seemed to enjoy the book.

"Are you hungry?"

"Yes. You were right this is an interesting book."

"I told you so." Denise had a smile that a doctor couldn't remove.

"My mom should read this book." The book was a story on morality and meeting certain people and taking certain paths. The book had grabbed at the very heart of Dillion and that was why Denise had picked it for him to read. Over lunch Denise began a book club type discussion with Dillion as she was very familiar with the book's content. She made the discussion something Dillion enjoyed, and the doctor appreciated watching the exchange. As they continued in their talk, mentioning things and characters in the book, Dillion was compelled to offer up something he heard.

"You know, my grandmother said that someone in a fancy car came to the house yesterday asking for me. She didn't know who he was, but what she described was almost like one of those characters the pilgrim would run into. She was glad I was going away to this camp." Denise's eyes opened more as she slowed the chewing of her food and turned her head towards the doctor.

"What? Did you know about this?" With as much shock, the doctor looked at Dillion with an astonished look.

"No, I did not! Why didn't you say something?"

"Well, until now I didn't think about it. Grandma said something, but it was quick, and I just didn't think about it. I had to pack, and my mind was on the camp. I went online and spent a lot of time looking up the activities. I guess I just forgot." Denise's gears in her head were grinding as she wanted to have a conversation with the doctor but knew it would have to wait until the ride home.

"Who was it? Did your grandmother say?"

"No, she didn't know who it was, just that it was a man named Don and she didn't even open the door." The doctor's fears that he had been keeping on a backburner became apparent. The protections he was putting in place were now a necessity. No longer was he dealing with an assumption. A new fear for him would be those he loved not listening to him.

The potential for this to spiral out of control was now a reality, especially with Denise's suspicions. Her involvement would now be certain, but her potentially unpredictable actions would have to be controlled. This was something the doctor was concerned about.

"Well, it was probably nothing, especially if it wasn't anyone your grandmother knew." The doctor moved to get off the subject. He didn't want Dillion to think it was a big deal or Denise to overthink the situation and get wound up.

Denise said nothing. Her mind was rolling with thought, but she said nothing and just continued looking at them both. The doctor knew the ride back home was going to be intense.

Lunch moved rather slow as the conversation applied itself to things other than what was on the minds of Denise and Dr. Richards. Dillion mentioned the things he had seen online at the camp and expressed his enthusiasm about participating in them. The doctor could see Denise was having to force a shared excitement with Dillion as other things were competing for her attention. She was shaken by what she had heard.

Back in the car for the remainder of the trip, Denise closed her eyes and attempted to sleep. The reality was that she was too restless and had nowhere to escape. Dillion was still too naive and young to understand things. He just sat in the backseat reading the book he had been given and time seemed to fly until they pulled into Hunt, Texas at the site of the camp.

"Wow, look at that!" The doctor could see the beautifully clear waters as the noonday sun pierced into its depths as they crossed the mighty Guadalupe River on Farm to Market Road 1340.

"Are we there yet?" If there had never been any kid that asked that question, Dillion did it for all of them. His total being was set to the tune of a thousand harps. His amp was turned up to eleven. He wanted to open the door at the full speed of the car. He couldn't be more thrilled as his expectations were still being imagined. Denise was able to let go of some of her frustrations as she appreciated Dillion's attraction to his newfound tabernacle.

"Wow, are we there yet, I would say so. Doctor, I have never been to the Hill Country before. It is gorgeous." Denise was impressed herself.

"It sure is. I can't wait to get in the water. Is there fish in the water?" Dillion was ninety to nothing with his speech. He wanted more answers than he had questions. As they pulled up to the camp, the doctor got out and went to get Dillions bags from the back of the car.

"Dillion, get over here. I'm not carrying your bags by myself."

"Yes sir." Dillion had almost forgotten himself as he wanted to immediately start exploring. Quickly he rushed to help get his own bags so they wouldn't be delayed any longer. Denise and the doctor walked in with Dillion behind them. They began the process of checking him in. Within an hour Dillion was turned over to a counselor and the farewells were said.

"Now you take care, remember that even though you are here to have fun, you have to behave. Don't skip on brushing your teeth and try to be helpful." Denise had an instinct of motherly affections.

"I think he will be fine. Do as she says and we will both be fine." With the doctor's statement, Dillion hugged them both and was gone in a flash.

It was past 1:30pm and they were ready to hit the road. It was only expected for a long straight talk to begin and last for the duration of their trip home.

"Did you know about this?" Denise wasted no time in asking the doctor about Dillion's encounter.

"Denise, I promise I did not. I have had some very credible suspicions but not any real justifications to act on up until this point."

"What do you mean, justifications and acting on? I'm not understanding you doctor. You are talking like someone I don't even know." Denise was talking as sincerely as she could. Her emotions had been overwhelmed for much of the drive up and she was beginning to tear up as she spoke.

"You really don't to a certain point. When Melinda was murdered, I was crushed. I learned a lot about myself at that time and since meeting you and the boy I have learned a great deal more. I have also had to suppress many of my feelings through all I have learned working with you, the department, the scum we have encountered, and the system that doesn't seem to work. I still believe right is right no matter what the circumstances may be and that standing up for that is a right as well." The doctor's tone was one that Denise had never heard before. There was a part of her that agreed, another part that felt empathy for him, and yet another part that gave her a feeling of fear.

"I think we should get the authorities involved. This is becoming too dangerous."

"Denise, I think we should wait before we do anything like that. I want you to meet a friend of mine. That is why we are going out on the boat next week."

"That trip was planned, so you *did* know about this."

"No, I did not! I heard that Luis's people were nervous because they had heard Dillion was questioned by the police. That's all. If I had known they were going to come to his house, I would have got him out earlier. I certainly wouldn't have let the authorities do that for him. He might have gotten hurt under their guidance. That is why I think we need to talk to this guy I know."

"Is that what the detective told you to do?"

"No, in fact he didn't like the idea just like I don't think you do either. Denise, you need to listen to me. You will get hurt from this guy if you try to beat him within the limits of the law, because he has no limits. At least be smart about it." The doctor pleaded his case without a concession from Denise.

"I don't know. I just don't know." Denise gave the doctor an answer he didn't want but would have to live with for now. The rest of the drive home was long and lonely. As they pulled into the Dallas city limits the doctor asked Denise if she wanted anything to eat before taking her home.

"No thank you."

"I'm sorry for all of this, Denise. The last thing I want is for you to get hurt. That is why my concerns are leaning me in this direction. I'm not going to let it happen to me twice." Denise's hand remained over her face until they pulled up to her house. Her makeup had smeared and she looked less presentable with the forming of small tired bags under her eyes. "Are you still interested in going to meet my friend?" The doctor was short and to the point. He had to know.

"Do I have a choice in the matter?"

"You always have a choice. I'll just have to change mine."

"Sure, I'll go, but I'm not committing to anything. I never imagined my work would become so depressing."

"It won't be if we triumph in the end. This I promise you." They hugged each other with the doctor's hand holding Denise's head. His intention was to see her safely through all of this. She felt protection coming from the doctor. It scared her to wonder how far he would go to maintain it.

Chapter Fifteen
The Struggle of Her Good Conscience

It was an early start to the day as Dr. Richards met his brother Matthew at the marina at 7am. They would go over a few things for the doctor's planned outing, and also spend some time together. It was a Wednesday, the middle of the week, and although Matthew was a busy man in real estate, he was the boss and loved his freedom to exit work at any time he wanted. The doctor had gone boating with his brother on many an occasion and had even operated the boat. He was well skilled in the process, but he and his brother felt it to be a good idea to go over everything prior to his weekend excursion. This would be the first time the doctor went out without his brother.

"Joey, you are looking good. Are you hungry? I'm going get a breakfast sandwich in the marina before we go out. I can grab you something." Matthew was the type that was always fast and on the go. His business fit his personality.

"I'm good, Matthew. I ate a little early this morning."

"Ok, we'll be back before noon anyway, and can eat a bite before leaving. I have to be back to meet up with Karen this afternoon. She and Julie Lynn are shopping. They have to get a few things before we go to Cancun next month."

"Matty, where is he?"

"Karen dropped him off at a friend's last night. He is like me, can't stand to go shopping. We just trust our girls to get what we need." The doctor laughed as he knew his brother's nature. The son was much like his father.

"It's gonna be kinda funny if they have you two looking like double-mint down in Mexico."

"No chance. One thing Karen likes next to looking good herself, is her boys looking just as good. You know that, Joey. Do I ever look bad?" Matthew laughed a bit as he was joking, but there was a side of him that truly liked himself.

"Yea, you do look good," the doctor said it with a slice of sarcasm.

The morning consisted of them taking the boat out and moving about the lake. The doctor controlled the entire trip. Matthew talked continually about business and their upcoming family vacation. His trip to Cancun was more than just a vacation. It was a business opportunity as well. He was looking into acquiring a vacation rental for himself. He even tried to recruit the doctor to go with him and possibly invest in some property down south.

"You know it would be good for you to have another hobby. I know you have the money for it Joey. Besides it will help you get away from this stuff you are messing with." Matthew was a fun person to be around. He always kept the party functioning on a high level and had a personality that attracted all. He was also a lot to take in and seemed to always be on the scout for a hustle. His appreciations weren't the same as the doctor's.

The doctor loved his brother. He respected him for who he was, but knew they were two different individuals. Their ride was completed as the doctor spent much of the time listening. They parked back in the marina and grabbed a quick bite before saying good-bye.

"I'll let Karen and the kids know that their uncle Joey loves them. They would love to see him in Cancun, but I know you can't go. Maybe another time. I might buy a property down there, so we can plan a trip when we visit next time."

"Another time. I just have too many things going on now, but we will do it one day."

"I hope so Joey." Matthew looked up to his brother, as Dr. Richards embodied the character of their late father. He had been a man of spiritual thought and calculated actions. These were the two hardest attributes for most men to acquire and apply to doing the right thing. Most of the time they get misappropriated, based on interference by emotion.

The day concluded and they separated. The doctor set his cruise control and headed back to the DFW area. He turned the radio down and spoke to the console.

"Siri, call Mace." The phone rang a few times before a tired sounding Manus picked up.

"Hello Doc. What's up?" It was midday but for Manus it was just beginning.

"You sound a bit sleepy. Late night last night?"

"Yeah, I guess you could say that. I was out with a lady friend. A bit of drinking and dancing. I happened to bump into an old friend of mine that had some interesting news to tell." Manus was starting to move about. The doctor could hear this as it sounded like he was getting out of bed and becoming more awake.

"Something about Luis I suspect."

"Yeah, Luis, no doubt. That pig is nervous. They can't find the boy. He sent his boys to look for the kid and now the kid has gone missing. They even got Stacy calling her mom to find out where he is." Manus was fully awake and was now a bit charged in the conversation.

"Did they find out where he is?"

"Not from what I heard. I think they think that girl you work with might have sent him somewhere."

"You mean Denise?"

"Yeah, Denise. Don't worry though. Those assholes ain't gonna mess with her."

"I hope you're right Mace. Look, I just left my brother's boat. I have everything set up for Sunday. I hope you can still go with Denise and me. I want to discuss these things a bit more, and especially now, let her know what all is going on." The reality of how complicated things were becoming was frightening to the doctor. He knew Denise's good conscience would be a true challenge to overcoming the false stigmas of society.

"I'll be there. This guy thinks everyone should listen to him. He is crazy."

"I just want Denise to understand that we can't take chances with Luis. She might think she can act a certain way and be protected by the law, but that is just not the case." The doctor had major concerns for her.

"You're right, she needs to know how this guy works. He is a real scumbag. Now he moves on the family. He won't stop until he gets what he wants, but that crap is gonna stop."

"At least as far as I'm concerned. I won't be offended again. Denise must understand that." The doctor cut the conversation short. His mind was in a constant twist putting truth and justice against reality and fears. The remainder of the ride he thought about calling Denise to reaffirm this Sunday's outing but refused as he felt their conversation needed to be face-to-face. He decided to drive by the office as there was still time left in the day. He would see her mood and talk to her according to how she appeared to be. *Had it been a hard day? Had the day gone well? Was she still holding reservations from their last conversation?* He needed to see her and feel her out.

When he showed up at the office he found out she wasn't there. The receptionist let him know she had left early. She told the doctor that Denise hadn't been feeling well. The doctor wondered if it was caused by the pressures being felt from Dillion's situation. The new discovery that Manus laid on him would only complicate matters. It was vital he got to talk with her to make sure she would be on the boat Sunday. Not knowing if she was sick or just dealing with emotions, he called to hear from her.

"Hello."

"Hello Denise. This is Dr. Richards."

"I know." Denise sounded depressed. The doctor needed to choose his words very carefully.

"Well, I called up to the office and they said you weren't feeling well. Is everything alright?"

"Yes, I just feel a bit overwhelmed. I needed to come home and rest. I should be back tomorrow."

"Ok. Is there anything you need from me?"

"No, I think I'm going to lay down." Denise's tone let the doctor know she didn't feel much like talking.

"I just wanted to check in to make sure you are still planning on meeting up with me on Sunday."

"I think that is why I felt like leaving today. My mind has been racing and I can't think of anything but that, well I mean Dillion."

"So, what are you saying, will I see you Sunday?"

"Yes. I am just beginning to worry much more about what is going on."

"That is why we need to discuss things. My friend I have coming knows some things we need to consider. Trust me, the more we know, the better things can get for all of us, but we need to figure things out for ourselves first."

"I understand. I'll be there."

"Good. I know you to be good and wanting what is right. That is my only intention. Get some rest dear. I love you."

"Love you too, doc." They hung up and shortly after the doctor pulled into his driveway. It was still early, but the doctor felt tired as well.

He wasn't going to retire immediately but decided to change for bed. He would spend a few hours on a new book he had started. It was on the Lost Ten Tribes of Israel. His interest in the history of the Bible was becoming more significant in his life. He was beginning to see a vast difference in man and his Creator. It was apparent to him that the scales of justice tipped differently between the two. He read until he couldn't keep his eyes open anymore. There was much to consider before Sunday. He would have to decide what direction and how far in that direction he would be willing to go. As he faded to sleep these were the thoughts going about within his head. The dreaded Sunday wouldn't get here fast enough.

The rest of the week was spent with the doctor avoiding the office. He called Denise everyday with surface talk, not amounting to much passing of information. It was more of an attempt to lift her spirits without mentioning the elephant in the room.

Sunday came and the plan was to leave the marina at 10:00am so they could enjoy the best part of the day. Riding through to a late afternoon on a beautiful setting had to be in the cards to offset the obvious difficulty they were confronting.

Manus would be meeting them at the dock. He had traveled up the day before and spent the night at a casino. He favored the lifestyle of chance, and it profited him sometimes. Denise was riding up with the doctor and both of them knew it would probably be a long and quiet drive.

Before arriving at Denise's house he picked up two coffees. As he pulled into the driveway, Denise was standing by her front door. Without the happiest of looks on her face, she still looked so pretty to the doctor. He admired her so much because of her convictions. She was facing fears she didn't want to, as well as holding true to her code of helping and protecting those whom she loved. The doctor got out of the car and helped Denise with her bags. She had a cooler packed full of food and drinks that the doctor reached for first.

"Well good morning beautiful."

"I wish I felt as good as you see me." Denise was still worn down by the situation.

"You will. Today is about moving forward, making progress. No one is doing anything wrong. We are just figuring things out."

"I guess so. Are we picking up your friend?"

"No, he went up last night to do some gambling. He will meet us at ten."

"Oh, he is a gambler?"

"No Denise, he is my friend that wants the same thing we do. Things to be right. You need to not be so apprehensive."

"I'm sorry, I'm just concerned. I called up Mrs. Metzner and asked about the encounter Dillion told us about. She told me Stacy was calling asking where he was. She doesn't know much but had the mind to not let Stacy know anything. She is worried a bit that she might get a return visit. Without divulging too much to her, we have arranged with patrol to go by their house from time to time."

"Good, that is good. Stacy is probably being probed for information."

"That is my guess, and my guess is that this friend knows more about what's going on."

"You are correct."

The conversation continued but seized on that subject. Denise began to have a more relaxed attitude as the drive was peaceful. There weren't many cars on the highway as most of the people were undoubtably in church. Denise took command of the exchange as she brought up her nephew's baseball game she had just attended. They were right in the middle of the season, and she was one of their biggest supporters. She showed the doctor a couple of pictures she had taken with her phone. Some of them were action photos and some of them were of course, "Princess" posing for her aunt. This also helped Denise's spirits become uplifted. The doctor took a portion of its medicine too.

It was 9:40am when they parked at their destination. Manus was already there. From the look on his face, the doctor could tell his night at the casino was a success. The doctor smiled as his suspicions made him happy. Denise, not knowing Manus, was less impressed.

"I guess that is your friend?"

"Yes, it is, Denise. Don't try and know who he is before you get to know who he is." The doctor could tell Denise had prejudices, and rightly so. She didn't want to waste time with things that compromise one's energies. Manus just seemed to fit that mold on all landscapes. "Well, let's do this. I hope you are right about him."

They got out of the car and approached the dock. Manus was smiling ear to ear.

"Let me know, how much did you win?"

"How do you know I won?"

"The incredible smile on your face." The doctor was smiling as he was inquiring.

"That obvious huh. I beat the house out of $7,600. Not bad for a couple of hours of blackjack."

"No, not at all. Mace, I want to introduce you to someone very special to me. Her name is Denise Wilson. I have told you about her and her about you, but now you two get to meet."

"Wow doc, you never said she was pretty." Manus's demeanor and speech habits were a bit rough, and he wasn't setting the best of tones for Denise to accept him. It would take her conservative personality a while before warming up to him.

"Hello, nice to meet you." She did the polite thing and stuck out her hand to shake his. It was an extended reach as to not enter that zone that some take as an invitation to hug. She had reservations about him and wasn't ready to engage in his buddy system.

This wasn't anything new for Manus. His character had been dealing with these types of attitudes his whole life. He was well adjusted to proving himself.

They loaded up everything on the boat, went through the routine of lifejackets and what to do in the case of an emergency and then set off for a day of great expectations.

The air smelled like nature, pure and clean. As they raced out to find a place to anchor, Denise sat where her face could feel the wind and consider the most appreciated things in life. The doctor drove the boat as his job always fell on taking command in one way or another. The curiosity of Manus had him exploring throughout the boat and asking questions. As Denise was listening to the doctor and Manus's conversation, she would have preferred more peace and quiet as the real conversation hadn't begun. Right now, it was useless to her as she was just seeing him as an immature kid that she would have trouble trying to appreciate. She knew the doctor had vouched for his character and was working with her own hesitations to try and accept him. A bit of laughter was kept to herself as she continued to listen to him as he never really shut up.

The doctor found a spot that seemed off the beaten path and peaceful enough for them to sit and talk. He anchored the boat and employed Manus to help set things up for the day.

"Can you move the table and chairs more towards the back of the boat? I'm hoping for a little sun today."

"Yeah yeah, I got it. Where do you want to sit? Next to me?" He was giving Denise a jab.

"There is only three of us, so I guess you have to." Manus could tell Denise wasn't a huge fan of his and dealt with it the way he knew how, all open.

"That's ok I'll sit right here." Denise was getting up and claiming her chair. She was smiling this time at Manus as his silliness was truly laughable. They all sat down, and Denise reached into the cooler she brought and pulled out a container with some fresh fruits and sat it on the table.

"Anybody hungry, help yourself." Denise set it out for them, not hungry herself.

"Well, I guess we need to open this meeting."

The doctor began a more in-depth conversation, telling Denise how he came to know Manus. He talked to Manus about how Denise and he built their relationship. To the doctor, he wasn't trying to make a sale. He felt the need to express what he was discovering within himself, and the reason for its existence. He talked about his deep affections for her and her family as she seemed to come into his life and filled a void that had left him in many ways helpless. Each shared stories of themselves that went beyond their own person. Explanations of themselves involving family of who, and why they were who they were, opened each other's eyes. It was a slow process that ventured into a few beers and a glass of wine, but respect began to develop between the group. Slowly, the topic of Luis and his operations took over the floor. None of them would have ever cared about what he did, but now he was an effrontery invading into the things and ones they loved. His drive of pure shameless greed was what they were being forced to confront.

"I'm sure that he isn't going to let up until he speaks with the boy, and then no telling what he might do to make a point." Manus was aware of Luis's parties' ruthlessness.

"If he thinks he is going to do anything to Dillion, it will be to his undoing. I will face him myself."

"No, you won't." The doctor quickly attempted to shut down Denise's admirable stance to protect the boy she so painstakingly dedicated her time to. In many of her thoughts spent alone during the last few days, an unknown courage was emerging from within her.

"You will not confront him on any level. I forbid it. If anyone is going to deal with him, I or someone Mace knows will have to. You will not get involved like that."

"You can't tell me what I can and can't do. You are not my father." The doctor looked down when she said that. Maybe he realized he had spoken too abruptly. Maybe he needed to cool off as the volume of their conversation was elevated. Maybe he realized she was right, and he didn't have a claim to her even though he felt it.

"You're right, I'm not."

"I didn't mean it to sound so mean, but I'm not some little girl that has no interest in the matter." Denise was tired of being told what to do and felt she needed to put her foot down and show some authority. Manus felt the need to diffuse the tension by speaking.

"Look you two, we just need to keep Dillion away. If Luis's men start pushing at his family, we need to do something. Getting the law involved might get a reaction from them we don't want. I do happen to know a few folks that have other ways of doing things, but with that comes an amped up game we might not want to play." Manus was capable and willing to set things up for the doctor to make a move on Luis's operations. It wasn't discussed how illegal or even if it was. It was implied that to beat him, they would have to be willing to cross certain lines that had been drawn with the marker of morality.

"Where does he hang out? Is he ever in the public eye?" Denise wanted as much as Manus knew of Luis to be made known to her.

"Not really, he and his goombahs are sometimes seen at the 'Cardenal', it's a small Mexican restaurant located on the west side of the inner loop by the Trinity River. Not just anybody goes in there."

"Which means we don't go in there." The doctor was being indirect, but his comments most definitely included Denise. She didn't say a word but bookmarked this location in her head. She had plans to at least take a look for herself. "We are all in agreeance, right?" The doctor spoke again about them not making a move yet.

"I know you are talking to me. Yes, I agree. I'm not going to go there." Denise was beginning to feel much like the doctor had been feeling for some time. There was an answer to this madness. There was a cure for this corruption, but it wasn't inside of the things they were brought up to trust in. The old saying of "if you want something done right, do it yourself" was a reality that was turning all lawful presumptions on an about-face.

"I will see if I can find out any more about where Stacy's case is going. If she is going to get off, none of this might even matter." They had been on this subject for some time now. They had all been snacking and drinking through the afternoon and the discussion had reached its potential. They were all but beating the dead horse of their emotions now.

"Look at that sun behind those clouds." The doctor chose to change the topic. "Isn't it beautiful?"

"It is. It's a shame life can't be that way for all." Denise's heart was becoming content with the acceptance of the things she couldn't change and believing in the things she could.

"It's not that way for some because that's the way they want it. It is a hard thing to realize and even more hard to accept sometimes." The doctor's philosophy hadn't necessarily changed. It was just made more manifest as his life's circumstances had drawn it out of him, making it much more clearly seen.

"You are quite the psychologist. You know, you ought to write a book." When the conversations got to a level of sentiment, Manus refrained from speaking, but here he felt compelled to comment. As much of a clown as he portrayed himself to be, he recognized truth when he heard it.

"Thank you for your encouragement, but I don't have the time. Well, I think we need to be getting back before the sun goes down on us."

"Me too, it's been a day." Denise agreed with the doctor and they set the short course back to the dock.

Once they pulled in, they cleaned up the boat, pulled the trash and loaded all they had brought back into their cars.

"I had a good time. I have to go. I'm meeting some friends back at the casino tonight. I hope you don't mind but I'll see you guys later." Manus was ready to leave and kept things rather short.

"Goodbye, Manus. It was nice to meet you. Sorry if I came off as standoffish this morning."

"That's alright, most girls who like me take that approach." Manus just couldn't give up his natural comedic routine.

"Is that what it is, I'm glad you let me know." While Denise was smiling, she gave Manus an easy hug. He patted her back to show it was mutually accepted. "You take care, Mace."

"Will do, you too doc." Manus jumped in his car and was gone.

"How do you feel?" The doctor looked at Denise with a solid stern stare. It was a question deeper than just how she was feeling.

"Better. Sometimes I think I complicate things by rejecting what is obvious and right because of the price I think it might cost or because of an emotion telling me different. I am having to do a lot of growing and fast. You know, if I would have known that this is the road I would have been going down the day I came to your door, I might not have knocked." Denise was rambling faster than she was thinking. They were her thoughts, but had she considered them, she would have kept them reserved. "That's not true. I would have come anyway."

"I know you would have. I am so thankful you did. I am a beneficiary to this union as much as you are. There are reasons for our path's crossings outside of our understanding. This I fully believe."

"You are probably right, doctor."

They started their drive back to Dallas and left all that had been said to rest within their minds. The music was set to a soft level in the car and Denise rested for the entire trip home. She had come to a place of recognizing the things she had feared. She had to take a hard look and overcome those reservations. Her last days of naivete had finally come and gone. It is sad that the days of innocence have to end in order to face a true degree of maturity. Knowing the depths of evil isn't an acceptance of them. Rather, it is an acknowledgement of their existence. No more would she see things as she had before.

Chapter Sixteen
The Making of His Strong Conviction

Separated from the harsh realities that were looming, Dillion's enjoyment wasn't without its own challenges. As he was learning to swim, horseback ride and partake in things such as obstacle courses and archery, the trials of petty juvenile immaturity were also making their rounds. Dillion was by nature a standout. His life had been given over to a look of defeat. He wasn't a child of great self-esteem, although Denise and Dr. Richards had been moving him to understand these things.

The camp he was attending wasn't in the price range of the modest and most of the kids attending were of an affluent background. They didn't take too kindly to outsiders, much less people they considered lower or even a charity case. They had a way of spotting these tokens and thought of them as an intrusion on their spot-free life. Dillion was struggling to take in such a great advantage he was given while at the same time hiding much of who he was. This task seemed impossible with the three inseparable campgoers who regarded no one but themselves. Dillion's insecurity and programmed embarrassment fed the boys' creativity to demean his innocence.

The self-made leader of the bunch was naturally the shortest. His name was Byron Ryder. He was the loudest and most arrogant of all the kids at camp. The two he had handpicked for his gang were boys named Paul Stoddard and Danny Simpson. They were both bigger but much less outspoken than Byron. Had they ever decided to take the lead of this band, there wouldn't be one vote cast. Either one could easily find themselves doing so, but they were content to let Byron have the reigns.

Upon his lead, the group made Dillion their subject to express any vanity they wished. The pressure mounted on Dillion as the aggravation pressed forward a little more every day. The boys had targeted him from the first time they saw him. They learned of his name and their torment was continually pushed by the leader as often as they could.

"Dillweed, do you miss your mommy?" Dillion ignored Byron as his cronies stood by laughing at his side. Not knowing his home life, it was by chance they were pushing buttons on Dillion's heart. Unaware of its impact they continued to taunt him for their own greed.

Dillion's difficult situation was a matter the boys didn't know about. If they did, it probably wouldn't have prevented their behavior. They were immature and selfish. Incidentally, their actions would only force him to break, or see to it that he might break something.

"What's the matter Dillweed, your mommy told me to tell you not to miss her and I can let her know how you are doing when I see her tonight." Dillion began to hurt a bit and walked away from the boys before they could see his eyes begin to water. He was mad and frightened at the same time. He was also establishing a hatred for these boys. When Byron saw that Dillion was walking away, he pursued him. The one thing Dillion didn't understand was that the bad guys only hit harder when seeing defeat. "Don't run away when I am talking to you, boy." Byron went after Dillion, and his buddies kept pace at his side.

"Leave me alone." Dillion wasn't going to say much. He wasn't a boy that had overcome anything like this. It was always a thought that his life was what it was. Now with the doctor and Denise being influential people in his life, things felt different. But situations like this destroyed all the progress that had been made.

Byron, who received no discipline at home, was thought of by his parents as a little angel. He was extremely smart in the art of deception. He was able to tell them exactly what they wanted to hear. His parents' confidence in him was so strong that they blindly defended him many times when he was in the wrong. He could do no wrong in their eyes. The fact that they had money and prominence added to the score that their boy kept. He couldn't get in trouble.

A loud buzzer went off throughout all the camp. It was an announcement that everyone needed to get to their next activity. Fortunately, Dillion wasn't going in the same direction as these boys. As quickly as the buzzer went off, Byron and the boys forgot Dillion. They immediately shot off to their class.

Keeping up appearances was a priority. As they ran off to enjoy their scheduled pursuit, Dillion spent his next hour with a depressed attitude.

Unfortunately, people without regard towards others don't understand the lasting effects that gross negligence can have. They can't see what they are doing. They would only detest it in reverse. What had started out as great expectations for the boy, was turning into a dreaded activity.

Denise and the doctor were unaware of what he was dealing with. They would never suspect that all their careful planning was being compromised within its own elements. It was a commonly overlooked reality that no one ever totally escapes torment, as it exists all around us.

The swing of work seemed to get back on its course. Stacy was locked up. The lawyers were hard at work. Dillion was safely tucked away in the Hill Country. Denise and the doctor were growing in their perceptions and understandings. They were seeing harsh realities and how it is not always the proposed solution that best serves justice. They would strive to deliver an acceptable outcome for Dillion, despite the many obstacles they were up against.

They focused their attention on other cases for the next couple of workdays to allow time's blessing to fall upon Dillion's case. If all the pieces fell according to their wishes, there would be no need of having to negotiate their judgments. Even with all the boundaries they were considering crossing, a just outcome, without the introduction of their own influences, was preferred. These were definite thoughts, not being discussed.

"Doctor, can you get me some more paper? My printer is almost out." The doctor wasn't doing much as Denise was printing off forms she needed to fill out and get filed.

"Sure, I'm going to get some coffee while I'm up, do you want any?"

"No thanks, just the paper." The doctor had been on his phone looking over some emails, most of which were junk. He was cleaning out his phone and continued as he walked down the hallway to where the paper was stored. Inside the supply room, the doctor saw what he thought needed some attention. There was absolutely no organization to keeping things neat in this room. It was a shared supply room and for that reason, no one ever owned its responsibility. Boxes weren't stacked. Three of them had been opened to get paper out, without emptying the first box. The straps that hold the boxes closed for shipping were left on the floor just a ring toss away from the trash can.

While the doctor could keep a good composure, these were the things that added to his frustration. He turned from getting the paper and went to get more coffee as he planned on spending a bit of time cleaning up in the storeroom. His attention to Denise's request was averted by his concentration of the disorder in their office. As he began the task of setting the room up the way he thought it should be, fifteen minutes went by, and it still needing attention.

"Doctor, my paper?" Denise stuck her head in the room to find the doctor working, moving things around in the storeroom.

"Sorry, Denise. I got stuck on something else. Here you go." The doctor handed her a ream of paper. "If you're good, I am going to finish cleaning up in here." Everyone in Denise's office appreciated the doctor for this very positive trait he had. He was known for wiping the counter every time he got coffee. He took the trash out quite frequently, as the maintenance crew was stretched between different buildings.

"It's alright, I had to stop what I was doing. We got a call from a counselor at Dillion's camp. Dillion is wanting to come home."

"What! What did they say?"

"He told the counselor he wasn't having a good time and missed being home." Denise explained to the doctor what she was told with a confused and disappointed look on her face.

"Something isn't right. That boy was so excited when we drove up there last week, and now he misses home. Did you talk to Dillion?"

"No, the counselor said that he asked for her to call us."

"Well, I'm going to call Dillion. Something isn't adding up here. I'm going to find out what it is." The doctor left his project of arranging the supplies. He had to switch his focus to a situation he thought was in order.

Circumstances were causing a constant awareness to be placed on Dillion. Unforeseeable forces were becoming manifest and causing disruption. This was just another complication the doctor would have to grasp. Every turn, every corner had an obstacle waiting to take its own turn. It was as if a higher power was making a move on his every play.

"Did they leave a contact?"

"Yes, it's on my desk, her name is Cecilia. The number is on that sheet of paper. I think she is the camp coordinator."

"Good, I will call her. I want to speak with Dillion."

The doctor called the number and spoke with the counselor. She sounded warm and didn't indicate there was much of a problem at all, just that Dillion wanted to go back home.

"It is that way sometimes with kids. Independence doesn't mature as fast for some." She took Dillion's request as simple homesickness. Without having heard from Dillion, he could tell the counselor wasn't that perceptive. He, having known Dillion, knew that something was causing him to want to leave the camp.

"Is Dillion around? I would like to talk with him. I would like to encourage him to stay, especially if it is because of a little homesickness."

"He is out canoeing right now, but they are due back to eat lunch at 11:45am. They don't go to another activity until 1:05pm. I can have him call after he eats."

"That will be fine. Have him call this number. I will be here. Thank you."

"You're welcome." They hung up. The doctor thought that the lady at the camp wasn't that good at her job. Someone working with kids should have a better intuition to decipher the deeper needs that kids sometimes tend to resist coming out. While this wasn't a camp for troubled youth, that might be acceptable, but the doctor's thoughts were that all children have some sort of a need that requires attention. He was sure she had well intentions, just not the skills to expose those problems that need solving.

Dr. Richards promptly went back into the supply room and before restarting the organizing of the room, he brought back a paper ream to Denise at her desk.

"Thanks, but you handed me one when you left the room to come and call Dillion. That's ok though, I'll take one more, because I'll need it eventually." The doctor set it down and went back to the supply room to occupy the next hour and a half before expecting the call from the camp. After setting all things in order and knowing it wouldn't look like that in a month or so, he went back into Denise's office. Denise was still at her desk, now eating a sandwich and some fresh vegetables.

"Do you want some of my lunch?"

"No thanks, I ate two granola bars while cleaning up in there."

"Oh my, you know that every so often someone tries to do what you did in an effort for people to change the atmosphere of that room, but it always goes back to looking like that."

"I figured as much. It's alright, I'm ok with it. I needed something to do. I'm just wondering what is eating at Dillion."

"I know you think it is something else, but it also might be he feels out of place and wants to come back. Remember, it took a while for us to get him to accept our company, and we worked exclusively with him. There he is just a number."

"I know, but my instincts are telling me it is something else bothering him. I need to talk with him. We can't have him coming back. You know this!"

"I know, I agree, but if he wants to leave, perhaps we need to come up with another plan." Denise's suggestion of Dillion's departure from camp was not a good option for the doctor, but he allowed his patience to wait for the phone call. He would first have to figure out what was really happening and then resolve the matter within his own powers.

"I'm going to get a water from the vending machine before the call comes in. Do you want one?" The doctor asked Denise as he was getting up.

"No thanks." *Ring ring ring.* The phone suddenly rang, and Denise looked at the doctor. "You better cancel that order." The doctor walked around the desk and picked up the phone.

"Hello, Dr. Richards speaking."

"Hello doctor. I was told to call y'all."

"Yes, we were told you wanted to come back already. Is there a problem?"

"No." There was a pause as the doctor thought he might have more to say.

"Well, what is the matter? You have only been there for a week. Is something wrong?"

"No." Again, Dillion wasn't saying much and the doctor had to continue talking. Denise was looking confused as she could tell it was a one-sided conversation.

"Is something going on at the camp?" This time Dillion didn't speak. The doctor's intuition began to make its presence known. "Are you not wanting to speak?" Dillion remained silent.

"Dillion, is someone in the room with you and that is why you don't want to talk? Just say yes or no. Is someone in the room?"

"Yes."

"Is that why you aren't talking?"

"Yes."

"Is it Cecilia, the counselor?"

"Yes."

"Ok. Put her on. I am going to talk with her and then you and I are going to talk."

"Ok." Dillion told the counselor that the doctor wanted to talk to her. He began explaining that Dillion needed to talk with him in private. He didn't want to divulge into much of Dillion's situation as it wasn't any of her business. She was most understanding and expressed they could have the conversation without her in the room.

"Absolutely, honey you could have asked me for privacy, that would have been no problem." She was on the phone and had answered the doctor but turned towards Dillion explaining to him as well. She handed the phone back to Dillion and exited the room.

"Dillion, what's going on?"

"I want to leave. I don't like the people here."

"They can't all be bad. Cecilia seems very nice and accommodating. Do you mean 'some of the people?'"

"Yes." Dillion's answers were short, and the doctor was losing his patience. Denise was listening and looking at the doctor with a puzzled look. The doctor wasn't liking the fact that his perfect protection plan was unraveling.

"Talk to me Dillion, what is it? Are there kids that are getting at you?"

"Yes." Another pause took place.

"Talk to me! You are four hours away. I need you to talk to me if I'm going to help you! Talk!" This time the doctor's frustrations were made apparent. Denise raised her hand and began to motion downward to show the doctor he needed to lower his voice down. This didn't seem to help with the doctor's frustrations.

"There are these boys that keep messing with me, they talk about my mom. They won't leave me alone. I just don't want to be here anymore."

"Were you having a good time before they started picking on you?"

"Yes."

"Put the counselor back on, I'll get this thing straightened out."

"No no no. Please don't do that. That will make things worse. If they know that I complained, then they will only do it more. I don't want to be around them." Denise started to get involved and spoke to the doctor while he was on the phone.

"Tell Dillion that is what needs to be done. The right way to get over this is to have the counselor deal with those boys." Dr. Richards was feeling empathy for Dillion as he heard his plea and then Denise's solution to the problem. This was more of the same justice that was continuing to not get served.

"Dillion, hold on. I'm going to put you on hold."

"Ok." The doctor put Dillion on hold and talked with Denise for a second.

"I'm going to talk with the counselor and get her to take care of this for us. Can you do me a favor and run to my car? I have a prescription of heartburn pills in my console. This has given me extreme heartburn. Can you please go get them and I will deal with this?"

"Well, I guess so." Denise looked at the doctor as if she was getting pushed out the door, and that was exactly what the doctor was doing.

"Thank you, I appreciate it." As soon as Denise took his keys and walked out, the doctor took the phone off of hold. He knew he had only a few minutes to convey a strong message into this young man's mind, but it was high time for him to hear it.

"Dillion!"

"Yes."

"Listen to me very carefully. I'm so mad I could cuss. That wouldn't do justice to the lesson I'm about to try to get you to understand. Listen carefully. How many boys are messing with you?"

"Three."

"Is the littlest one got the biggest mouth?"

"Yes. How did you know that?"

"Those little insignificant small men are always the ones that attempt to puff themselves up by taking someone down, and they don't do it alone because they CAN'T! Do you hear me they CAN'T! Don't you fall for this Dillion. Most times it's out of jealousy that they do these things." The doctor was on edge. The last thing he needed was some group of immature brats compromising Dillion's safety by scaring him back home to a really scary situation. The doctor was tired of defeat and had to teach Dillion he needed to fight back too. "Listen, the next time this boy approaches you, I don't care, you get up in his face and tell him straight up- YOU ARE GONNA KICK HIS ASS! Did you hear me?" There was a pause and Dillion didn't know what to say. "These boys don't know you. They don't know your mom.

They are trying to boost their ego at your expense. I will tell you that Denise and I have been working too damn hard for you, for these boys to come in and wreck things. I need your help. I need for you to help yourself!"

"Well, what if they all jump me?"

"They won't. They are bullies. They are weak. Besides if they do, whip them all. Don't confuse matters Dillion. Fighting is not always the best answer. Most times it's the wrong answer. But when it is warranted, it is wrong to withhold from it."

"What if I get in trouble?"

"You may get in trouble at camp, but if you put that bully in his place, I'm buying you ice cream every week for a year." Dillion let go of a laugh that he so desperately needed. "Oh, and by the way, I had to talk to you in private too. Denise left the room, so don't tell her what I just said. Our secret right?"

"Yeah." Just then Denise walked in the door and asked the doctor about the conversation.

"What did the counselor say?"

"I didn't have to talk to the counselor. I am still talking to Dillion. He is going to see if he can make friends with the boys by showing them some respect." Dillion could hear the talking between the doctor and Denise.

"That is some change from when I left. Can I talk with Dillion?"

"Sure, here he is. Dillion, Denise wants to talk with you." The doctor handed the phone over to Denise. "Dillion, what's going on?"

"Not much. The doctor talked to me about dealing with these boys."

"And what did he say?"

"That they are just bullies and I don't need to let what they say bother me."

"And that's all?"

"Yes, and to just enjoy myself while I'm here."

"Ok, well you let us know if you need anything. We are always available. You know that?"

"Yes." The doctor was motioning that he wanted to talk with him before she hung up.

"Well, the doctor is waving his hand. I guess he has something important to tell you that you two haven't already discussed." Denise had thoughts there might have been more to their conversation as the two scenes were different from one another. She handed the phone to

Dr. Richards with a look like he was guilty of something.

"Dillion, I will check in with you tomorrow. I will let the counselor know we need to talk during your lunches until we know you are going to be ok. Alright?"

"Yes sir." The doctor could detect a spark of confidence in his voice. It was a sign of maturity for the boy to realize it is ok to stand up for yourself.

"I'm proud of you boy. It's ok for you to be proud too." Again, Dillion thanked the doctor with a sir and called the counselor in to talk with the doctor. He explained to Cecilia that Dillion was good to stay, and he would be checking in on him. He gave the counselor confidence that it was just a bit of homesickness but that he would be fine. When he hung up, Denise was sitting with her hands crossed, waiting for her turn to speak.

"Well, it's nice that you two got everything figured out. Am I becoming a fifth wheel?"

"Not at all Denise. You are my boss. I work for you." The doctor felt better about everything and put a big smile on for Denise to see.

"You know you make it hard for me to sometimes get mad at you, especially when I think you are up to no good."

"I know, but trust me, it's all better now."

Dr. Richards and Dillion both knew it wouldn't be long before Dillion's test would be set before him. Byron, Paul and Danny were also counting on it. To them it was going to be more of the casual routine of picking on the helpless to satisfy their own selves. Their only problem was they were unaware of the certitude that the doctor helped to convince Dillion of. These boys would no longer pose a threat to Dillion. While Dillion had certain fears of fighting, he was confident that what the doctor had told him was true. He trusted in his words and was willing to follow them. Facing the situation was something Dillion played over and over in his mind as he slept throughout the night, knowing the next day was most assuredly going to be a trial.

It was breakfast time, and all the kids would gather in the cafeteria to eat prior to going to their assigned classes. This was a forty-five-minute time period where the kids would eat and could talk a bit depending on how fast they ate. Most used this time to brag, tell tall tales, share jokes and some to boost their egos.

Dillion was eating his breakfast alone. Perhaps his loner status was partly to blame for him being a target. None the less, he didn't dish out the trash so it was wrong for him to receive it.

When Byron laid eyes on him, he grabbed his friends to go cause a little morning havoc. Dillion saw them and continued eating his breakfast. As Byron walked up to Dillion, he was laughing and talking to his buddies, most assuredly making some sort of a joke. Dillion began to feel nervous and cornered.

"Well, well, what are we having for breakfee Mr. Dillweed?" Dillion ignored him. He had it in his mind that he was going to put an end to this harassment, but pulling the trigger had to feel right. "Did you hear me? Huh, do you hear me Mr. Dillweed?" Dillion kept quiet. Maybe a bit of fear was doing it, but anger began to fester from within. "Look at him. He thinks he can make me invisible." Byron looked at his friends as they were laughing and cheering on his useless efforts. "Are you wanting to make me go away little baby? You think you can ignore me? Huh? Can you ignore me? Well, ignore this." Byron's friend's chanting, along with his abuse of power and missed perception of Dillion being weak, pressed him to cross the line. He reached over and slapped Dillion's hand as he was eating cereal. The spoon he was holding turned over and spilled on the table where he was sitting. Dillion put the spoon down and stood up.

"Don't you ever touch me again! Do you understand?" As Dillion pushed forward to stand up towards his aggressor, Byron took a step back. Paul stuck his hand out between the two of them to stop any escalation. The three were all surprised at Dillion's reaction, as no one had ever dared push back against their antics. With the aid of one of his buddies Byron felt protected enough to not submit.

"What do you think you are doing boy? You're gonna get hurt!" Byron, shielding himself with Paul's arm, shouted at Dillion while lunging his face forward and raising his fists to frighten him. Dillion didn't flinch and kept his eyes pierced at Byron.

"Don't you even ever talk to me again." After speaking his last piece, Dillion walked off from the table. Some of the kids had enjoyed the morning entertainment, but in its rush, didn't allow enough time to attract the usual crowd. Byron was left standing a bit confused and bruised on his ego. He knew he looked foolish starting something that he was now having to question if he wanted to end. He did the standard act of any bully and began to make excuses to his friends by putting down Dillion.

By answering the impulses that desire the stroking of one's vanity, he had put himself into a position that would require another attack. This hand would be forced by the friends he had performed for. They would obligate him to a second act, one that he would now have stage fright with.

Lunchtime came and after Dillion ate, Cecilia walked him to the office to get the promised phone call from the doctor. Dillion was anxious to tell the doctor what had happened that morning. He was feeling like it was finally over. While sitting there, the counselor asked him about the camp. She asked if he was enjoying himself and began talking about some of her past camping experiences. She expressed that she too had been homesick and that many people have those feelings when they first come there. Dillion just entertained the conversation as she perceived it was, knowing to himself that homesickness wasn't the culprit. It didn't take long, and the phone rang. Cecilia left the room as before and Dillion talked with the doctor. The doctor called from his cell phone away from Denise. These conversations were better off without her knowledge.

"Well, how's it going? Did your friends pay you a visit?"

"They sure did. I don't think they expected me to snap back either, but I did."

"Did you get in any kind of trouble?"

"No."

"Good, what about the boys? Did they get in trouble?"

"No."

"Good, well hopefully that's that." Dillion began to explain all that had happened. The doctor could tell the boy was quite proud of his accomplishment. His confidence was beginning to climb. Before he could get to a sentiment of boasting, the doctor offered wisdom.

"Now Dillion, what you did was good as long as it serves the purpose to stop what is wrong, but it profits you nothing if wrong just moves to another location, namely yourself. Feel good that he stopped, don't feel good that you made him feel bad. Because then you are like him. Do you understand?"

"Yes sir. But what do I do if he comes at me again?"

"The same thing I told you the other day. YOU KICK HIS ASS." Again, Dillion chuckled a bit to hear the doctor talk that way. Dr. Richards wasn't advocating anarchy, to the contrary, he was promoting order. "Are you going to be alright?"

"Yes sir. Well, I have to go. The bell is about to ring."

"Ok, take care. Do I need to call you tomorrow?"

"I really don't think so."

"Ok, I'll tell you what. Write me and Denise letters from camp."

"Really?" Dillion gave another one of his less enthusiastic responses as writing didn't seem to spark interest in his mind.

"Yes really. I would very much enjoy having your thoughts on paper. Denise would too. It is a thoughtful gesture."

"Well, ok. They actually told us if we want to do that to let them know and they have all the stuff."

"Good, I'll expect a letter next week."

"Ok." The conversation didn't go much further and both parties were satisfied. The doctor was most proud as Dillion seemed to be overcoming fears. It was a task he knew would be a more severe learning in his future.

With about fifteen minutes left in their lunch Dillion left the office with much of a skip in his stride. He was walking with the confidence of a champion. He grabbed a drink from a water fountain and went into the bathroom as lunch neared its end. Little did he know that Paul and Danny had pushed Byron to redeem himself. This time the group didn't want to fare as bad as they had that morning. They watched him go into the restroom and followed him in there.

"There he is. Now are you going to take care of this or am I going to have to." Paul was now acting as the aggressor and making the issue for Byron to step up. Byron stood there looking at Dillion in a stance to fight but made no move or mention. Dillion just stood still watching as Byron didn't look so confident as he had before. "Do I have to show you how to do this?" Paul started to approach Dillion. Dillion felt a streak of adrenaline shoot from his back up to his head. "Watch this." Paul set his arms in a motion as if to swing. He was attempting to scare Dillion, when everything came to a head. Dillion, faster than he could think, swung and hit Paul square in his nose. Paul made a yelp like a dog getting hit with a rolled-up newspaper. He grabbed his face and his eyes immediately started making water. Danny backed up quickly. What had been funny to him before had lost all its humor. Dillion didn't stop. He quickly charged Byron and grabbed his head pushing it into the wall.

"Stop, stop, let me go." He was squeezing his head and tightening his grip, pulling, and pushing on his hair.

"You want me to stop? That's what I've been telling you. You don't want any of this is what you're saying?" Paul was standing back and holding his nose as it bled. Danny was standing back as well. They were both amazed. Their fearless leader whom they were beginning to doubt had now lost all his credibility. "Answer me. Did you hear what I said? Answer me. Say it. Do you want me to stop?"

"Yes. Stop!" Dillion remembered what the doctor said and let go of Byron. He pulled him off the wall and pushed him over towards his friends. It was clear Byron had begun to cry. Dillion stepped towards all three of them with courage and confidence. He raised his hand and pointed his finger at all three of their faces.

"No more. You will not pick on me or anyone here anymore. I'm not going to mess with you, and you aren't going to mess with anybody. If you want to and that's what any of you want, then I want you to know I'm gonna serve it up, and I'll give it to you the way you want, bitch. I'm giving you the choice to decide." All three boys were silent as Dillion turned to leave the bathroom.

This would be a problem that would never come back to haunt him. It was a turning point in his growth. Up until this day, Dillion had only come to the point of knowing and accepting the depths of hard truths in life. He had never seen much good or justice or its application to rectify. His ability to interpret and deal with situations often left him beat. This kind of growth was something all men must come to understand. Life is full of choices. Some men's answers break them down. Some men's answers edify them. Some men's answers are never to answer, which is the worst of all. Recovery can only take place with solutions. Solutions come from answering questions, even the ones about ourselves. Once a man finds the answers, he can stand on a firm conviction. This was the character building this young man needed.

Chapter Seventeen
A Strongarm Armistice

Taking no break from the concern of the new young subject, Luis sought how to fight against an unknown. The law firm hired should have been sufficient for adequate protections, but his mischievous mind allowed for his voracity to have its own freedoms. Not being able to get to Stacy and relying on others for his desired outcome was causing him to experience a worried nature. This just brought about anger within him. He was like an addict that lost control and control was his drug of choice.

Questions had arisen from the lawyers as to what might possibly give the prosecution a chance to run with any grounds of circumstantial evidence. Tying Mr. Maldonado to Stacy in any way whatsoever would not be acceptable to him. The team of Lucas and Abrams were aware of this issue. They were extremely cunning and drew hefty sums for their services. It was a double-edged sword, as they could charge well for their services but were held to a guarantee to win by the clientele they attracted.

In a couple of scheduled meetings with Stacy, the goal was to lay out a plan that kept all members in a state of belief that each was unaware of the other's knowledge of the real truths. Concealment was crucial. They knew Stacy's careless nature could let things out of the bag and part of their job would be to keep it from getting out.

Answers from their questioning would be tempered to not allow an assumption from Stacy to appear. If one doesn't say or speak of certain things, then those things are considered non-existent. They wanted to manipulate her story without telling her what to say. They also wanted to know everything she knew that could be crucial to the case and, at the same time, prevent her from giving unnecessary information. Stones not needing to be turned over should be left untouched. Only the things they knew were critical, and convincing her of their story without spelling it out was the art they excelled in. Attempting to keep her mind on the track they wanted it on was the goal.

It was talking on the surface with imaginary lines being drawn. The sad truth is that they were masters of lies and achieved much, beginning with lying to themselves. That was the truth, but it spoke highly in their trade as they set the bar for greatness.

Stacy had been locked up for several months and was feeding off the environment she was surrounded by. She had adjusted to her situation. Doing time didn't have the same effect on her as it had on a decent and upright person. Instead, it brought about the mawkishness of a spoiled child. She complained about how unfairly she was treated, and that the food wasn't what she liked. She convinced herself she had earned a constant grievance on her poor persecuted heart. Nothing filled her soul about the deaths of the people involved in the situation that she was facing a trial for. She was fit to be tied.

It was their third visit and the lawyers had learned much about Stacy's character. They had developed a distaste for her company. Still blinded by her sheer ignorance of all things, she thought she held standing in their eyes. She was completely oblivious to their true thoughts. They were more than courteous to her as their job was dependent on her cooperation. While that may have aided in her ignorance, she felt connected to them. They felt repulsed by her.

"Well Mrs. Brown, I think we can demonstrate comfortably to the jury you had nothing at all to do with this drug deal, because you didn't." The Q & A was more of an informative session. Stacy wasn't of a mind to object. As long as she could see freedom again, she was content. Her confidence was sparked as the two well-groomed lawyers appealed to her pride.

"I'm glad at least someone understands." Her guiltless gluttony disgusted Lucas and Abrams even though they needed her participation to carry out this lie.

"Given the lack of proof the prosecution has, we expect a fairly swift trial. We have heard that they might pursue questioning those who know you to see if they can establish any connections to anyone who might be behind this deal. Are you aware of anything we may need to know?" Mr. Lucas was the determined questioner. He felt that these were areas they would need to inquire about. Her character was an unpredictable mess that had to be dealt with.

"No." Stacy was quick to give an answer. She gave no consideration to it. Whether she did or didn't lack any memory of possible slips of her tongue, she knew herself too well, and feared answering with any great amount of thought.

"Are you sure? Because unless I know everything, I might not be able to help you." Mr. Lucas was determined to get all possible information that she knew.

"No, well I think if they ask my oldest son, he has probably heard some of the names of some of my friends that I hang out with, but he doesn't know anything that he could tell them." This was what the lawyers wanted. They needed her to open up in a controlled fashion. Without mentioning Luis's name, they wanted to know if it had been mentioned before. They knew Stacy's carelessness was more than enough to have left a mess unattended.

"Friends like who? We need to know what might be said so we can be prepared to protect you."

"I'm not sure. I just know that he is sometimes around when I have been on the phone and might have heard some things." Her answer was quick as she fidgeted, wanting the subject to move on. Mr. Lucas asked more poignantly.

"Now, think carefully. It is our job to see to it that you aren't convicted of a crime you didn't commit, but we can't very well do that if you aren't forthright with us. Is there anyone, any names that your son might bring up that could be detrimental to your case?" Stacy paused and began looking around. She already knew the answer she was safeguarding. Her squirming was all they needed to see to make the determination to continue to press and hopefully purge out any concealment of her carelessness. "Who could your son possibly mention that might put you in a compromising position?" It was ironic that they asked that question. The truth the attorneys were seeking, they had already predicted. They just had to have her say it without themselves volunteering the name.

For her, it was the real compromise to her situation. The name Luis was what everyone was thinking, but no one would dare mention.

"Stacy, you are pausing. There is something you are not telling us. If you want, you can get a court appointed attorney if this is the way you want to do things." A change in tactics was what these men were good at. Strategy was their art and victims were useful mediums for them to display their skills.

"No, no, I'm thinking. He may have heard me mention Luis's name a few times. You know who he is?" Both lawyers looked at each other and knew immediately that their questioning would now open

Pandora's box. Stacy was sure they knew him, but formally there had never been that discussion. The less Stacy knew of their knowledge, the whole situation would be better.

"Ok, now we have something we can work with. This is good. We weren't aware of any of this, so now we need to know what might have been said. Anything that might have taken place. We need you to come forward and be clean with all you know." A conversation about Stacy and her involvement began to unwind and download into the notes of the lawyers. Skillfully crafted and on the clock, they meticulously documented all the information that Luis would expect them to get back with him on.

Lucas and Abrams were well aware that many of their clientele had operations that dealt outside of the law. They were just a branch of their reaching to keep things as clean as possible. In this case, it didn't surprise the attorneys upon learning about Stacy's confession, that she might be getting a settlement out of court.

For the meantime there was the issue at hand that must be dealt with. What had the boy heard and would he be useful to the prosecution in a conviction that might lead to a connection to Luis by way of Stacy saving her own hide? Would the prosecution attempt to put a son against his mother? While justice should be served, many people think there are certain lines that should never be crossed.

"Looks like we are finished here today. It is important that you don't speak to anyone about anything we discussed here today. Not with family, not with friends, not with any of the inmates here. Keep all things in your case confidential for your own safety. Do you understand?"

"Yes sir. I won't talk to anyone." Throughout their conversation, she had mentioned how she tried to get Dillion to talk to her about what he might have known regarding why she was locked up. With Dillion, it was like pulling teeth. The lawyers advised her to not even reach out to him. She was never the mom that had allowed her son to trust in her, let alone have any real meaningful exchanges. They saw any interaction between the two as potentially hazardous. The overall comprehension of everything was still without sufficient answers.

Not knowing what the boy knew and who he might have talked to, would most certainly lead to harassments for answers. Luis's team wouldn't be satisfied with the conclusion of information retrieved by the lawyers, so inside interrogations would have to take place.

It wasn't within their knowledge or concern that the boy was content on leaving all that his mother represented to him, in a distant rear-view mirror. They were only affected by the possibility he could cause them problems. Even if this move was orchestrated at the hand of another, he was considered enough of a threat.

Denise was feeling the pressures of her long days compounded by the relentless forces they foresaw could perhaps engage Dillion. It was causing her to break down, and she was in a fight, refusing to accept it. Her mind was slowly wrestling with the idea that she was losing a grip she had always taken for granted.

The sanctified lifestyle she had been protected under wasn't in the cards for everyone. This was a troubling truth she strived to work through. How could she overcome this battle? What could she do to make things right? Was there a part of her that was failing to recognize that some people's destinies are doomed? She knew she couldn't save everyone, but it was too hard to watch this one fall. It was too close to home. She could admit that life's tragedies were a natural process, but everyone seemed to stop short of accepting them when it involved a loved one. This one was causing too much pain to allow in.

Her phone rang. It was the doctor.

"Hello."

"Denise, I guess you know by now, I'm not coming in?"

"Well, I figured as much. You know you have used more vacation than any new employee I have seen hire on here." Her attempt to hand out quick wit was a mask to her inner emotions. She was aching inside.

"Yeah, give the old man a hard time. Well, I was here at the house and I'm thinking about what to do when Dillion returns from camp in a week and a half. I spoke with him two days ago and he is doing a lot better. He is really enjoying his stay there."

"I'm so happy for him. Although, I am also concerned like you about him coming home. I hate to think about it, but there is a real threat to him from those who are uneasy about what he may know."

"I know, that is why I'm thinking of what we need to do. Sending Dillion away was a good plan but it was only temporary and we knew it."

The court systems were slow and wouldn't allow for a decision to be made in Stacy's case for some time. Dillion's security would be in limbo until his mother's fate was answered. Until that time, keeping Dillion safe would prove to be a juggling act.

"I know I have badgered you about not overstepping bounds, but someone needs to set an agreement in order that Dillion is off limits. The poor guy doesn't even know anything." Denise surprised the doctor with her suggestion.

"What do you mean?"

"I mean, someone needs to confront this guy. Someone needs to tell him that no one is after him. We will leave him alone just as long as he leaves the boy alone."

"I'm afraid people like him don't negotiate."

"Well, he is going to have to compromise. I am willing to make a truce as much as I can. Otherwise, your thinking has begun to rub off on me. Perhaps the answer lies outside of the law." The doctor for the first time heard Denise express her frustrations.

He didn't expect her to act on any of them. The doctor had a feeling of empathy flow through him. He connected to her concerns, knowing she was embracing deeper considerations in the battle of what was right and wrong. It was a realization of discovering the truth and recognizing its importance. It also brought with it a sense of fear in the doctor. He knew those opposed to true justice, sought to silence it.

"Denise, you know you must stay grounded and protect yourself. We can't be much good to Dillion if we ourselves are in trouble." The doctor knew that if Denise got hurt, it would open doors for him, that people are generally afraid to look behind. Any job requiring an act such as one Denise was subtly suggesting, would only be done by him. Denise's safety was paramount to him.

"I mean it doctor, no one is going to mess with him."

"Ok, I agree. Let's just take things a day at a time. We still have some time to figure out what to do." The doctor did his best to maneuver their speech away from its current position. He had to get Denise's mind removed from thoughts that promoted her being vulnerable.

Their conversation continued a while and drifted into less concerning issues. They ended with a commitment that the doctor would be in the next day, and they could discuss things further. After getting off the phone, Denise's curiosity decided she would take an alternate route home. She remembered the mentioning of the restaurant where Luis was known to eat, in the conversation with Manus. A call to a friend that worked downtown, answered some questions about the location that housed the restaurant. It seemed to be tucked away in an unexposed area. Her inquisitiveness had her wanting to drive by for a simple look. A courage within her was reaching farther than she would have ever dared.

Sharing this thought with the doctor would be a cause for his concern. She knew his feelings for her. Lately he had been expressing them more stringently. Denise felt his knowing would be unnecessary as today she was just planning on driving by.

Before she left she looked up the place Manus had mentioned, Restaurante El Cardenal. Much to her surprise, it wasn't what she expected. Denise thought it would be a gangster's hideout and in fact she was wrong. It was a favorite with the local Mexicans, known for its authentic flavors and alluring ambience. On its website it appeared to be an elegant place to dine. Knowing this, her mind surmised greater challenges to face. If she was to confront him to attempt an armistice, it would have to be in a place in the public and one she could be comfortable in. Even though the thought sounded good for a second, she knew she would be a fish out of water.

Why couldn't there be an easy way to express her concerns for Dillion and her intentions of causing no trouble for anyone. All she wanted was for Dillion to be kept safe with a promise. She knew he wasn't a good person but her wishful thinking had her wanting to believe that even people like him can come to understand the devotions of others. Dancing with the devil was something Denise hadn't considered. If she were to appeal to Luis, it would have to come at a cost. He only negotiated for things he wanted and most times it was one's commitment.

As she drove by, the place was set just off of IH35 East, close to a Park. Seeing the place and what she saw online had her entertaining the idea of having a meal there. Talking to the doctor about this hadn't been decided yet.

Getting the chance of seeing this man might satisfy a hate she was beginning to love. She could experience good food with the hopes of seeing him and simply remain obscure. This restaurant would provide that cover. It was every bit the authentic Mexican eatery. If someone desired the cultural embrace from south of the border, this looked to be a choice stop. Pricing on the menu showed that much of the riffraff wouldn't be entering the place. Entrees started in the $40 price range, with drinks averaging $15. It was not your typical Mexican restaurant.

She was convinced that she would have to start making a much more proactive effort in Dillion's protections. She was content to resolve things by letting everyone mind their own business. However, she was also aware that some of the parties involved didn't share that same opinion. Taking a stance against them would be done only if she was forced to. She knew her heart was stronger than her backbone.

One of the reasons she looked at the doctor with so much trust was because she knew deep down, he was desensitized to compromising emotions interfering with true justice. It wasn't that he didn't care, in fact it was the complete opposite. He cared very much.

As she drove past the place and started back home, she processed many thoughts. After much of a tug-o-war inside herself, she decided she would be going into the establishment. She would plan a date and stick to it. Would she go alone or ask the doctor to go with her? She knew once she did this, the possibilities were endless, and the outcomes couldn't be changed. It would all depend on how things went through the course of the next few days and how she would deliver her thoughts to the doctor.

Chapter Eighteen
Restaurante El Cardenal

Days of contemplating the risk of asking the doctor if he wanted to join her for dinner, bounced within her. It was a catch twenty-two. On one hand, the doctor might object to her idea of inquiry. His protection of her would steer that thought. On the other hand, if he were inclined to go, the doctor was much more of a deliberate man than any she knew, and he would be the best person for her to be with. Given the doctors past, she knew he had grown into a much more methodical individual and would adhere to anything he felt was justified. More recent conversations had sculpted that into her head. Reservations about his invite were also coming from what she might not know about him. Some might think it bordered on thoughts of unhinged behavior, but she understood that his pursuit of what was right was what drove him.

All these thoughts she could afford to be lost in her self-conversations. She knew his convictions were born out of many trials. They were noble and his character remained committed. Her past beliefs had her failing to pass any judgement towards him now, as she was starting to sympathize into seeing things the way the doctor saw them.

It was Friday, about 3:30 pm and everyone was filtering out of the office. Denise had been careful not to mention anything about the restaurant during the week. Sitting at her desk, she thought about whether or not to invite him. Indecision had her waiting until the last minute to say something. This would help in the decision. If prior engagements kept him from going, it wouldn't be on her. At least she would have mentioned it, even if at the last minute. She wouldn't have to deal with questions or lectures from the doctor.

"Doctor, what are you doing about supper tonight?" She threw a quick probe into his dinner plans.

"Not much, I'm really not all that hungry. Why do you ask, though? I don't mind hanging out." The doctor never really passed on the opportunity to be around Denise. She was in a sense his only child.

"I was wanting to try out this Mexican restaurant out by Pike Park. I heard it was good. It's called El Cardenal." Denise's attempt to spark the doctor's memory slipped right by him. He had forgotten about Mace's mention of the place.

"Never heard of it. I'm not really hungry, but maybe I'll have an appetizer and a drink." The doctor was content with just having an evening with Denise. It was about a week and a half before Dillion was due back and plans had become stagnant about what was to happen next.

"Good, do you want me to pick you up? I'm not planning on drinking, so you can enjoy yourself. I'm just gonna eat."

"That sounds fine, what time should I expect you to show up at my house?"

"Well, let's leave now as most everyone has and I'll be at your place in a couple of hours, before six."

"Sounds good." They both put away some papers and went home to get fixed up for the evening. Denise was still thinking about how she was going to mention her true motive for this dinner. What would she do if Luis happened to show up while they were in the restaurant? Each one of them would recognize his face as it had been examined by the both of them since his introduction into their lives. He had a despicable look, especially to someone who knew about his enterprises.

Denise knew she would have to tell the doctor before entering the place in case there was an encounter. She knew it wouldn't be fair to the doctor not to let him know. How she would introduce it to him was the issue she was having. She knew it would have to be sellable to her if she was to expect him to buy into it.

Denise pulled into the doctor's driveway at 5:40pm. She was good at being early. She was going to get out and go to the door, but the doctor had been watching for her from his backyard and motioned to her through his garage as he closed the door and came out through the house.

He was dressed up and ready for an evening out. For someone who knew the doctor, they would say he was going through some changes. He allowed for a five-o-clock shadow to sport sometimes, along with a longer style of hair. It wasn't unkempt at all. He remained well put together. He was just changing his appearance some.

"Well, hello dear." The doctor greeted Denise as he got into her car. His cologne made a bigger presence than he did.

"You smell nice."

"Thanks, it's a new smell for me, something different. We have about forty minutes, right?"

"About, just enough time for me to prep you."

"Prep me, is that a joke on my appearance?"

"No, not at all. I need to be more forthcoming on my intentions." Denise's tone gave way to a serious mode. The doctor looked at her waiting for the joke, but none came. "Luis likes to eat at this restaurant. I found that out and wanted to go there." The doctor looked at Denise with a surprising look.

"Stop the car."

"What, you don't want to go anymore because of that?"

"No, I forgot my wallet."

"That's not a problem, I got it."

"No, I need my wallet!"

"I don't think they are going to ID you."

"Dammit Denise, can we just go get my wallet please?" The doctor was surprised by Denise's announcement. His wallet was the first thing that came to his mind for going back to his house. He needed an excuse for that, as now he felt he would need to be guarded against these threats that exist in society.

"OK, alright, I understand, we can go back and get your wallet. I thought you might get upset about my reasons for wanting to go here, not about needing your wallet."

"Sorry, maybe his name triggered me a bit." The doctor wasn't about to let Denise know his intentions.

They pulled back into the driveway and as the doctor got out, Denise's curiosity never escaped one detail as she noticed what appeared to be a bulge on the doctor's back pocket. With a few minutes passing by, the doctor returned, this time with a dinner jacket on.

"Sometimes the restaurants get too cold for me." The doctor offered up an excuse for the jacket. Denise had suspicions, but because of fear and her not coming forth at first, and all that had accumulated, she let it go.

The drive to Pike Park was set to heavy fast traffic. Everyone was out and apparently seeking their own weekend pleasures. They were moving well without invites for Sunday drivers. Denise could hold her own behind the wheel. Her concentrations moved in and out of the lanes passing the cars, while developing a sense they were just out cruising. Both of them avoided talking about the mounting and ever-present topic, knowing it would certainly occupy dinner's conversation once there.

When they arrived, the doctor was impressed.

"Looks and smells wonderful. Man, you sure know how to pick the places to eat."

"Funny Doc, you know why I wanted to come here."

"Why, for the same reason as me, the food." The doctor smiled with great confidence as they entered El Cardenal. Denise was walking alongside the doctor and brought her arm around to hug on the doctor as they entered. Quickly, he did a side-shuffle acting as though he was getting the door for people leaving but his intention was not wanting Denise to feel underneath his jacket.

"I don't have cooties."

"I know, just helping others out." Now, in a better position to control the hug, he redeemed himself. "See, I don't think you are poisonous. Now the food here, is that a different story? Seems like the kind of place one might be done in." Making a joke about the obvious, the doctor and Denise walked in and were quickly seated.

At first, all conversation was bouncing off anything but the obvious. Possibilities were making them avoid recognizing a truth. As they looked at the menu, it was only time before the real conversation would begin, and they knew it would have to, especially in the case that he walked in.

"This isn't a cheap place by far." The doctor noticed the prices were far from what he expected.

"I told you earlier and I am still sticking with it. Tonight's meal and drinks are on me. So don't even think about paying."

"I won't. It's yours, I promise. So, what's with the idea of coming here? We kind of got sidetracked in our discussion." Just then a pretty little Spanish waitress came to their table.

"Hello, I will be taking care of you this evening, can I start you two off with a drink?"

"I'll have just water. He is going to want something stout I suppose." Denise was making good on her offer, letting the doctor take in on the libation.

"Do you have a particular flavor you like?" The waitress was ready to assist in his drink order.

"I have kinda taken a liking to those Mexican Martinis. Let me get a top shelf one of those."

"They are good, aren't they?" Denise had to agree.

"Excellent choice, I'll get that right out with some chips and chile' sir." The waitress ran off, leaving them both to think about what to say. The doctor started out first again.

"Well, what are you going to do if he shows up? I mean, why do you want to see him? I'm sure you aren't going to do anything."

"I know, I wanted to ask him to leave Dillion alone. That's all. I just want the boy's safety to be guaranteed."

"And you would trust this man's word as a guarantee? I think not. Seeing him here tonight will probably make the inevitable more palatable for me."

"What does that mean?"

"I will probably be able to see firsthand what this man truly deserves." A young Spanish boy brought them a bowl of warm salsa and warm chips, followed by the young waitress with their drinks.

"Are you ready to order?"

"Sorry, not yet, can we have a few more minutes?"

"Yes, take all the time you need." The subject changed as they discussed the menu items. The menu was expansive compared to the regular Mexican restaurants they were used to. One item on the menu that caught their eye was the "Cabrito en Rojo." It was half of a baby goat, flavored in a red sauce, and grilled over an open flame. Served with rice, corn, charro beans, pico-de-gallo, guacamole, and tortillas.

"You know, I said earlier, I wasn't really hungry, but if you want to split this, it's a meal for two, I will eat it with you. It sounds really good."

"That sounds good, let me look a little more, maybe." As they looked and discussed the many selections the restaurant had to offer, the inevitable happened. Just as fate would have it, Luis, Manuel, and Saul entered the restaurant. Neither Denise nor the doctor missed their entrance as their vanity strolled in before them as if it were a red carpet. They were unashamed and had a loud presence. The staff was well aware of who they were and scurried to seat them in a booth that seemed to be reserved for them.

What was unknown to the doctor and Denise at the time, was that

Luis had become aware of who Denise was. His prying into Dillion's whereabouts brought him to understand all those involved in his life. Finding out that Dillion was being tended to by the system was a part of that detail. Naturally, he wanted to know the players involved, as they would have an importance in his life, probably more so than his family.

He was aware of the quality of Dillion's family and figured the system was the one that was championing any care he was receiving in his life. Luis's knowledge was one of a visual learning. Faces were how he catalogued information and he had Denise's memorized.

As the men were seated, attention to the details of their surroundings was a must. During his initial scan of the room was when he laid eyes on Denise. Seeing her there aroused his defenses. Never making eye contact, both parties knew of each other's occupancy.

"I don't believe it, he showed up. What luck?" Denise was in shock. Her breathing took on a jogger's pace.

"You're not going to confront him! I can tell you that right now!"

"I don't want to, but I feel like I have to."

"Denise, if this all gets out of hand, no one is going to appreciate what happens. I think it's best to leave it alone. I'm prepared to deal with them if I am forced to, but I don't want to so don't provoke something you might regret later!"

"What does that mean?"

"It means exactly that, they will get their due from me, especially if you are harmed. You better believe me." The look on the doctor's face as he spoke was one of a cold and deliberate nature. Denise felt scared and protected at the same time.

While the conversation was going on, anyone watching could notice the unease on Denise's face. The one that took the most notice was Luis himself. As he and his companions discussed who Denise was, he delighted in the obvious discomfort she displayed. He assumed he was causing her unease with his mere presence. Many times in his life, fingers pointed in his direction to place blame. Although it wasn't without cause, it was an automatic suspicion he had worn for years. Many wanted to see to his demise and Denise had a reason. His arrogance had him wanting to provoke Denise as he knew her attendance wasn't coincidence. She had to be here because of concerns for the boy.

"Denise, let's just eat and we can re-think this out another way."

"I'm not even hungry anymore. I've lost my appetite."

"Ok, well let's just sit for a while, we don't have to order anything, and then we will leave." The doctor got her to calm down as the emotional eruption was totally unexpected. Going to the restaurant with intentions of seeing him soon became the reality of a bad idea.

After a few minutes, the doctor managed to get Denise to settle herself. In the entirety of the situation, no one had yet stepped out of line. Nothing could really be done.

Asking a favor from this man wasn't necessarily a stock choice, given his nature. It was the familiar impasse; the right can only react, until a wrong is committed. Then and only then can you do anything. Prevention of crime lies useless when directed towards a determined evil. There is no changing of that mind.

"Here comes the waitress. I'll tell her we are just going to finish our drinks and we have decided to go." The doctor wanted to get Denise out of there and into a more comfortable environment.

"Sir, I know the lady is not drinking, but the gentleman wants to buy you drinks and thanks you for taking care of his boy." The waitress said these words as she motioned to Luis and his henchmen, who were all smiling with their glasses raised towards the doctor and Denise. They had found it in their hearts to do what they did best, flaunt their vanity.

In an explosion of disbelief, Denise shoved the table from off of her seating and began a shouting that had the doctor floored.

"You son of a bitch, you do one thing to harm that boy and it will be your ass! I mean it. I don't want to see you anywhere near him! Your drugs got busted, and your boys shot up, but not because of him, so you better leave him alone." She approached his booth as she was berating him loudly in the establishment.

The doctor managed to set himself between Luis's booth and Denise as she approached the men. As the doctor was holding Denise back, his eyes never looked away from Luis's men.

"Back up, Denise. Let's go. This isn't right. We got to go." All three men sat comfortably as if not bothered. Saul had placed his hand inside of his jacket to show he could end this faster than one might want.

"My generosities are often overlooked. All I wanted was to offer a friendship, but I see your woman is too unruly. Take her away from me before I have her removed." The doctor now had reason to speak towards Luis.

"You don't know me, but don't ever threaten my loved ones, ever. You WON'T live to regret it."

"Get out of my face, you piece of shit, you don't even know who I am." The doctor was having to manhandle Denise at this time as her outrage had turned to kicking and thrusting about. With Denise's words unharnessed, she continued to shout at their table. Luis continued smiling with short replies.

"Get the hell out of here."

The doctor, never taking his eyes off the men, kept his words directed at Denise and her comfort.

"Let's go, I'm gonna take care of this. Trust me."

"You're finished, Luis, you're going down." Denise's emotions were all expressed. With a few last choice words, the doctor managed to get her out of the restaurant and into the passenger's seat of her car. She was in no shape to drive. The doctor got into the driver's seat and started to leave as he used his right hand to rub on the back of Denise. She was slumped over and crying hysterically.

"It's OK. It's gonna be OK. Calm down. I'm taking you home with me. I'm not dropping you off to be by yourself." The doctor's concern for Denise was mainly due to the emotional frenzy she was in, but he now knew she had threatened someone that could bring about repercussions.

"No, I'm fine, take me home. I can't believe he said that. He wanted to provoke me. That son of a bitch did that on purpose. How evil of a man!"

"Calm down, Denise. You are in no condition to be alone. You are going home with me. I'm taking care of you. We can de-escalate at my house. I'm calling this shot." The doctor wasn't about to budge.

"What if this gets out? My job could be on the line! I can't believe this just happened." For much of the ride to the doctor's house, Denise cried profusely. Her understanding of just how evil worked had finally reached a deeper level. The doctor had been pressed to understand one must not balk on being deliberate. This encounter had proven this to be true as he entered it with the gun he carried.

Never did he want to brandish the weapon, because doing that was a sure decision to use it. He also got to re-experience a taste of revilement, as Luis showed him that nothing escapes the wicked in their pursuits. Getting Denise home and asleep was now priority one for the doctor. Many more tasks were to now be put on the list, but taking care of her was tonight's main objective.

Once they arrived at the doctor's house, he walked Denise into the spare bedroom and had her lay down in the bed. The doctor walked out and returned with a glass of water and a pill to aid her in a much-needed rest. Denise obliged the offer and as the doctor sat by her side holding her hand and rubbing the side of her face, she fell fast asleep.

Luis and his men were left with quite a different conversation. As always, he assumed within his own mind the role that he was the good guy. The restaurant manager was told all that was damaged in the melee would be happily put on Luis's bill and that he apologized for his friends getting a little out of line. They ordered their food and ate, never having any intention of leaving, even after being involved in such a loud altercation.

"Boss, who was Denise's old man?"

"I don't know, but I'm thinking we will meet him again. He seemed to have an interest in her, so he will probably be affected by what's going to happen. Saul, *asesinato esa puta*."

"*Si*," Saul answered without disturbing the enjoyment he was receiving from the food he was eating.

"She knows too much already, *mantenerla viva es una amenaza excesiva*." Casually, they continued with eating their meal, while making a decision about someone's life. This solidified proof of their ruthlessness and lack of compassion for anyone. The doctor would have his work cut out for him. In spite of all the protections being placed on Dillion, now Denise's life would be in jeopardy too.

Chapter Nineteen
Going Home

It was a week that had gone by fast. Dillion's return home was due by a flight the doctor had arranged. Much of the time had been spent looking over Denise and a drive back to the hill country wasn't about to take place. All concerns with her work were fine. No one in the department had heard of the incident that had taken place. He wasn't sure how her recovery from the encounter would progress, especially with Dillion returning soon.

The doctor would be picking up Dillion from the airport in Dallas with Denise, and they had arranged for him to stay with the doctor for a few days after his arrival. Forced by the hand of circumstance, Dr. Richards called and talked with Manus about what had happened. He wanted his opinion on what could possibly lie ahead after this encounter with Luis. The doctor was concerned about the volatile nature he knew Luis possessed. Manus reserved nothing with his instructions about what to expect.

"You know doc, you might end up having to claim self-defense."

"I'm not worried about myself. If he decides to go for Denise or Dillion, he will wish he hadn't." The doctor was less concerned about himself. His will to live now, was for others. He would sacrifice himself if the circumstances presented themselves.

"Does Marlioni know any of this?"

"I don't think so. He would have reached out to me already. I don't even think the incident was reported."

"Probably not. Much of what goes on around Luis, never is." Manus and Dr. Richard's conversation became deep, exploring the questions most people are afraid to ask with any true sincerity. Not that people haven't seen or heard such things, but never with real considerations are they looked upon. It seemed to be what fantasy is made of.

Manus talked of happenings in his past that would make an individual want to remove their friendship from him. Dr. Richards was understanding. He could appreciate an affection towards these kinds of actions in an effort to create a balance in society. It was long overdue that evil triumphed over good.

"Well, are you going to talk to Marlioni, or do you think we'll keep this in our bag?"

"I'm not mentioning this to him. It might complicate things. Dillion is going to stay with me for a while. Stacy's trial is expected to start soon and I'm hoping if we let things just ride, the system will work once for the good guys."

"You never know. Luis is the most unpredictable in the equation and he probably doesn't have much in the way of patience."

"You're right and that's why I'm not talking to Det. Crawford."

"Good enough. Let me know if you need me in any way."

"Thanks." Their conversation ended and the doctor was left feeling satisfied with any decision he might have to make for the sake of his loved ones. A reminder of his wife and the commitment he had towards those he loved, gave him a feeling of confidence as he thought through the unavoidable terrors of this world. He had done all to make his mind up that he wouldn't fail them.

Time was the healing agent for Denise. Not that it removed the hardening of her character, but it seemed to have given her a higher level of maturity. She was realizing truth and accepting the fact that some things are out of her control. Her control of her actions was what she was responsible for and finding peace in believing in justice was what she had to keep in mind. These growth steps in her life were good, yet they removed some of the things people loved about each other, like innocence and our ability to trust others. Life hardened, was a wisdom that comes with compassion lagging so much farther behind than we would desire. Denise was growing into her own. Unbeknownst to her at the time, her first encounter with the doctor had set a course that was molding much of what her identity was becoming. Her love and passion hadn't changed. Her tolerances had been adjusted and were now set to new levels.

The doctor was getting ready to go to the airport to pick up Dillion. Earlier discussions in the week had coordinated picking him up. Denise was going to come to his house, and from there they would depart together.

Outside of what Dillion was coming home to, his experiences at camp had him facing difficulties. After a short run with adversity, his time was spent being youthful. He had learned much of what is to be valued in life. Standing up for what's right and enjoying the goodness set before us with appreciation. He learned it sets a standard that can carry one through a successful life no matter one's circumstances.

The concern now was for his next setting. A series of harsher lessons awaited him, and the doctor and Denise wanted to shield him from them. Getting him home was the first step. Every step after that would be done one at a time. They were anxious to see their boy for many reasons.

"You know, it seems like it's been so long since we have seen him." Denise looked at him sort of like a nephew.

"I know. With all that has happened, and now looking back, it does seem like a long time."

"I know, but I don't want to mention anything about the obvious. Let's just enjoy time together. He is staying with you for a few days. Let his head unwind from camp and next week when he goes back home, we can talk more about his mother's trial to him."

"Agreed. Are you going to stay for a while when we get back?"

"Maybe for a while."

"Come on, I'm going get some pizza delivered and order a movie online. It will be fun."

"Ok, let me think about it." The remainder of their drive wasn't bad as traffic for the rush hour hadn't yet begun. They talked a bit about what would be a good movie for Dillion to watch. The doctor suggested 'The Princess Bride' as a way to convince Denise to stay over. "You know that's my favorite movie! You're just trying to get me to stay for your little plans."

"Maybe." Denise was smiling as she knew the doctor wanted the three of them to hang out. It would be therapeutic for all of them, and she felt the tug from him pulling at her to stay. "Well, I guess I'll stay for that movie, but do you have ice cream? I'm feeling like indulging. The shoes will come off and a blanket on the couch will be calling my name."

"I have Homemade Vanilla and chocolate syrup just for you."

"Really?"

"Yep."

"Well, I don't very well have a choice not to stay. Hope there's enough for you two."

"There is." They both smiled and laughed as they talked the rest of the way to the airport. It was a moment of clarity to who they really were and the connection they had. After parking they went in to wait for Dillion's arrival. They had gotten there twenty minutes before his plane was due to land and surprisingly to them, it was scheduled to be on time. The airport was bustling in its usual fashion. They were both glad to be getting Dillion back.

Amongst them in the crowds of people were everyday walks of life. The doctor and Denise had both become accustomed to making judgements. Mostly to provide a shield of defense. Their experiences with society and seeing much wrong lurking in its midst required them to set up guards. If they left themselves unprotected, they knew the world was good at producing victims.

Most of the people they saw walked with purpose and were unintrusive. Some, on the other hand, reminded them of the ever-present malicious part of society they were dealing with. Through the traffic of people and the many conversations, they heard Dillion's plane's arrival announced.

"He's here. I can't wait to see him." Denise was more excited than the doctor.

"I bet he had a good time." The doctor was thinking about the lesson he knew he had learned at camp. Dillion's letter to the doctor explained how things turned out after he finally confronted the bullies. Denise had been left in the dark by the both of them from the beginning. Her need to know now wasn't important, although her attitude had been adjusted to better understand the advice the doctor gave Dillion. However, its relevance wasn't important anymore to even bring it up.

"Look there he is! Dillion!" Denise left the doctor's side and moved swiftly towards Dillion as he emerged from the crowd coming off the plane. She waved her hands in the air. "Dillion!" Dillion spotted her as she was the most noticeable person in the airport. He wasn't taken back or embarrassed by her display of enthusiasm; on the contrary, he embraced her excitement.

"Denise! I'm back!" Dillion skipped towards Denise with the biggest smile they ever saw the boy make. They made it to one another, and Denise grabbed him with a hug that she struggled to lift him with.

"I am so glad to see you. I think you gained 10 pounds and grew 3 inches."

"Man, I had a good time."

"I'm so glad."

"You look good, boy." The doctor finally reached their reunion and was just as happy to see Dillion. "Are you tired?"

"I was, on the flight, but now that seems to have all gone away."

"Did you have any more trouble?" Smiling, the doctor winked at him.

"Not at all." Dillion and the doctor knew what they were talking about. Denise knew it was to remain with the men.

"I don't even want to know." She just rolled her eyes at them.

"Ok, we agree." The doctor smiled at her, but with all love and sincerity his answer was how he felt. "Well, I'm ready to get to the house and relax. Let's get your bags and we can make for home. Denise is coming over tonight for pizza and a movie and most likely staying over, right?" The doctor didn't want her to have to drive home at such a late hour.

"I never promised that."

"I know you didn't, but it will be best if you stay. There is no need in you going home."

"I'm sure I'm gonna want to go home."

"Oh well suit yourself. We're gonna crash after the movie while you have to drive home." The doctor and Denise's razzing of each other was just part of their relationship. They loaded Dillion's suitcase and all he had brought back from camp and were on the road to the doctor's home in no time.

They quickly drew out the plan for the evening by deciding on the kind of pizzas to order. They pulled into a grocery store for sodas to drink, bananas and strawberries for splits and antacid for the doctor. They asked Denise if she needed anything, just in case she spent the night, and her answer came with a final decision.

"NO. I appreciate you guys wanting me to stay over, but you need to appreciate me wanting to go home and sleep in my bed."

"Ok, alright, I get it. I was just trying to make it easy on you. You know you are always welcome." The doctor finally understood.

"I know and thank you." Denise understood as well.

Even though she wouldn't stay, that wasn't about to damper the time they would have.

Once at the doctor's house, Dillion was led to the guest bedroom to put his stuff up and get ready for bed as he would be going to sleep after the movie, if not before. The doctor's plans were no different as he prepared for bed on the front side of the movie.

When the doctor came back in the den, Denise was like that big kid they loved so much. She hadn't lied one bit. With shoes off and a throw blanket on her, she had banked much of the cushions to one end of the couch and rolled herself up like a taco against them. She was all ready for someone to come in and turn the movie on for her. Doctor Richards had already ordered the food for delivery and sat in his Lazy Boy with remotes in hand to put the movie on. Dillion came in the room to see everyone in position with the stake they had claimed.

"Oh no, you can't have all the couch. Doctor Richards has his chair. Where am I going to sit?"

"With me. Come up here." Denise had come from a family where affections were never hidden. Dillion had never had much experience with that. She, however, was the big sister he never had, and he found himself more able to relate to her. He grabbed a cushion, laid it on her legs, lay on the bottom portion of the couch behind her with his head resting on her. She reached her hand back and began rubbing the side of his head.

Doctor Richards started the movie but could hardly watch the show. Although it was a favorite of his and Denise, and Dillion would be learning to love it, the doctor was distracted. He had too much to be grateful for as he observed those two enjoying the time as siblings would. He was truly in love with the family he now had.

Thirty minutes of the movie went by, and the pizzas finally showed up. They paused the show long enough to get some food, a drink and come back and assume their spot. The doctor couldn't complete the movie as everything was feeling so right in his life. It had been so long since he had known such a thing. Luis and all that trouble could be forgotten, if only for a while. He slowly drifted into a sleep as Denise and Dillion watched the movie and enjoyed sundaes towards the end of it. As the movie concluded, Denise spoke with great expression.

"Did you enjoy it?"

"I did. Look, the doctor's asleep."

"I know, he has been. He has been snoring for some time. Doctor! It's over. I'm going home," Denise spoke to the doctor, and he opened his eyes.

"I'm going to bed. I suggest you go too, Dillion."

"I am, I'm pretty wiped out."

"Denise, you call me when you get home."

"Ok, I will." Denise got up and hugged Dillion before he walked into his room to go to sleep. The doctor walked Denise to the door.

"You've done well with the boy."

"No doctor, you've done well for the boy, and me. You are an amazing man. I think of what you have had to endure and to see where you have taken your life today, you are truly a selfless man willing to sacrifice yourself to make a change for the better. I am blessed to be working with you."

"Well, it was you that helped me to change and see the direction I wanted to go after the death of Melinda, and I am forever grateful to you for that. You have replaced a loss in my heart with the best daughter a man could ask for. I love you."

"I love you too."

"Don't forget to call me when you get home."

"I won't." They hugged and she got into her car and headed for home. The doctor shut and locked the door. He went to check on Dillion. Dillion had just finished brushing his teeth and was getting in bed. The doctor came to the entrance of the room and told Dillion he enjoyed the evening they had spent together. He mentioned how proud he was of him for making the decision to stand up for himself and that he was having to learn some hard lessons at a young age.

"Denise and I are going to stay committed to you and our goal is to see you become a fine, mature young man."

"Thank you. I appreciate all you all are doing for me."

"We know, we can see that. Just stay the path and we'll be right there for you."

"I will."

"I told Denise and I will tell you. I love you guys."

"Thanks." Dillion wasn't accustomed to expressing too much emotion but was understanding and beginning to grow a bit more.

"I'll see you in the morning."

"Yes sir, good night." Dillion lay down and the doctor went back into the den to pick up any mess that was left. A few paper plates in the trash, glasses in the washer and a quick fold up of the throw blankets and he was ready to go to bed.

While straightening up, he noticed that Denise had left her sunglasses on the end table. He figured her to be halfway home and she was due to call him upon arrival. He decided to be proactive and get the call out of the way. He was tired and would let her know about her shades. Her phone rang a few times.

"Hello," she answered the doctor sounding perturbed.

"Denise, you left your shades."

"Aw, oh well. Dammit."

"It's not that big of a deal."

"No, not that. There is a car that has been tailgating me close and its night. You know how the lights can be blinding."

"Well just let them pass you, just slow down and move over." Denise sounded very frustrated. The doctor could tell she was excited. "Just pull over."

"Shit, now they are flashing me. What the hell? I'm pulling over and they are slowing down behind me." The doctor flashed into a set of fear.

"Denise, don't pull over! Get out on the road! Where are you?" The doctor began shouting loud enough that Dillion came back into the room.

"Doctor, I'm driving off. They are following me…. Fast!"

"Where are you?" The phone connection began to go in and out. "Denise! ...Denise! She's not answering. Denise!"

"What's going on?" Dillion asked the doctor with a look of an unknown terror in his eyes.

"Denise!" The phone cut back in.

"We are hauling ass! They are coming around my side!"

"Keep going, get away from them. I'm coming after you. Where are you? Denise! Denise! Denise!" No answer was heard. Her phone had disconnected. He looked at Dillion and forcefully told him to get in the car. As he rushed out, he continued to dial her number. He could only reach her voice mail. They left his house and followed a pattern that would take them to Denise's home the shortest way possible. What they would end up learning, would change everything for them from now on.

Chapter Twenty
Farewell My Love, Again

Dr. Richards' blank stare was cutting through the wall. An emotionless face was a façade for what lay beneath. He sat at his kitchen table, dressed in a black suit. More thoughts than any conversation could ever process were playing within him. No questions of why, just meditations of purpose and justice. Desperately needing to, he couldn't manage to cry. Unlike the first round of losing someone, this time his experience happened under circumstances well-seasoned. He wasn't without sensation. It was just different, managed and controlled. His actions would need to be applied in a productive way. The balancing of the scales in his mind would be measured and with intent.

Denise's services were set for 10:00am at Leary Funeral Home with the interment following at Memorial Gardens. The weather was set to be nice, and the doctor had already stepped outside to view it. Despite the day's appearance, it didn't bring about any great outlook.

Part of the doctor's thought was in much anticipation as everyone's thinking was. Awaiting the details as to who was responsible was only a pretense. The doctor was certain of who was responsible for her death. The whole department was grieving, especially because of the conditions of her murder.

Being shot up at close range while driving in her car was in close competition to her killing with the concrete bollard she hit traveling at 57 mph. She was dead when first responders showed up. Unfortunately, for all of those who loved her, pictures and memories would be their last glimpse at her, due to a closed casket.

The doctor knew everyone would be seeking closure of one degree or another. His consideration for this was contemplated much differently than all those with concern. This didn't stop him from gathering what he wanted to know. His close ties to the force gave him updated information as it became available.

Detective Crawford knew that everything he could find out, the doctor would expect to know. He also suspected the doctor would be in a quest to obtain a better justice than he had seen before. This had the detective sympathetic as well as cautious. Even though Dr. Richards wanted to hear from the detective and Det. Crawford wanted to talk with the doctor, they were still reluctant to reach out. Both of them knew of the other's convictions and now more than ever dared not question them. The one that knew the doctor would be contacting him, was Manus. He knew there would be no honorable solutions or restitution coming from the established system. He also knew it would require a deeper commitment and compassion to truly see any indemnification. This was what the doctor was seeking. Manus's insight saw it coming from the doctor before Denise's departure. The doctor's words and reckoning weren't up for any debate and those who could appreciate him saw and agreed with that. Manus would have a role to play, and he knew it.

The doctor, with much reserve, got himself up and went to the funeral home. Facing the Wilson family wasn't what he wanted to do. Wanting to or not, he had to, as he was sitting with the family. They considered him to be a part of them, knowing how he and Denise shared the same zeal in life. The many outings they had together, the family gatherings he had attended, and her input to the family established his placement. Dillion, the other piece to their puzzle, was being dropped off by his grandmother and the doctor was looking forward to seeing him. He had been shaken up by the sudden loss of Denise.

Just as so much progress had been made in his life, tragedy struck with no mercy. One thing that was carved in stone now, was Dillion had a concentrated hatred for all things criminal. His disgust for the wrong things in life, borderlined a criminal element itself. The irony of it all was that Denise's death sealed a purpose for Dillion much as the doctor's wife did for him. She succeeded in her goal to get him fixed and set him on a good path in life and in doing so forfeited hers.

All of this was swimming about the doctor's head. No radio was playing while he was driving. It was only his thoughts, resonating in his head. The closer he got to the funeral home, the more he had to suppress his emotions of anger. As he pulled into the parking lot, he saw Manus there. He was smoking a cigarette and distanced from anyone standing outside, as a courtesy. Manus nodded at the doctor when he saw him and waited for him to park and get out. He knew the doctor would want to talk. Walking up to him, the doctor displayed a look that would make any man precautious.

"Doc, I am so sorry." The doctor refrained from comment. "I know it was that piece of shit, although we'll probably never get that told to us." Looking down he still remained silent. "That whole situation at the restaurant you told me about has got to be why. I know it was him."

"I do too, and he is finished."

"What are you going to do?"

"I'm going to be generous towards him." The doctor's demeanor was slow and methodical.

"What do you mean?" Manus was a bit excited hearing the doctor talk.

"I'm going to put him away with your help. No more will he live in this world."

"Whoa, slow down doc! I know and agree with you, but I'm not gonna just go blind and do something to get in trouble. This isn't a decision you make just right here, right now."

"I know. I made it the other night. I thought about it for a while, but I'm not going back on it. I'm not considering anything that will possibly change my mind. All I want from you is information. I am owning all of his death."

"Doctor, you sound scary."

"No, just unwavering. I'm going in. The Wilsons are expecting me. You expect me to call you. Very soon!" The doctor walked off and entered the funeral home.

When he walked in, what he saw was enough to break his heart. Desmond was holding a weeping little Candace on his hip, his wife standing beside them with her arms around them both. Next to the closed casket, they were staring at numerous pictures of Denise. Some were of her as a youth. One was a professional photograph. Some of the pictures were taken at family gatherings. They even placed a picture that Denise had of her, the doctor and Dillion from their trip to the entertainment house, amongst the rest. It was all the doctor could do to keep from crying. It was now four years since his wife's death and over two years since Denise came into his life and all of it was over.

"Doctor, good to see you," Desmond spoke and Dr. Richards just buried his head into the Wilsons and put his arms around them. He felt little Candace put her small hand on his head in an attempt to pull him in and that was all he could take. He burst into a cry that showed he was still worthy of healthy emotions. He raised his hand to hold on to princess's hand. She was all that was left of a reminder of Denise. A solid minute went by and he spoke.

"I'm going to sit down." There wasn't much of a need to carry on. He walked over to the family and shook the hands of everyone and then sat in the place they had reserved for him. He felt honored, heartbroken, bitter and responsible all together. Now, engrained in him, was the worth of a venture that would eliminate the causes of such pain. Now more than ever was there a need for that.

The doctor saw Dillion come in and walk directly to him. He had been crying. He had grown a bit since the doctor first met him, but still had the face of a young boy and now it looked beat.

"Sit down Dillion." The doctor put his arm around him. He could feel the boy shaking.

"Why?" That was about all he could get out.

"It's evil, son. It is good for nothing. It only causes pain."

"I hope they catch who did this and they get what they deserve."

"I'm sure of it. You need to make sure you do what is right and keep going the way you are. You know, she was very fond and proud of you."

"I know. I liked her too. I just wish she was still here."

"That's why you need to understand that by doing right, you make good out of her death. She wins. It was what she was working for." Dillion understood what the doctor was saying. This was by far the hardest lesson he had ever learned, but it would remain with him forever.

The funeral was performed by a preacher they all knew growing up. He had stories of her that he told from personal experience. It was good to let a laugh relieve the pain that was ever present. Scriptures were read to assure everyone that she was in a better place and that at the appointed time of her resurrection, she would meet her Creator, and that peace would be afforded to her for an eternity.

Their church also had an amazing choir that sang about the homegoing and lifted the spirits of those gathered. Fellowship and food followed. Comfort and peace seemed to come into the hearts of everyone as her services were a complete display of it. The doctor felt it throughout his body, so much so that he was never more convinced of the mission he now must complete.

After the services, he drove Dillion home. Small talk filled the ride. The doctor had plans to continue with Dillion and told him so. Getting things lined out with the department would have to be done, but whatever it took, he would see to it. The truth of the matter was in few more years, Dillion would be grown, and their relationship wouldn't need to be monitored through a system. Dillion thanked the doctor and went into his house. As the doctor pulled away, he got on his phone and called the detective out of curiosity.

"Hello, Joseph."

"Marlon, have you heard anything yet?"

"No, I spoke with the boys working the case. They sent in some casings to ballistics, but without a gun or a person to tie it to, we have nothing."

"What about surveillance videos? No one had any around there?"

"No, nothing we can find as of yet, no witnesses have come forth. Nothing."

"You know who it was!"

"You think you know who it was and I don't blame you, but let's see if we can find out. Give it some time Joseph. I know you want to know. Just give me some time."

"I will. Let me know if you hear anything."

"Alright, goodbye." It was important they talk, although the doctor's mind was already made up. Exhausted from the stress of the day, he went home and found himself going to bed early. The stress was harder and more draining on his person than physical labor by far. If the doctor was to perform his greatest act ever, he must remain healthy. Rest would provide the rejuvenation his system required.

Luis was living a life uninterrupted. The order on Denise's life hadn't fazed him in the least. Reading about it in the papers illustrated the power he felt he had. He knew people reading this might bring about anger, but not without its counterpart, fear. This comforted him, as he knew word would reach Stacy. She would understand any time in prison would now belong to her as she could at least live as opposed to facing the fate Denise did.

All of this chaos surrounding Luis and his operations gave him a sense of safety. For everyone else it was horror and disbelief. The doctor would put an end to this. He wasn't waiting for the law to go through its obstacle course, but would give the grapevine a chance to confirm. Time would be allotted for news and preparations. The doctor wanted his part to be done with precision.

Three days went by, and as fate would have it, word about Luis's involvement in Denise's murder reached Manus's ear. Acquaintances that he had heard of Luis's involvement by knowing a friend of the driver of the car that night. Manus called the doctor with the information the second he received it.

"Hello Manus. I suspect you have news for me. Being that I was feeling the need to call you."

"I do. It was Luis who ordered the hit. Not provable in court, but it was him."

"We don't need the courts. We will settle out of them. I need you to find out a location where I can meet up with him. Where he hangs out and where he feels comfortable. Maybe where he conducts his business. But this location must be private."

"I already have an idea. They say he has an old warehouse where he and his boys go. I'm not sure of the outlay, but I'll find out. You ain't gonna be able just to walk in on him."

"I am, and I'm going to. He thinks he is over everybody and that nobody can even challenge him. I'm going to be his first real challenge, someone who isn't afraid of dying."

"Look here, don't go in there acting stupid. You do this, you do it right. Let me see what I can find out and we can go from there."

"Detective Crawford is going to want to talk to me after it is discovered that Luis is dead if everything works out the way I'm planning."

"And so what, we'll clean everything up. No mess for anyone to know about." Manus was set to do all he could to help the doctor. He wanted no physical hand in the dispatching of Luis but would be glad to assist with the set up that needed to be performed.

"You find out his location. Stake him out if it isn't too dangerous. Find out his habits and inside info to when and where he is supposed to be. I will make my plans based on what you find out."

"Wow Doc, once this is set in motion, we might not ever talk again."

"Whether or not I speak again doesn't matter. What matters is neither will he. We will both be ending up in different places I assume." Manus could tell the doctor had a much different outlook on life now. He wasn't dark by any means. He was reserved for justice. Love was the driving factor that filled his passion to do what he deemed as right. Knowing his life might soon come to an end, he had one thing left to do.

While Manus would be gathering what the doctor needed to plan his event, the doctor would spend one more evening with Dillion. He wanted to let him know that he cared for him deeply and that no matter what happens in life, one should always be in pursuit of what is good and right, no matter the consequences.

It was a Thursday evening and the doctor picked Dillion up to go out for a burger and a shake. The doctor wanted Dillion's focus to be on making good out of the situation. Through the doctor's daily reaching out to Dillion, he could tell the boy was dealing better with the horrible passing of Denise. Prior to all this, there were activities that Denise had helped line up for him. He was going to be starting off in the tennis program at the high school. It was always something he had an interest in, just nobody to push or encourage him. They had also had conversations about his future, what he wanted to be. Although he never pinpointed anything, they danced around the idea of an architect. He seemed to take an interest in some of the things Denise had discussed about design and buildings. The doctor's idea of meeting was to make sure he stayed focused even if he wouldn't be around.

"Well, what do you want?"

"Just a cheeseburger and a vanilla shake."

"Me too. That sounds good. Dillion, I wanted to say how proud I am of you. I know you have heard me say that before, but one thing you now know is that nothing in life is for sure. Denise's passing has shown that to you."

"Yes sir."

"Well, I might not always be around to make sure you are working at what you need to. So I want you to remember the lessons we have both taught you."

"What do you mean?"

"I'm just saying you are your own man. You have to guide yourself."

"I know that. I was thinking. I know now what I want to do."

"What's that?"

"I want to get into law enforcement. Maybe become a US Marshall."

"I think I know, but what brought that on?"

"Denise."

"She had you interested in other things."

"I know, but now she's gone, and I think the best way to honor her is to fight against what took her from us. I hate those kinds of people who did that."

"Don't confuse matters by learning how to hate. It is a habit that once man develops, he can hardly break."

"So how am I supposed to think about them?"

"With love. There is a side to that many never learn to know."

"I guess so. I just want things to be right."

"You sound like me. I understand exactly where you are coming from. Don't make the mistake of becoming proud in your efforts though. Most men never come to understand that. It is humility that gives way to proper discernment, unlike its popular counterpart, vanity. Through pride, men think that mere wanting and desire can produce truth, but in fact it doesn't and this is hard for people with egos to ever see. Death is a teacher of whom we don't want to follow, rather eradicate." Dr. Richards had learned this lesson as it was taught by the ways of the world. He had always had much of the same convictions, but now he possessed a clearer sight on how things worked. "It will be alright. I think you will make one hell of a fine US Marshall. Just don't come arrest me." The doctor made a comment that one day the kid might understand, but today it made him laugh as he thought it to be silly.

They wrapped up the evening with good food and a couple of stories about Denise. The doctor kept reminding him not to dwell on the negative. He told him that Denise would want them to continue on in her absence. The boy had a mature attitude and accepted the doctor's advice. They left and the doctor didn't know if that would be the last he would ever see the boy again.

Two days passed and the doctor got a call from Manus. He detailed out information of Luis's whereabouts and when he was expected to be at these places. He explained the entourage he was with, which was known already, and a layout of their "meeting place."

"Look, I'll get everything lined up for you to go see them. I'll need a few days. Don't make a move until I say it is clear. You have to trust me on this."

"Right now, you are the only one I can trust. You just set things up. I'll take care of the rest."

"Never would I have thought this was for you when I first met you. You seemed different, but the more I think about it doc, you haven't changed. What you are doing is right. What I see now has always been in you. It just came out from all the things that have happened."

"You have a good perception. I don't feel as though I have changed. Maybe developed more, more mature, but my values are still the same. I'm reframed, that's all."

"I'll call you in a couple of days, we'll discuss the plan and then it will be to execute."

"Hopefully." They hung up and the doctor was left to concentrate on his composure. Overthinking might cause distortions within his emotions. He would have a few days to contain them. Thought would now be his preparation until the call came and then the plan would come to fruition.

Chapter Twenty-One
Judgement is Rendered

The night had left the downpour to be forgotten. There was a northerly breeze that came in and removed all thought that there had been any rain. The cool front provided a dry blistering wind that blew over the dampened earth, making the air appear colder than it was. The sky was now clear of clouds and the moon had almost waxed to its full potential. The visibility was crisp, and it was a perfect night for this job.

Though not being quite cold enough to permit a winter jacket, the weather seemed to have come early in the season. Most folks hadn't acclimated to these conditions yet. Outside of that, people seem to want to safeguard with clothes sometimes and with this setting, things just gave an eerie appearance.

It wasn't a holiday or even the weekend, but no one seemed to be out and about. Most everybody was in for the night. It was as if the climate was providential in its manifestation.

Dr. Richards was enjoying the moment. He felt in his heart that he was about to make a substantial gain in eradicating a long-overstayed evil. The doctor sat outside with a couple ounces of Irish Whiskey in a tumbler. He was looking up in appreciation of the firmament and all the glory he perceived to be surrounding him. Everything felt right in his mind. His convictions were unbreakable. He had a mission that must go on without any disruptions. It had been thought through. The entire event was contemplated for all of its unpredictable variables. He traced down all possible scenarios, leaving nothing to the imagination. The possibilities of "what if" can leave the mind hopelessly wondering. His concentration was above that level. He meticulously reviewed potential situations, guarded against his vanities, and with precision and deliberation had decided upon his actions. He was committed to excellence. It was time for justice to be rendered. His breath drew deep the cool of the night and exhaled a slow rolling fog, tinted with a brush stroke of whiskey. Heavy were the thoughts that sat inside the doctor's heart. The confrontation looming in the immediate future was the doctor's meditation.

Sitting next to him on a small outdoor table were his keys, cellphone, and a semi-automatic nine-millimeter pistol with fifteen hollow tip cartridges in the magazine. A spare clip was loaded as well. He was wearing a black suit with a long sleeve pressed black t shirt and black leather dress shoes. His hair had managed to grow out more so he could now comb it back. He seemed chiseled and yet unrecognizable. His image was licensed without papers. Moments seemed to be moving at a slower pace. There was still time before the call would come in, but that wasn't reason for him to walk away from his phone. Attention to detail never escaped his mind.

He picked up his cellphone and walked in his back door. The house was lowly lit and an aroma from a spiced pumpkin candle was lingering in the air. He would light one when a feeling of relaxation was necessary. It reminded him of Thanksgiving. It directed his heart back to the simple days with his wife. Remembering the important things was much of the foundation to his dedication for this occasion. It was justification to any contemplating. It kept him going, without regret, and he needed to feel thankful for tonight.

Looking back to the loss of Denise, could make someone question 'was it all worth it?' He never wanted to see her leave and was never more convinced that he couldn't stop now. He was well satisfied he must continue, or else it would have all happened in vain. To finish was to complete what was right.

There was no lacking of hurt inside him, but it was part of the construction of his character he had now grown into. Its presence legitimized the assignment.

He passed through the living room on his way to the liquor cabinet. He would have a second drink, but no more. Nerves that become numb don't feel, and this job required affection. His passion for fairness mustn't be renegotiated. These men were to die tonight. The countdown would begin once Mace called.

As he poured his second glass of whiskey, he looked over at the mantle where he had strategically placed a picture of Melinda next to a picture of Denise. Oh, how they would have enjoyed each other's company if life had only let their paths cross. Tonight would be set apart for them. He wouldn't question whether or not either one of them would approve of his remedy to the situation. It really didn't matter to him.

"The one thing I can always count on, is that you will always end up doing the right thing." He remembered the words he heard on more than one occasion from his wife.

Denise had spoken similar words to him. "If I need to know what to do, I know I can always call you."

He had their confidence and that was all he needed to satisfy any concern he may have about them with regard to the decision that was being made tonight. Taking Luis Maldonado out of this world would be a right decision in all aspects of life. The doctor took a sip of his drink and slowly meditated thoughts that were important to this mission. He wasn't to take in any satisfaction in dispatching Luis and any henchmen who may be fortunate enough to be cleansed from this lifestyle. He was just carrying out something that must be done, like taking out trash to be disposed of. Once it is done you think no more of it. His relaxation was inside of considering all that can be cured and healed from this elimination. As he reached for the picture of his wife, his phone rang. It was Mace, the time was 8:43 pm.

"Hello, this is the doctor. Am I set to make a house call?" His tone was calculated and deliberate. There wasn't room for any other interpretations.

"You are correct. You will be visiting with three of them. All of them are sick. They should be ready for your appointment at their waiting room after 10:00pm." Mace told the doctor everything he needed to know and then hung up.

The doctor finished his drink and walked back out into his yard. He picked up his pistol and placed it in a shoulder holster inside his suit jacket, grabbed his keys, the spare magazine, and stepped out the front door of his house.

He sat inside his car and turned it on to warm up. He was leaving in enough time to get there 30 minutes ahead of his subjects. He paused as the engine idled. He didn't want a feeling of being rushed or anxiety to enter in his mind. He immediately began to concentrate on those whom he had loved in his life. Reaching down he turned on the radio, to the 70s channel. This would most certainly take his mind to a place he and his wife had been. With the words "I love you" coming softly through his lips, he put the car in reverse and backed out of his driveway to leave.

He knew exactly where he was going. It was an old warehouse that

Luis owned and where he conducted most of his business. It was located on the north side of Mountain Creek Lake. Most people knew not to enter in the building. It was littered with NO TRESPASSING signs everywhere. The talk about it was that inside there was a plush room that was outfitted for their criminal enterprise, but no one would suspect it by the condition of the exterior of the structure.

Mace had secured a safe entrance for the doctor to walk straight into the meeting room. This had all been planned on paper, so the doctor would be opening doors and laying eyes on territories unknown. He went through everything in his mind that he and Mace had discussed about the entry. His undivided attention reviewed all details of the room that had been told to him. He wasn't thinking much about the drive as his knowledge of the streets of Dallas had over five decades in the making. Muscle memory made the drive as if the car was in autopilot. Movements through the streets were just blurs to the clear picture he was surmising in his mind. The trip seemed almost instant as his thoughts were focused on other things.

It was 9:27pm when he parked at his designated vantage point. He made sure and sat in his car with no interior lights on. He wanted to disguise his presence from any set of eyes that might be around. He would now only have to wait on the arrival of his patients. Their route was as usual as their nature. They didn't veer off from much of what they knew. They would be driving in and entering an automatic garage door in two different cars. Their arrivals and departures were always at the same time. This had been the common practice to minimize traffic and attention to the warehouse, although departure wasn't going to be in the cards for them tonight.

Once they were inside, the doctor would enter by way of an adjoining warehouse. He would take a flight of steps to the roof and cross over to an attic doorway that was fixed as if locked. Once entry was made, his descent to the encounter would need to be swift and accurate.

Having never been inside and or seen the layout meant he had to have trust in Mace. It would most assuredly be a determining factor in the outcome of this situation.

In the distance he saw headlights as they pushed through the landscape of buildings. His heart began a thick, heavy pounding. As calculated as the doctor was about this obligation, it was still uncharted waters for him. He wanted no room left for error. Two cars approached the building and the garage door opened for them. No lights came on inside the warehouse, and once the cars entered, doors shut, no more lights could be seen. It was time for the operation.

He allowed five minutes to pass before exiting his vehicle. He reached into the glove box and put on a pair of black leather gloves. He took a cloth and alcohol wipe and wiped the gun down as a precaution to losing it in a struggle. The gun had been acquired by Mace so it could not be tied to the doctor. He was ready.

Exiting his vehicle and shutting the door were steps that took longer than normal, as noise couldn't be a luxury. His time now to the appointment needed to be taken with great caution. As he walked up to the building, it had an unwelcoming appearance. Although it appeared structurally sound, it was abandoned and gave an impression of no kind of welcoming.

He would have to walk up five flights of stairs before coming out on top of the roof. He took his walk with dedication, as all sounds in the warehouse seemed to amplify. The acoustics were right for music, but not for stealth.

Finally, as he approached the roof, he felt relief, as if he had been holding his breath during the entire walk up the stairs. He paused to collect himself together. At this point he was having to resist anxiety.

Stepping over onto the other roof top he was now only moments away from his destination.

The door was his next challenge. Would it make any noise when he pulled on it? He wouldn't know until he did. Hesitantly he slowly gripped the handle. With his hand on the knob, he turned it, and heard hardly anything. The door was set to open from the outside, but not turn from the inside, to appear as locked. Now to pull it open was the next test. The doctor began to apply a bit of pressure to pull the door open, but it wouldn't budge. He placed two hands on the knob and pulled a bit harder. It took him a few times of slowly tugging on the door before it gave way to opening. When it did, it made a slight noise of release. The doctor froze. Although it wasn't that loud, it appeared to be as it broke the continuous background noise of the night.

Suspicious is the nature of a criminal, and the doctor knew that if Luis or his men thought they had heard something they would investigate it. He left the door ajar and walked away to hide on the other rooftop for a moment to pass. He couldn't be too hasty. A few more minutes spent waiting wouldn't change things now. It would give the doctor a moment to meditate and focus on the task at hand and provide him with reassurance of the job's importance.

With no indication of them being privy to his entering the building, he continued to push forward. The supposed occupied room was located on the second floor, so the doctor would be on a quiet descent down a few flights of stairs.

This was the uncertain part of the task. Would all members of Luis's team be inside this room? This could require some adjustments on the doctor's part. There was no option for leaving anyone alive. Every step the doctor took was slow and his eyes constantly scanned all of his surroundings for any movement. Upon reaching the second floor, he saw what he expected. The room was boarded up from the inside and released no light with a few exceptions of the door jam and window seals.

As he approached the door, he could hear a television on with the volume on a low setting. The men were talking. He undoubtably recognized Luis's voice as being the commanding force in the room. From what information Mace gave him, the doctor was somewhat aware of the room's layout but could only guess as to where everybody was.

Listening to them talk, the doctor determined Luis to be on one side of the room with one of the men and another at a distance from them. Their speech appeared to be jovial, so a threat wasn't expected on their part. The entry would have to be swift and carry the element of surprise with it. Hesitation would only complicate matters.

The doctor had been holding his pistol ever since he entered the building. He had already chambered a round and was ready. As he stood facing the door, he paused to collect a few last thoughts. He was convinced beyond any change. His decision was more than a thought. It was a conviction. He had no other path to take. With one last "I love you" to those he thought most of, he raised his leg.

CRASH, he kicked the door in and, with both hands securing the gun, entered the room. As he located everyone, his peripheral vision was in tune to his direct focus. He kept the gun thrust forward panning back and forth between the distance of the men. Any sudden movement would be to their demise.

"Hands up." The doctor's arrival caused total disbelief and shock to all three men. Luis and Manuel were sitting on a couch with a coffee table in front of them. Saul was behind a bar appearing to make drinks.

"Get from behind there and come join your friends." The doctor was cautious about them being spread out. Saul slowly moved toward the couch to join the other two. The doctor's intensity was dedicated, there was no compromising it.

"So, you came to fix things. Are you here to give me what I deserve? You probably need to re-think your decision. You know that no matter what happens, if you shoot, you will be shot. So, you might as well put that gun down and maybe you can have your life spared," Luis spoke with such a defiant tone. There wasn't much fear in Luis's voice as he didn't think the doctor had the nerve to kill. He placed the doctor in a category outside of the elements he had been brought up in. He wasn't aware of the doctor's fortitude and commitment to justice. Dr. Richards despised hearing his voice and it only reaffirmed his commitment.

"Unfortunately for you Mr. Maldonado, that is not going to be an option. I want to allow you to know why I'm here and why I am going to kill you, although you most assuredly already know. You have forfeited your life by the evil you have invoked upon society and it will no longer be accepted. I am here for one particular crime, but I'm sure the many people you have terrorized would give their support to me for ridding this world of your worthless self." Luis's face began to twitch ever so slightly as he perceived a cold chill to the doctor's statement.

"So, what then, now you are like me? A killer is a killer. You do this, you do what you hate." Luis's tactics were confused and scared.

"Never like you. Choice is what has made the difference between you and I. You do what you do with malice and hatred. You act out of self. I do what I'm doing here today with the hand of help and love. Consider your dispatching as an act of kindness towards you. It is better that you go to the grave, no longer able to commit such crime." The doctor then proceeded to walk around to the front of the couch to take better aim. Fear began to overwhelm Luis as he realized this was it.

"You pull the trigger and you will be shot!" Luis screamed, indicating one of his henchmen would draw and have a credible chance to shoot the doctor.

"I know. That is not of any concern to me. I am content as to where I will be going. You and your men, however, need to be worried. My choice in life has given me purpose and a destination. Unfortunately for you, your choice has given you its terminus."

As these words were spoken, Manuel jumped back off the couch, reaching for his pistol. The doctor rotated his position and discharged his weapon, hitting him in the abdomen. As this motion took place, Luis and Saul pulled their guns out and jumped towards the back of the couch.

The doctor began a blaze of gunfire, shooting in an attempt to hit each one in consecutive order. Countless shots rang out as everyone was aimlessly firing and moving for protection.

The doctor was hit with return fire and he managed to slip behind the bar to have a barrier between him and the men.

Gunfire ceased for a second as no one was sure who had been hit or even killed. The doctor could feel a pain in his left side that was generating a lot of heat. He knew this could be life threatening. The noise from the TV was all the sound in the room until Luis spoke.

"You better stay down or else we are going to kill you!" His voice rang out with a hint of fear. The doctor knew he had been shot. The question he was evaluating was if the henchmen were still a threat.

The doctor lay still and didn't make a noise. If he appeared to be dead, whoever was left would eventually reveal their status to him.

"Did you hear me you son of a bitch!" Luis spoke again, with an impatient nervous sound. The doctor knew of his own wound and wanted to seek help. He was just as sure that the same was true for Luis, but nothing would take precedence over the job at hand. The doctor just sat quiet, and his resolve was torturing Luis.

He could hear movement of someone attempting to get up with difficulty. The doctor was on the ground with his head positioned near the end of the bar. He managed to crawl ever so slowly as his pain began to increase. Never having lost his gun, he situated himself to having a view of the couch from the ground.

In all the exchange of gunfire that ended as fast as it began, he lost track of how many shots he had fired. He was holding another full magazine, but changing clips would take time he wasn't sure he had.

"I'm going to kill you, you bastard." Luis was still trying to get a response from the doctor with no effect. Dr. Richards could see one of Luis' men laying dead on the ground with a shot to the neck. He never made it to the back of the couch. "If we die here, you know we are both going to hell. I'll see you in hell if you aren't already there!" Luis's attempt at seeking the doctor's condition wouldn't let up. His desperate attempt at intimidation exposed that he knew he needed medical attention. The doctor could now tell this for himself as well. He had to make a move if he wanted to preserve his own life.

The doctor got in a position to get ready to stand up. The pain of moving was almost unbearable, but his adrenaline was overriding it. He grabbed a bottle that had fallen in the melee and threw it to the wall behind the couch. Following the explosion of glass, he heard a failed attempt to discharge a weapon. An empty click let the doctor know Luis was out of bullets. This wasn't a part of his plan, just a tactic to get the movement back in play and end the job.

The doctor forced himself up and with his gun panned forward, slowly rounded the couch to find Luis holding his bloody arm and his leg having received a hit. The other gunman was lying face down in a pool of blood.

"Alright, you got me. You won. Now if you let me go, I can give you what you want." Luis was rambling shallow words with no substance. Anything he said was to save himself at any cost.

"Look at you. Was any of it worth it at any time? The pain you caused, the lives you wrecked, and just to get ahead. Now you sit like a dog, dying of your wounds, and ask for mercy. I have to say, my nature is to show mercy. And because you ask for it, I will give it." The doctor said the words with much affection and then pulled the trigger. Before Luis could respond, he was void of any thoughts that he might have once possessed.

The doctor, knowing it was over, started becoming faint. He had been bleeding and was in need of care. As he looked around the room, it began to fade into a grey and the doctor collapsed.

"Doctor, doctor, are you alright? I'm taking you to get help." In a cloudy haze the doctor looked up and saw Mace. It seemed as he was in a dream, but the presence of pain let the doctor know he had a chance to make it.

Mace managed to wrap a t-shirt into a makeshift bandage around the doctor's waist and get him to his feet. They started a descent down two flights of stairs to get into Mace's car to go seek help.

"Doctor, I need to know where to take you." The doctor was in and out of consciousness. He couldn't respond, much less think. "Doctor, you need to listen to me. I can't take you to the hospital. Where can we get you help?" Once again, the doctor wasn't responding. Mace quickly got the doctor down the stairs and into his car. As Mace ran around to get in, the doctor had slumped over in his seat. Mace reached over to feel the doctor's heart and it was still beating. He turned on the car and started dialing on his cell phone.

He put the car in gear and sped off. The doctor would have to live to see another day. Manus had contacts and would pursue the doctor's well-being. There were too many reasons he had to live for. Inside the doctor's mind, he had decided earlier, if this was it for him, he was content that his life would end. Others would certainly want him alive.

Manus, being one of them, ripped out of the parking spot to a destination he didn't know yet. Only knowing he needed to save his friend's life was the direction he focused in. Mace started a series of phone calls as the doctor reflected in what might be his last thoughts. Only time would tell his fate.

In a haze, he thought about those affected by the situation he had come through. They would be left to see the choices he was forced to confront. Truth and justice had been compromised by self and vanity. Evil had challenged love and emotions were set on a scale left to choose for themselves what was right and what was wrong. This was what had ultimately led to the failed justice system made by man.

Life and death were the ultimate decision that had to be made. He hoped that this understanding would come to those who would choose life. It was to live with the intent of all things to be good. It was what made all things good. It was selflessness, and when that is adopted, all can feel a sense of belonging. For those who dwell on self, there was no regard for anyone else. That was the pattern that led to destruction. It was death. For those who chose death, it was a forfeiture of their own life that they embraced. The doctor wanted to live, but whether he did or didn't, he desperately wanted the meaning of his life to continue to live on without him. That fate would lie in the lives and choices of the ones that would remain.

About the Author

Born and raised in the small town of Lockhart Texas, Carroll has always enjoyed the simple things in life. He has been married to his wife since 1995 and they have two children together. He has worked in the Utilities industry for 30 years, is an elder at his church and enjoys writing in his spare time.